CENTER THE CROSSHAIRS

by

Gene Klark

PublishAmerica
Baltimore

ISBN: 1-60836-055-5
PUBLISHED BY PUBLISHAMERICA, LLLP
www.publishamerica.com
Baltimore

Printed in the United States of America

ACKNOWLEDGMENTS

I want to give a special thanks to my wife, Mary, who puts up with me on a daily basis. For her support and inspiration to follow my dreams.

To my daughter Anna Klark, for providing initial edits, re-works and wise suggestions, thank you for everything.

To my youngest daughter Mary and my sons, Nathaniel and Kristopher, thanks for sticking with me while I was writing this book.

To my father-in-law, Norman L. Boling (Ike), who passed away before the publishing of this novel, thanks for your support and encouragement.

PROLOGUE

...Evil brings death to the wicked;
Those who hate the good are doomed.
The Lord ransoms the souls of his servants.
Those who hide in him shall not be condemned.
Psalm 34

November 12, 1991
Ormoc City, Leyte Island, Philippines

The room carried the dank smell of dirt and putrid water. A makeshift table and three chairs sat off in a far corner against a mildewed canvas tarp that separated the kitchen and living area from the sleeping quarters. Several opened cans of food lay strewn about the floor amid the piles of rodent feces. Stepping inside, the officer buried his face in the crook of his arm to suppress the gag reflex that erupted from the pit of his stomach.

"What's that god awful smell?" he said, between gasps of air.

"Rats, mother-fucking rats," was the reply. The recent flooding and mudslides had caused the rodent population to leave its' flooded quarters and seek shelter in the vacated shacks above the flood line.

"Any witnesses?" he asked, more out of formality to follow the guidebook than an expectation of an affirmative answer.

"No Sir," was the reply, hastily given. "When he didn't show up for chow this morning, I sent a couple of his guys to look for him. They said they found him just like that," he said, nodding in the direction of the corpse, its' raw flesh revealing hundreds of rodent bites.

"No note either, I suppose?"

"No sir. Nothing."

"His service revolver?"

"Yes sir. No one touched anything. I called you as soon as I came in and saw the body. There's a shell casing next to the body. My assumption…He put the weapon in his mouth and pulled the trigger."

"That how you see it Lieutenant?"

"That's how I see it sir. His weapon, one bullet, one shot, no witnesses. Looks like he checked himself out."

CHAPTER 1

Sunday, March 30, 2008

With an ETA of less than forty-five minutes, the Boeing 727 began its descent from its cruising altitude of thirty thousand feet. Less than half full, it was only a matter of time before the airlines would combine this flight with an earlier one or cancel the flight completely. The cost of jet fuel had almost doubled in the last twelve months. The US economy was on a decline. With the increase in airfare and higher costs of consumer goods, people weren't flying as much as they had in the past. Two months earlier, SKYBUS and Eastern were forced to close their doors, seek protection from the Bankruptcy Courts, adding thousands of displaced workers to the long list of unemployment statistics.

Fifteen minutes later, NORTHWEST FLIGHT 1712 entered Washington airspace and lined up on final approach into Reagan National Airport. The interior cabin lights came on and the captain started the announcement requiring all passengers to remain in their seats. The events of September 11, 2001 brought about many changes and procedures in security measures for domestic as well as international air travel. Washington D.C. was especially hit hard by these stricter regulations. The Department of Homeland Security required all passengers to remain in their seats for the last thirty minutes on arrival flights as well as the first thirty minutes on departure flights when traveling to and from the Nations Capital. The Boeing 727 was in route from Minneapolis-St. Paul after a short delay while the ground crew de-iced the plane twice prior to takeoff. A late winter storm had dumped two feet of snow on the twin cities in less than four hours causing numerous delays and cancellations of flights. Air traffic controllers worked diligently to manage the heavy traffic in patterns above the busy airport while ground crews cleared the runways with plows and dump trucks. Snow wasn't unusual for early April in that part of the country but the weather reports had predicted that the storm would miss the Twin cities as it swept the country farther south. The mayor had implemented emergency services, calling for every available worker and maintenance vehicle to be put into service until conditions returned to normal. This storm showed signs of old man winter grasping at straws trying to hold on to the last remnants of a season past.

His flight had originated in Bismarck, North Dakota earlier in the evening, connecting through Minneapolis on his return to Washington after the short Easter recess. Serving his third term in the United States Senate, Senator Clayton Powell was the senior senator from the State of North Dakota, serving as the Chairman of the Senate Armed Services Committee. He had spent the past week with his family in his home state. It had been a difficult decision but he and his wife Sally had decided when he was elected to his first term to keep the family in North Dakota. Sally and the two children would receive support from their extended families and friends while he would make the five hour commute as often as he could. The senator had taken an apartment in Washington in the early years but had recently purchased a small colonial in Georgetown, just a short commute to the Hart Senate Office Building and the U.S. Capitol Building.

"Senator… Senator Powell," she whispered. "I'm sorry sir. We are almost in Washington. Would you please put your seat back in the upright position?"

He had been sleeping soundly for the last hour. Having taken this flight many times, he knew he could get at least an hour of rest on this final leg. He looked out the window as the plane started its descent into Reagan National.

Off in the distance, the lights on the Washington Monument and the Lincoln Memorial shined brightly against the dark sky. As they crossed over the Pentagon he observed the flaps on the wingtips move back and forth as the pilot prepared for landing. Sheets of ice broke loose from the edges and caught in the wind currents, cascading over the wings like panes of broken glass. He heard the thud of the wheels as they descended and locked into position for landing. He smiled with a sense of pride. Next to his family, he loved this job more than anything else. The separation had been difficult but he knew in his heart that they had made the right choice. The plane touched down softly, using the entire length of the runway. Within minutes, it had taxied to the gate and passengers crowded the aisle, pulling their carryon luggage from the overhead compartment, awaiting the opening of the doors. He waited patiently while passengers pushed ahead to get off the plane. He wasn't in any rush. Opening session wasn't until 9 a.m. the following morning and his driver would be waiting for him for the short drive to Georgetown.

Outside the terminal, in a 2002 Dark Green Chevy Tahoe, temporarily on loan from the long term parking garage, a man with a gray stocking hat pulled down almost over his eyes sat patiently awaiting the senator's arrival. He had waited in the passenger pick up area with the engine running for almost a half hour before pulling into the short term parking area, turning off the ignition and leaving to check the flight monitors in the terminal. Halfway down the main terminal, he found the arrival and departure screen displayed over the entrance to the carry-on security check point. Looking down the screen of delayed flights, he found the Northwest flight from Minneapolis that was due in at 7:30 p.m. The plane was on an hour delay which meant he still had a half an hour before the plane was scheduled to arrive. The weather in Minneapolis was causing real problems in the northeast with delays and cancellations of hundreds of flights. *Can't control the weather,* he thought. He resolved himself to getting a cup of coffee at the Starbucks kiosk on his way out the door before returning to the Tahoe to await the planes arrival.

Starting the ignition, he drove the Tahoe back to the waiting area outside the double wide doors, turned off the ignition and sipped his coffee, while he waited. At 8:15 p.m. a dark Lincoln Town Car drove past him and parked curbside in front of the double doors with the engine running. The security guard standing by the doors walked over to the Town Car and spoke to the driver. He couldn't hear what was said between the two but the Town Car was able to remain in the "No Parking" area. Twenty minutes later, he watched as the senator walked through the double doors and headed for the Lincoln. The driver stepped out of the car and ran around the front of the vehicle to open the door to the rear passenger area. He greeted the senator who handed him his carryon luggage. The driver placed it in the trunk of the Town Car before waving to the security officer and getting back into the car. Starting the engine, Stryker fell in behind the dark sedan, keeping his distance as they traveled north along George Washington Memorial Parkway, crossing the Potomac into Georgetown. They drove slowly through the narrow dark streets stopping several times to let the Georgetown college kids cross the street in front of them before finally coming to a stop at 455 Congress Way. He found an empty spot between two parked cars a couple of houses back, shifted into park, turned off the lights and let the car idle while the senator got out of the car and walked up the stairs and into his house. The driver followed with his luggage, placing it inside the open door and nodded to the senator before returning to the Town Car and driving away.

Slowly moving the SUV until he was directly in front of the house, he watched as the light in the room at the end of the hall came on. He knew from his uninvited visit a couple of days earlier that this was the senator's home office. Stryker sat there quietly for ten minutes, just staring at the house. Finally the light went out. *Not tonight senator, not tonight!*

CHAPTER 2

The morning sun pierced the blinds sending rays of dancing light directly into Jake Hunter's face as he fought to keep his eyelids closed for another couple of minutes. It was only six-thirty but he had not needed to set an alarm for over fifteen years. His internal clock went off every morning between six and six thirty.

Hunter had just completed a grueling six month investigation and trial on a devastating prank gone badly when two teenage boys kidnapped and eventually murdered three children from the state of Virginia. The two teenagers had been found guilty of felony murder since the victims had died as a result of the kidnapping, a felony offense. They had taken the victims just to scare them but had stored them bound and gagged in an old ice cream truck in the middle of a twenty acre junkyard outside Rockville, Maryland. By the time they returned for them, the children had suffocated in the back of the sealed truck. The FBI had been involved in the case because the crime occurred across state lines.

Jacob Alexander Hunter was forty four years old. Any fifty year old American remembers the day he was born. Jake was born on November 22, 1963; just one hour after President John F. Kennedy was assassinated in Dallas, Texas. At an even six feet tall, Jake worked hard to keep his weight between one hundred eighty and one eighty-five. He didn't enjoy going to the gym but he had plenty of equipment at home to stay fit. He no longer had the washboard abs that he had at thirty but fifty push-ups in the morning and fifty at night on his Ab Lounger kept his abdomen in decent shape. He ran three to five miles at least four times a week to maintain his cardio system. Jake wasn't always this way. Five years earlier, he had let his weight blossom, tipping the scales at two hundred twenty. He ate all the wrong foods and his exercise consisted of jumping off the couch during the T.V. commercial breaks to raid the refrigerator. On the weekend, he'd enjoy a good cigar with a couple of cold beers. His entire life changed one night as he was getting ready for bed in his apartment in New York City. At the young age of thirty-nine, he had trouble breathing, broke out in a cold sweat, and had numbness in his arms. He called 911 and was rushed to the hospital and admitted to the ICU. After numerous tests and more wires and tubes sticking out of him than he cared to remember, the doctor said he had suffered a mild heart attack. That scared the hell out of him. It was the wake up call he needed. Fortunately, the doctors said he didn't suffer any major damage to the heart muscle but cautioned him on his horrible eating habits and lack of exercise.

Jake was taking the week off to catch up on some long awaited rest and spend some time with his daughter, Sam. Samantha had moved to Alexandria, Virginia last year and worked for a government contractor in Crystal City. She had purchased a townhouse in Alexandria, ten minutes from the Metro Blueline. Jake had been a lead investigator in the New York FBI office for ten years before being reassigned to Washington in December. Jake was in New York City when the twin towers came down, the fear and horror that shook the nation still vivid in his mind. It was a time in his life that he tried to put away but the scenes kept coming back in his dreams. The devastation caused that day will long be remembered by so many who lost family members and friends. Jake had tried for several years to be relocated to Washington. Fortunately, another agent's forced retirement due to a shooting injury opened the door for him. Jake was selected from a group of ten to be the senior agent on the FBI's Task Force on Special Crime. His office was located in the Hoover building in Washington D.C. The Hoover building sat on the North side of Pennsylvania Avenue, equal distance between the White House and the Capitol. Jake had moved in with Sam, occupying the lower level of her townhouse. Due to the caseload he was working, he hadn't spent much time at home recently and had some father daughter time to catch up on.

Sam had taken a couple of days off to do some spring cleaning and spend some time with him. Today was the first day of the Cherry Blossom Festival, celebrated annually in Washington during the first week of April. They had planned on taking the Metro into the city and doing a four mile run beginning at the Capitol. Sam had finally convinced him after hounding him for the last three months to begin training for the Marine Corp Marathon at the end of October. Jake had been an avid race competitor during his younger days but had slacked off in the last ten years. He hadn't even run a 10K race in the past five years. Over the weekend, Sam had mapped out a training schedule on the internet that included numerous distance runs through the city.

After a healthy breakfast of oatmeal with skim milk, a banana and a couple cups of black coffee, they filled their bottles in their running belts with Gatorade and water before heading for the Franconia-Springfield Metro Station three miles away.

CHAPTER 3

The Metro was filled with passengers heading into D.C. to enjoy a day in the city. The sweet smell of cherry blossoms filled the air as Jake and Sam exited the Metro at Capitol South. The Mall was full of kite flyers and Frisbee throwers. Hundreds of students flocked around the Capitol building, touring the grounds, laughing and taking pictures. The Cherry Blossom Festival was a big draw for students from as far away as Ohio, Kentucky and surrounding states. Charter buses lined the streets while the students spent a couple of days in the nation's capital visiting the museums, touring the Capitol and usually stopping at the Gettysburg Battlefields on the way home.

Sam and Jake had decided on a run that would take them up Pennsylvania Avenue past the F.B.I building and White House and then through Foggy Bottom to Washington Circle before turning south toward Constitution Avenue. They were making good time, running at a nine mile pace until they came upon a group of students taking over the sidewalk in front of the Viet Nam Veterans Memorial. Taking a short detour further south behind the Lincoln Memorial to Independence Avenue, they crossed the Kutz Bridge and ran up past the Washington Monument back to Constitution Avenue. Jake's legs were feeling pretty heavy when they turned east on Constitution. They had about seven more blocks to go when Jake told Samantha to keep her pace. He needed to drop down a bit to let the old body catch up. She was waiting for him with a cold bottle of water when he got back to the starting point at the steps of the Capitol.

After they walked another block, his breathing slowed to normal and he felt like he was going to live to see another day.

"I don't know about you, but I'm whipped," he said to Sam.

"You're just out of shape pops," she laughed. "You keep this up and you'll be ready in October. You're not going to break any records but I guarantee you'll finish."

"I don't know. At the rate I'm going, I don't know if I'm ready for twenty-six miles."

"Come on dad, I'll buy you lunch."

They decided to walk to Union Station where they could get something to eat and also catch the Redline over to the Metro Statio.... One of the nice things about Washington is the great public underground transportation system. You can get about anywhere using the Metro by walking no more than a couple of blocks to a stop.

The students had taken over Union Station and they had to wait a little while for a table but put their names on the list at the America Restaurant and took a short walk around the station. Jake had a real passion for great architecture and always enjoyed the majestic ceilings, marble columns and passages leading to the trains. Someone really knew what they were doing when they put that system together.

They got back to the restaurant just as their names were being called. They were seated in the gallery section and both ordered healthy salads and ice water with lemon.

After a nice lunch, Sam and Jake caught the escalator to the bottom level to ride the Redline over to the Metro Station where they switched to the Blueline. The Blueline would take them all the way to the Franconia-Springfield stop where they had left the car earlier in the morning. Within minutes of grabbing their seats on the Blueline, Jake dozed off and didn't wake up until Sam shook him forty minutes later.

"Have a nice nap?"

"I wasn't sleeping. I was just day dreaming."

"Yea, I snore when I day dream too!" she laughed.

CHAPTER 4

Wednesday April 9

Stryker arrived shortly before noon and took a seat with his back to the wall in the outdoor seating area facing Pennsylvania Avenue. He had watched them from his car for the past three Wednesdays. They always came from the direction of the Capitol. They always came at the same time and sat at the same table. The Hawk and Dove Restaurant was a well known hot spot for the Washington bureaucrats, just a short three block walk from the Capitol Building. Its location was convenient and a favorite lunch spot for the Washington powerbroker set. When the temperature reached the low 70's several weeks ago, the owners set out tables and chairs along the sidewalk in front of the restaurant. These were the choice seats on nice days since the restaurant was not air conditioned and the ceiling fans did little but swirl the hot stale air. He waited patiently. He knew they would come. It was almost noon.

After placing his order with the waitress, Stryker glanced down at a copy of the Washington Post he had brought with him. Sipping on his glass of Coke and looking over the top of the newspaper, he saw the colonel coming down the walk in his green Army uniform. They always arrived in the same order, first the colonel, then the director and finally the senator. Within minutes of the colonel sitting down at his table, the other two arrived. They greeted each other with firm handshakes and took seats at the table next to him. The waitress made her way to their table, recited the daily specials and took their drink orders. Returning with their drinks, she took their orders. None of them decided to eat healthy, each ordering a greasy burger with fries. While they waited on their food, they talked about their children, upcoming vacation plans and the colonel's scheduled retirement plans for later in the summer. When their conversation turned to golfing, Stryker's attention picked up. He pretended to read his paper but listened intently to their conversation. The senator confirmed his 6.30 a.m. Saturday morning golf game at the Congressional Course in Bethesda. Stryker heard what he came to hear. He finished his lunch, paid the bill in cash and left the restaurant with newspaper in hand. His mission for the day was accomplished. He headed back up Pennsylvania Avenue toward the Capitol.

CHAPTER 5

Saturday, April 12

Stryker was up at 4 a.m. He had a half hour drive to the course and he wanted plenty of time to get set up. He had learned long ago to plan for the unexpected and be prepared to change the plan. He started the day with the usual 100 push-ups followed by 100 sit-ups. He grabbed a quick breakfast of oatmeal with bananas, two cups of black coffee and his daily ritual of vitamins and herbal supplements.

Before leaving the motel, he checked the weather forecast on the local television station.

"Morning in the low thirty's, high of sixty-five today and mostly sunny," said the newscaster.

He reached in the closet for the Taylormade golf bag he had modified to hold the Remington sniper rifle. The bag would hold everything he needed and still had several clubs sticking out of the top. He didn't want to draw any suspicion if he was seen by anyone. He carefully inspected the weapon for any loose parts and made sure the Nikon scope was seated properly in the rings. Comfortable with the setup, he carefully wrapped the weapon in a soft cloth and inserted it into the bag. He added a box of shells, a silencer and a pair of binoculars. He loaded the Blazer and headed north on the George Washington Parkway, keeping his speed under the limit. He didn't want any chance of being stopped today. Stryker had made a dry run last Saturday and had planned his entry and escape routes with care. He had calculated precisely how long it would take him to get from where he parked the car, over the fence, across the number five fairway and to the clump of trees separating number four and five fairways. From this location, he calculated two hundred seventy-six yards on the range finder to the center of the tee box on hole number four, a par three shot over water.

He arrived shortly after six a.m. and parked the car in an area on the service road that would not draw attention but would enable him to get out of there in a hurry if needed. He grabbed the golf cap from the passenger seat, slung the golf bag over his shoulder and quietly climbed the eight foot fence, dropping to the ground. Keeping low, he walked to the edge of the number five fairway.

Damn, it hadn't been mowed yet. Last weekend, the temperature was in the forties at this time in the morning. He hadn't counted on the cooler morning temperature. There was dew on the ground and his footprints would be seen. He sat there, hidden beneath the pines thinking through the plan. They played every Saturday morning that he was in town. And, they always had the first tee time which was at six-thirty a.m. By the time they got to the number four tee, it was an hour to an hour and fifteen minutes. They should be on the tee around seven thirty. He had planned on being on location an hour before they arrived on the tee. He waited patiently, knowing their tee time would be delayed as well. He just didn't know how long that would be. Then he heard the Kubota tractor coming down the third fairway. It would take four passes with the 18 gain mower and the driver would be done with number three fairway. With the pond on four, there wasn't any fairway to mow so he would come immediately over and do the fifth fairway. Stryker looked at his watch and waited. After sixteen minutes, the Kubota was finishing his last pass on three. The driver stopped, picked up the mowers and drove the tractor through the rough to the fifth fairway. Stryker stayed hidden in the tree line as the tractor made its first pass by him. He checked his watch as the tractor continued to make three more passes then stopped at the end of the fairway. After a couple of minutes, with the tractor still stopped, the engine running, Stryker peered out from under the trees to see what was going on. He saw two maintenance men in a golf cart talking with the tractor driver. He couldn't risk being seen if he chanced crossing the fairway now.

"Come on, Come on," he said to himself, losing patience. It was already after seven and he didn't know how long their tee time had been delayed. Thankfully, he had given himself that extra hour for circumstances just like this. Then he heard the tractor leaving and saw the golf cart heading away toward the clubhouse. Quickly, he picked up the golf bag and made his way across the fairway. He slid between the trees and found his spot. From his location, he could see the entire tee box but was hidden by the pines on either side of him. He took out the ATB binoculars and glassed past the number four tee down the number three fairway. He could see two golf carts about halfway down the fairway and coming his way.

They had only been delayed about fifteen minutes. Quickly he pulled the rifle out of the bag and screwed the silencer into the end of the barrel. Grabbing the range finder, he looked through the view finder until he spotted the tee markers at the far back of the tee. He calculated the distance at two hundred eighty seven yards. He sat there quietly while they approached the green. From his vantage point, he could see them laughing and carrying on. He checked the distance on the range finder one more time before stowing it in a side pocket in the golf bag. Picking up the rifle, he waited.

They were now on the green and putting. Less than five minutes and it would all be over. He watched as they finished putting and replaced the flag. Three of the golfers "high-fived" the taller man as they made their way to the golf carts. *Must've been a good hole, he thought.*

The taller man walked the short distance to the tee as the other three brought the carts around. He obviously had honors, given the celebration on the prior green. He stood there looking over the water at the flag waving 180 yards in the distance and shouted to his cart mate for a club. When all four players had made it to the tee, the taller man took center stage, said something funny to the other three and took a practice swing.

Stryker sat motionless downrange. He looked through the scope and held the Remington steady. Holding his breath, he watched as the golfer took his backswing.

Squeezing ever so gently, "Pfft", the bullet entered the forehead, midway between the eyes, exploding the back of his head, sending gray matter on the remaining three golfers standing behind him. He lay lifeless before his ball hit the green rolling within two feet of the pin. *"No birdies for you today, Senator."*

CHAPTER 6

Jake had been tossing and turning in his sleep for the past several weeks but last night was exceptionally difficult. Even a couple of Melatonin didn't give him the rest his body so desperately wanted. He watched his digital clock flip through the hours, catching solitary moments of rest before he found himself starring blankly again at the ceiling fan rotating above his head. The hours came and went but at four a.m., he finally decided it was a lost cause and climbed out of bed.

As he walked from the bedroom to the study, he realized how quiet the house was at night. For the first time, he heard the water shut off in the bathroom as the toilet bowl filled and the ice dropping in the refrigerator ice-maker. He hadn't really paid much attention to these sounds in the past.

Jake had been trying to read a biography of Winston Churchill for the past two months and thought maybe trying to muddle through the dry details would make him drowsy but after fifteen minutes of reading the same paragraph over numerous times, he decided this was going to be a waste of time. He put the book down and checked his email messages. Nothing good, only garbage that seemed to elude the scam filters during the night.

Jake turned on the Cuisinart coffeemaker and flipped through the remote searching for CNN while he waited for the coffee to brew. After two cups of coffee and catching up on the latest news, he looked for his Asics running shoes. He had decided during the night at one of his many awake moments to run in the morning. He had missed the last two days and needed to keep to his training schedule if he was going to make the Marine Corp Marathon in October. He planned on getting ten miles of hard roadwork today before it got too hot and humid. At five-thirty, it was starting to lighten up enough to avoid being hit by any cars but still beat the busy morning traffic. Jake found his nylon running shorts, his Nike running hat and his "Tru-Fit" knee band that he wore below his right knee to stabilize the joint which he had injured twenty years earlier in a high school wresting meet. He laced up his Asics, double knotting them to keep them from untying and disconnected his IPOD from the computer after updating it with another hundred songs. He bought himself the IPOD Scrambler for his last birthday, finding it easier to run when he was listening to music. Before leaving the house, he put his cell phone in his zippered pocket and slipped his Springfield 9mm backup piece into his fanny pack. Locking the door, he stretched his hamstrings on the outside railing before heading down Wendron Way toward Van Dorn Avenue. He had decided to warm up by running the half mile around the lake at the bottom of the hill before venturing north toward Old Town, Alexandria.

A dense fog hung low over the lake, the cooler night air mixing with the warmer water below. As he ran along the lake, Jake couldn't see the frogs but heard them splash as he passed, leaving ripples where they entered the water. Twice he had to move to the high grass to dodge the geese that had taken ownership of the path. Jake was in no mood to argue with them at this time in the morning. The mornings had always been Jake's favorite time of day. It had rained a little through the night and the air had a wormy smell. Although there were many running and bike paths in the area, he still preferred the streets but that meant staying alert and dodging crazy drivers. Sam accused him of having a death wish and refused to run with him when he hit to the streets. Traffic was light on Van Dorn as he crossed over I-95. He was about two miles into his run when a glance at his Nike running watch indicated that he was on a nine mile pace. If he could keep this up for the next seven miles, he would be satisfied with his progress. His goal was to run the 26 mile October race in under four hours.

Jake completed the run in good time without any collisions with cars or bikers and decided to walk around the lake again to cool down before heading back to the townhouse. His phone rang just as he slowed to walk. It was Sam. She was out of town on business for a few days and called him every morning for their daily "chats". "So, what are you doing?" she asked when he flipped open the phone. "Did I wake you?"

"Not quite," he responded, still trying to catch his breath. "Hell I've been up all night. Couldn't sleep so I decided to go for a run this morning. I just finished ten miles. You would be proud of your ole' man. I made it in a little over an hour and a half… An hour, thirty-two to be exact!"

"That so," she said. "You sound pretty proud of yourself."

"I am," he said. "Hey, hold on a minute, I have another call coming in."

After taking a thirty second call from his office, he reconnected back with Sam.

"Gotta go Sam. There's been a shooting at the Congressional Golf Course and all hell is gonna let loose. I'll call you later."

CHAPTER 7

Jake glanced at his watch as he entered the front door. A ten minute delay in his arrival wasn't going to change the outcome of this case. He grabbed a bottle of water and decided to take a quick shower before heading out to Bethesda. As he walked by the study on his way to the bedroom for a change of clothes, he heard the CNN newscaster break in for a special announcement. There had been a fatal shooting at the Congressional Golf Course. No mention of identity of the victim but the word being passed around was that it was someone "really important". That could only mean someone in the Washington political scene. The Bethesda PD would handle the usual homicide in their area. The FBI would only be called in on special cases.

In less than ten minutes, he had showered, shaved and was dressed in a navy blue suit, white shirt and dark tie. He grabbed his Sig Sauer P229 .40 SW and shoulder holster from the hook inside his closet door. After much debate, the FBI had gone to the Sig Sauer with 12 shot capacity for law enforcement several years ago as it's handgun of choice. Taking another bottle of water from the fridge and a couple of granola bars, he closed the door behind him and jumped into his Infinity G37 for the thirty minute drive to the Country Club. This was going to be a long morning and he could feel his stomach grumbling already.

Jake knew by the time he got to the course that the network and cable stations would be broadcasting the events of the day from vans with their satellite antennas reaching above the trees. Media coverage on this kind of news would be excessive. Reporters trying to get the latest updates would be swarming the place for any bit of information that would give them an edge. He decided to take the I-495 Capital Beltway around instead of the shorter route on the George Washington Memorial Parkway. It was a couple of extra miles but would keep him out of the tourist traffic that would be starting to build up through Arlington and D.C. at this time of day.

Thirty minutes and several cell calls later, Jake pulled off the beltway and turned off onto River Road to the entrance of the Golf Course. As he expected, cars and vans were parked on both sides of the road leading to the entrance to the course. Local newscasters jostled for position, jamming microphones in front of anyone that would give them a scoop or headliner that they could later call an exclusive on the evening news. TV cameras were everywhere you looked. Jake recognized newscasters from CNN, Fox and some of the network affiliates. The Bethesda PD were holding the crowd back and trying to keep the entrance clear for emergency vehicles. Jake found a place to squeeze into behind a Washington Post van and left his car for the short walk to where two officers were checking ID's. He intentionally kept his head down and away from the crowd as he worked his way through to the officer in charge. Flashing his ID, he was directed to the clubhouse where Bethesda PD had set up a command post. On entering the clubhouse, Jake was introduced to Doug Warren, Bethesda's Police Chief who had been waiting for him. Chief Warren said he'd brief him on the way to the crime scene as he ushered him toward a golf cart. Jake jumped in the golf cart and grabbed the hand hold on the roof as they made their way through the course, leaving the cart path for the shorter route across a couple of fairways. The Medical Examiner had not yet arrived. She had been tied up with numerous fatalities from a jack knifed tractor trailer causing a 14 vehicle pileup snarling traffic for five miles on 270 North. The morning fog had been heavy but that didn't stop the excessive speeds and reckless drivers.

The course had been shut down and all of the players on the course had brought to the clubhouse for questioning. Fortunately, it was early in the morning and there weren't many golfers on the course. As they approached the third green, Jake could see that crime-scene tape had been stretched around the fourth tee. An ambulance was parked next to the tee. No siren, its emergency flashers blinking. The Crime Scene Unit from Bethesda was there snapping pictures and collecting evidence. The victim was a U.S. Senator, Senator Clayton Powell from North Dakota. Chief Warren said that the men playing with the senator were still there as he pointed in the direction of three men huddled together at the edge of the green. Other than draping a blue tarp over the body, the CS Unit was careful not to disturb the crime scene.

Jake approached the tarp, lifting a corner to look at the victim. The senator had been shot in the center of the forehead and was lying in a pool of blood. From what he could see, he guessed the victim was dead before he hit the ground.

"Helluva shot," Chief Warren said. "Don't know where it came from. Those guys over there are pretty shaken up. Haven't said much."

Jake finished taking a couple of notes and approached the men, introducing himself as Special Agent Jake Hunter with the FBI. When he started asking questions about what had happened, the younger man blurted out.

"I can't believe it! We were just playing a little golf. You know, horsing around a little and joking. The senator was two under par going into the fourth hole."

"He was up on the tee telling us how he was going to show us how to make a hole in one. The next thing I know, we're all splattered with blood and Clay's on the ground not moving. We didn't know what happened."

"Yea, it was so sudden. Didn't hear a thing," said another who had obviously lost his breakfast on the front of his shirt. "We ran for cover over by that tree but didn't know what the hell was going on."

"Did you see anyone else before the shooting?" Jake asked to no one in particular.

"We're the first group off when we play so there's no one ahead of us. The guy cutting the fairways a couple greens ahead and a couple of maintenance guys in a golf cart is all we saw until this happened."

"You didn't hear the shot? Didn't see anyone running from the scene?" Jake asked.

"Nothing, didn't hear anything."

Jake figured the shooter had probably used a silencer so as to not give away his position. At this time, he didn't have any idea which direction the shot had come from.

As Jake continued speaking with the three distraught men, a Black SUV made its way down the fairway and parked in the rough between the green and the tee box. A very attractive brunette jumped out of the passenger side and walked over to the tee. She removed the tarp and knelt down next to the body with a medical bag and slipped on a pair of latex gloves.

Jake asked the men to remain there for further questions while he made his way over to visit with the ME.

"Jake Hunter," he said, approaching her from the back. She looked up at him and smiled.

"Jillian Harris, Medical Examiner from Bethesda. I'd shake your hand but as you can see, it's a little messy right now."

Jake figured that by the time she arrived, she had already been informed of the identity of the victim.

"Without the hole in the center of his head, this guy could be a dead ringer for Senator Powell," she said, giving him a smirk.

"I'd say by the looks of things that the senator has seen better days," she added.

"So far, looks to be a single shot to the forehead. Pretty powerful bullet to take the back of his head off the way it did. I'll know more when my forensic chemist gets a look at it back at the lab.

"Any suspects?" she asked as she rose. "You can go on and bag him," she said to the two attendants who had arrived with her.

As they continued to speak, the two attendants lifted the corpse and placed a black body bag under the victim, sealing it with a zipper before putting it on a stretcher and rolling it to the back of the squad wagon.

She removed her gloves, putting them in a plastic bag in her medical kit and extended her hand.

"Well, I guess I'm out of here. I'm sure we'll be talking." She handed Jake her card and said she'd call him when the autopsy was completed.

Jake returned to the three men still sitting on the grass.

"Senator left or right handed?" he asked, trying to get a position on the shooter's location.

"He was right. Why? What's that have to do with anything?" responded the younger guy.

"Because if he was right…and he stood like this on the tee…the shot would have come from somewhere in that direction," Jake indicated, pointing to the tree line along the fourth fairway.

He finished up his notes with the players, got their contact information for any follow-up later and let them go. Jake didn't think they had any intention of finishing their round.

The chief and Jake jumped back into the golf cart and made their way over to the tree line separating the fourth and fifth fairway, looking for any indication that a shooter had been hiding for a shot at the senator.

When the chief stopped the cart, they jumped out and started walking along the edge of the fairway. The grass was still wet and didn't take long for the wetness to penetrate Jake's shoes, creeping up his pant legs. Grass clippings collected on his shoes.

"Unless the shooter was part of the maintenance crew, he wouldn't know where the tees would be placed in the morning so he'd have to plan on getting a good visual of the entire tee box," Jake said.

"Yea, you're right," agreed the chief. "You don't think it's anyone working here, do ya?" he finished.

"At this time, everyone's a potential killer," Jake said, continuing to look for footprints.

He walked along the tree line keeping the fourth tee in sight until he could get a good view of the entire tee box.

"Anywhere in this area would be about a 275 yard shot," he said, stopping near an area with a clear view of the tee.

Jake ducked under the branches of an evergreen and looked into a cleared area about five feet in diameter. The grass had been trampled and there was evidence that someone had recently been there.

"Over here," he hollered. "Looks like someone's been sitting in here recently. This area has definitely been disturbed. Looks like some boot prints," he said, pointing under an overhanging bush. "This would make a good hiding place. You're completely secluded in the back with these pines and you've got a full view of the tee. Someone could sit in here all day if they wanted and would not have been seen."

Jake crept low and scooted his way through the pines to the other side.

"Why don't you bring the cart around and we'll see what's over there," he hollered back through the pines.

The chief brought the cart around the pines and they started across another fairway to a clump of trees. Though the trees Jake could see a chain link fence. Outside the fence was a service road that ran up along the outside of the course.

"I'd guess that our shooter came from this direction," he said, pointing in the direction of the service road. "At that time in the morning, he could have left a vehicle here, climbed the fence unseen, ran across the fairway and hid in the pines over there until he needed to take his shot."

"Let's head back to the clubhouse and talk to the maintenance crew. Somebody was out mowing grass this morning and they could have seen something."

Before heading back to the clubhouse, they stopped at the tee to let the CS Unit know what they had found. The CS Unit would spend the better part of the day collecting evidence samples, taking photos, dusting for prints and making molds of the boot prints Jake had pointed out under the Pine trees along the fairway.

Jake spent the next couple of hours talking with the grounds crew including the fairway mower, the maintenance crew, two other foursomes playing behind the senator and a foursome that had not yet tee'd off. Other than golfers on the course, no one saw anything out of the ordinary and Jake didn't have any reason at that time to suspect that anyone working there was the shooter.

Jake didn't have a lot to go on but he knew that with a high profile victim, there was going to be a lot of questions and not a lot of time to come up with answers. The powers that be would want a suspect arrested soon and brought to trial. Fortunately, his partner, Sully Gilmore would be back from his vacation in Florida tomorrow. This case was going to take priority and Sully could be a bulldog when necessary. Jake called Sam to let her know he was going to be late and she would have to catch a cab when she landed at Dulles later that night. He finished for the day with Chief Warren, exchanging business cards before departing the clubhouse through the side door. He didn't have any answers and didn't want to face the cameras until he did. It was mid afternoon when he merged onto US I-495 South, heading for his office in the Hoover building.

CHAPTER 8

The smell of Hoppes No. 9 filled the room as Stryker sat in the middle of the floor running a three piece cleaning rod with a brass wire brush attached to the end up and down the barrel of the Remington. Gun powder residue fell out the end of the barrel collecting on the white towel he had taken from the bathroom. Exchanging the wire brush for a cotton patch, he saturated the patch with lubricating oil and repeated the procedure, leaving a light film of oil on the interior of the barrel. Cleaning the Remington brought back memories long forgotten; memories of early morning deer hunts in Ohio with uncles sitting around the kitchen table, drinking beer and taunting each other over who was going to get the biggest buck. He reached into his shirt pocket and pulled out a crumpled picture. The picture was old and the edges were frayed but it meant a lot to have it with him. A half eaten Subway and a crumpled Washington Post lay on the bed where he had been slouching all afternoon. Earlier, he flipped through the channels, listening to the newscasters speculate on the shooting of the great Senator Clayton Powell. It made him sick to see how patronizing they were. *You would have thought by their comments that the great senator was worthy of their praise.* There was talk of conspiracy, terrorist cells, mafia. He listened intently and smiled at their wild guesses.

They didn't have a clue!

Little did they know the real senator!

He waited in the room until dark before packing everything into the Subaru wagon he had borrowed earlier that afternoon from the long term parking garage at Reagan International. It was 8 p.m. when Stryker headed south on US I-95 out of town for the three hour trip to the Virginia beaches and a couple of weeks in the sun. Things needed to cool down a bit and he needed some quiet time to plan his next move. Setting the cruise at 65 mph, he tuned into the local country western station and listened to the music.

CHAPTER 9

Jake spent the remainder of the afternoon with Director Avery in FBI headquarters at the Hoover Building in Washington. The director was getting pounded pretty heavy by the Senate Committee on Violent Crimes and needed to give them something soon. Before Jake left the golf course, he had spent several hours talking with everyone who had been at the golf course when the senator was killed. The only lead he had was from one of the ground maintenance men who was raking sand bunkers that morning. The worker had seen a lone golfer walking along the tree line with a golf bag but thought that he was looking for a lost ball. Since the senator was in the first foursome, that would have had to be someone else playing behind the senator's group, who would have had to cross two fairways to be where he was seen. None of the other players who were on the course at the time were anywhere near that location. The CS Unit had taken pictures, dusted for prints and taken molds of a couple of partial footprints around the area that he pointed out to them under the trees. Jake wasn't very hopeful that this would amount to much.

By six o'clock, he had not heard back yet from the CS Unit or Dr. Harris who was doing the autopsy on the senator. She said it would be several hours before she had anything. Jake didn't have much to go until he heard back from the lab so he decided to call it a day and go home. On his way out, he left a message with the front desk to call him if Dr. Harris or the lab called.

Jake called Sam on his cell phone on the way home. The cab had just dropped her off at the house and she had not eaten any dinner either. He needed to kick off his shoes for a while and decided to pick up a pizza on the way home. A couple of beers and an "everything pizza" would just about do the trick.

CHAPTER 10

Sam and Jake sat on the deck overlooking the pond while they scarfed down slice after slice of pizza and chased it with a couple of cold Corona's. An outsider would have thought they hadn't eaten in days. Dr. Harris had called just as Jake arrived home. No great revelations. The bullet that took out the back of the senator's head was a 7.62 Nato Caliber, fired from a Remington M24 Sniper Rifle. The CS Unit had recovered the bullet using a metal detector. It had settled in the rough grass behind the tee after doing its damage. The molds made from the boot prints were not deep enough to get a good match for any type of tread. It looked like a small boot in the 8-9 size but that was just an educated guess. Dr. Harris agreed to meet Jake at her office first thing Monday morning. After the day he had, it felt good to sit back with his feet up. Jake just wanted to sit there for a couple of hours, clear his head and forget about everything else. The sky was clear and the night air had started to cool down. He closed his eyes for a couple of minutes but then drifted off into a deep sleep. A loud snore, more like a grunt, from within awoke him and he opened his eyes. The sky was clear of clouds and filled with stars. Sam had laid a light blanket over him and was still sitting next to him.

"How long have I been asleep?"

"Not long, probably close to an hour. You looked so peaceful; I didn't want to wake you."

"Did I talk in my sleep?"

"No. But you snored and made all kinds of weird noises until you woke yourself up. You sound like a bear when you snore. I don't know how mom ever put up with it."

"Your mom was a saint," he said. "If you only knew half of what she put up with. Do you miss her much Sam?"

"I really do dad. I think about her often. There are times when I think she's right next to me. It's kinda eerie. I feel like she's watching over me."

"I'm sure she is." Jake gently put his arm around her shoulders.

It was good to spend time with Sam. He had missed a lot of quality time with her while she was growing up. Jake was out of town on an assignment when Rachael and Sam were out shopping one Saturday afternoon. They had stopped for a drink at the Starbucks on the corner when Rachael suddenly suffered a brain aneurism and died before the squad arrived. Sam was only thirteen and growing up without a mother to help her through her teenage years was difficult for her. He tried his best to be a father and mother to her but couldn't relate to what teenage girls go through when their hormones are raging and their moods change from one minute to another. Sam had several aunts who tried to step in but Jake attributed Sam's independence and strong will to her way of coping with the loss of her mother at such a young age. He was so proud of her. She had completed high school a year early in the top of her class, graduated from college in three years and was commissioned as an Army Officer. She spent five years as an intelligence officer in the Army, serving in Bosnia and Iraq, before resigning her commission last year and moving to Alexandria.

At midnight they decided to get some sleep. Tomorrow was Sunday and who knows what that might bring.

CHAPTER 11

Monday, April 14

Monday morning started off bright and early as Jake rolled out of bed at 5 a.m. and started the coffee. He knew he had a busy day ahead of him. Dr. Harris was planning on releasing the senator's remains to the family this morning. Jake needed to get up there by 8 a.m. to speak with the senator's aid who was accompanying the senator's body back to South Dakota on a Delta flight at noon.

With coffee in hand, he fired up his laptop for a quick read of the front pages on the Washington Post, New York Times and Wall Street before jumping into the shower. Sam joined him on the deck for a quick breakfast before she left to catch the Metro to Crystal City. Jake loaded the dishwasher and headed out the door at seven to meet with the M.E. before she released the body.

Jake arrived at the coroner's office just as Dr. Harris was pulling in to the parking lot. Together, they walked towards her office.

"We really didn't have the chance to talk much the other day," she said. "With the multiple car accident on the freeway and then the call about the senator, I was pretty frazzled. I apologize if I sounded short with you."

"I didn't notice," he responded, looking down at her ring finger. She didn't wear a wedding band but nowadays, that doesn't necessarily tell the story. Her administrative assistant had already made the coffee and brought them a couple of cups while they talked. Sitting across the desk from her, he couldn't help but notice her piercing blue eyes. Her medical degree from John Hopkins was hanging on the wall behind her and he squinted over his reading glasses to read the year.

"1992," she said, startling him with her response.

"I'm sorry. I didn't realize that I was being that obvious," he blushed, feeling the heat and redness increasing in his face. *That makes you about 41, he thought to himself.*

"Not a problem. I do the same thing whenever I walk into anyone's office where they have a pedigree hanging."

"Here, I made a copy for you," she said as she handed him a copy of her autopsy report.

"You can browse through this while you're waiting. I have a couple of final things to do to get the body prepared for transport."

As Jake watched her walk out of the room, he took a quick gulp of his coffee and began to read her report, inclusive of pictures she had taken. Her examination had revealed a single gunshot, with the bullet entering the left frontal lobe before taking out the back of the senator's head as it exited. After about twenty minutes, she returned and handed him a marked plastic bag containing the bullet the CS Unit had recovered in the grass.

"Other than the trauma from the bullet, the senator was in perfect health; no prior broken bones, no evidences of prior surgeries, no organ disease," she said. "If it hadn't been for the shooting, the senator could have lived to be a hundred years old."

The senator's aide, John Carson, arrived a little after 8 a.m. accompanied by the local funeral director. While the funeral director spoke with Dr. Harris and made arrangements for the transportation of the body, Jake took the time to speak with John. He was going to accompany the body back to South Dakota where the senator was going to receive a state funeral and burial on Thursday morning. John would be back in Washington late Friday morning. He agreed to meet with Jake later Friday afternoon and provide him with a copy of the senator's schedule for the past couple of months and a list of the senator's contacts, appointments, phone records, emails and BlackBerry messages. Hopefully, something in this information would indicate a motive for the murder and give Jake a lead on the potential killer. He gave John his card in case he thought of something important on the long flight to South Dakota.

As Jake left the medical examiner's office, he decided to drive to Quantico and speak with Chuck Embers. Chuck was a ballistic expert with the FBI who had helped him several times while he was trying to solve a couple of murders earlier on in his career.

On his way to Quantico, Jake called Sully at the office to let him know he'd be in after his meeting with Chuck. Lynne answered the call and told him that Sully's plane was delayed and wouldn't be landing until later that afternoon.

Due to a vehicle accident, the traffic on I-95 South was stop and go. It took

Jake over an hour before he saw the sign for Exit 150, Quantico, Virginia, home of the FBI's Behavioral Analysis Unit (BAU) and the U.S. Marine Corp Base since its inception in 1917. He hadn't called ahead but fortunately, he caught Chuck just as he was leaving for lunch.

"Hey Jake, I was just getting out of here for some lunch. Why don't you join me? There's a quiet little restaurant just down the road a bit. We can talk there."

"Sounds good. I'll drive. My car's right outside the front door."

"You're on. I'll even let you buy."

"So. How are you doing Chuck?"

"I'm on this side of the dirt," he replied.

Chuck was fifty five years old and after two unsuccessful marriages, was a confirmed bachelor. He had been with the Bureau for the past twenty two years. Two years ago he was diagnosed with colon cancer during a routine physical. After a successful operation and three months of radiation treatment, he took life one day at a time. After looking over the menu and thinking about a greasy burger and fries, they both agreed to eat healthy and ordered salads with low cal dressing.

During lunch, Jake took the opportunity to pick Chuck's brain on the specifics of the Remington M-24 Sniper Rifle. Chuck had fired it several times over the past six months and was familiar with its characteristics. The barrel's unique rifling allows for reduced bullet deformation with much higher bullet velocities. According to Chuck, the military was now using it as the weapon of choice for sniper activity in Iraq and Afghanistan. Due to its unsurpassed accuracy at extended ranges, multiple-shot capacity and durability, many SWAT teams nationwide as well as government agencies, and NRA marksmanship schools had also switched over to the Remington M-24 within the last year. With this new information from Chuck, Jake now had his work cut out for him. He needed to get a list of everyone who had purchased this rifle in the last six months.

CHAPTER 12

Tuesday, April 29

It had been over two weeks since Stryker had taken a room at the Motel 8 on the beach and Virginia Beach was getting old. Eating McDonalds everyday was getting boring. Stryker kept up with the investigation by reading the daily Washington Post and watching the local news channels. According to recent reports, no one had been arrested for the senator's murder and there were no leading suspects. Stryker had paid cash for the room through the end of the week. Things had cooled down enough in Washington for Stryker to return. He decided to head back to Washington on Saturday. He turned off the television, grabbed his ball cap and left the motel room in search of a pizza shop. Walking south along the boardwalk, he found a Pizza Hut Restaurant a mile from the motel. Following the sign at the register that said to "Seat Yourself", he found an empty booth at the back of the room and sat facing the front door. The waitress took his drink order and left a menu with him while she left to fill his drink order. Returning shortly with a pitcher of coke, she took Stryker's order for a medium pepperoni pizza. He dug into the pizza when she brought it to the table, the steam rising, it having come right from the oven. The pizza tasted great, having filled himself with cheeseburgers and fries for most of the week. He finished all but four slices, his eyes being bigger than his stomach and asked for a box to take the rest of the pizza with him. Leaving half a pitcher of coke on the table with a three dollar tip, he paid cash at the register and left the restaurant, carrying the pizza box with him.

He decided to walk along the beach on his way back to the motel. At this time of night, the beach was nearly deserted except for a couple of teenagers setting off firecrackers farther down toward the boardwalk. The stars were bright against the clear dark sky and he kicked off his shoes, walking in the surf, the bottoms of his jeans getting wet from the tide running up the beach. A half a mile from the motel he left the waters edge to sit in the middle of a sand dune. He lay back in the sand and looked up at the sky trying to pick out the constellations. It reminded him so much of back home in Ohio lying in the farm fields at night, looking at shooting stars dart across the darkened sky.

CHAPTER 13

Jake had spent the better part of ten days going over the senator's schedule for the two months prior to his murder. John had filled him in on what the senator had been working on up until that fateful Saturday morning. The senator had numerous appointments with lobbyists, bankers, school officials, etc. With the help of his office assistant, Lynn Miller, Jake and Sully checked every phone call made or received from the senator's cell phone as well as his office and home phones. Lynn spent countless hours reviewing the senator's appointment calendar and BlackBerry messages. Jake had the forensic accountants at the bureau go over the senator's books, his private bank records and all political financial records. They didn't come up with any discrepancies other than a couple of minor balancing errors that amounted to less than a hundred dollars. In addition to chairing the Senate Arms Committee, the senator served on several other committees. He had been in office long enough to make a lot of friends as well as piss off a fair number of people. The senator was quite outspoken on a number of hot issues. He was a right wing republican that spoke openly against abortion, gay rights and same sex marriage. An ex-military officer, he was a strong supporter of the military and voted for sending our troops in to Iraq in 2003 and supported President Bush's efforts to "stay the course".

There was nothing in the senator's records indicating that he had received any threats. Jake and Sully interviewed the senator's staff before starting in on his calendar. Outside of his political commitments, the senator had a standing golf match three out of four Saturdays a month at 6:30 a.m. at the Congressional course in nearby Bethesda, Maryland. On the odd Saturday, he was in South Dakota, flying out there on Thursday evenings after close of session. The senator's personal life was pretty routine. He stayed in Washington for three out of four weeks a month, having recently purchased a historic home in the Georgetown area. His wife and children still resided in the family home in South Dakota. He flew there on the third Thursday of every month, returning to

Washington the following Sunday evening. According to John, the senator took the same Delta flight each time he made the round trip and was picked up by his driver at Reagan upon landing. Jake called Lynn and asked her to requisition a copy of the flight passenger manifests for his past four trips to and from South Dakota. He didn't know if that would lead to anything but he still didn't have any suspects. Everyone they spoke to about the senator's personal life indicated that he was an upstanding person; his moral compass always pointing due north, no hidden affairs, no problem with alcohol or illegal drugs and no secrets in his closets. That one bothered Jake. Everyone has some secrets from their past that they would rather not remember.

The senator met every Wednesday for lunch with two friends he had known for the past twenty years. They always met at noon at the Hawk and Dove, not fifteen minutes by foot from the Capitol. Colonel John Stacker was attached to the Pentagon and David Preacher was the current Deputy Director of the Central Intelligence Agency, having replaced Ben Johnson last year after Johnson resigned for personal reasons.

Jake got the phone numbers for the colonel and director from John and decided that he and Sully would interview them separately for consistency of their stories.

Colonel Stacker had a pretty busy schedule but invited them to meet with him at his office on Thursday morning. Director Preacher was traveling and was not expected back in the office until Friday afternoon.

CHAPTER 14

Thursday, May 1

Jake met Sully at the office early Thursday morning and they rode together to Colonel Hatcher's office arriving at the Pentagon at 8:30 a.m. for their 9:00 a.m. appointment knowing that it would take them about a half hour to get through security. After September 11, 2001, the security at all Federal buildings in D.C. had been intensified with concrete pavers lining the entrances to all the buildings to stop any bomb laden vehicles from getting within fifty feet of any building. Many of the buildings had Marine snipers on the rooftops, ready to shoot at any threat.

Pulling up to the entrance to the Pentagon, they had to show their drivers license, FBI ID's and badges before being able to drive through the security gate to the parking lot. After finding a parking space, they walked toward the front door where they were required to walk through a metal detector before gaining access to the building. Jake and Sully, having been at the Pentagon on numerous occasions, had permits to carry their service weapons within the premises and were cleared through without delay. Walking up to the front desk, they provided their ID's to the receptionist who called upstairs to the colonel's office to confirm their appointment. Hanging up the phone after making the call, she provided Jake and Sully with temporary badges while they waited on their escort who would take them to the colonel's office. The place was a madhouse with people scurrying everywhere. It reminded Jake of Times Square at lunch hour during his stint of duty in New York City.

After fifteen minutes which seemed like an eternity, a tall dark haired man who appeared to be in his early thirties with a muscular build that filled out his starched Army uniform, captain's bars on his shoulders, appeared in the doorway.

"Agent Hunter?" he said, lifting his eyes without even acknowledging Sully, the only other person in the room.

"I'm Captain Grissom, the colonel's XO."

"XO. What's that?" asked Sully.

"Executive Officer," he murmured, looking with disdain at Sully.

Jake extended his hand but the captain quickly turned to the door. "Please follow me sir. The colonel's ready for you in his office."

They rode an elevator to the third floor without another word being said, everyone starring straight ahead. When the door opened, they took a turn to the right and followed the captain down a wide corridor with offices on both sides and what appeared to be a large briefing room before entering a room at the end of the hall.

"If you'll wait here a minute sir, I'll see if the colonel's ready for you," he said, knocking on the door and then entering the colonel's private office.

"No problem," Jake said, looking at the pictures on the wall depicting soldiers and marines in various combat situations reflecting images from World War II through the current debacle in Iraq.

"The colonel will see you now," he said, re-entering the outer office and holding the door for them.

Jake and Sully walked past the captain and entered the colonel's private sanctuary. He was seated behind a large mahogany desk, a US Flag and an Army Flag, 1st Infantry Division were posted on either side of the credenza to his rear. Jake quickly glanced around the office noticing what appeared to be war souvenirs and combat relics sitting on the bookcases and side tables.

Colonel Hatcher rose as they entered the room, greeted them with handshakes and motioned for them to sit in the two large leather chairs in front of his desk.

"Agents Hunter and Gilmore," he started. "I'm glad you're here. What happened to the senator was despicable. I can't for the life of me come up with any reason why someone would do such a thing. Well, I've known Senator Powell for over twenty years. He was truly a good man. He did a lot for this country and the State of North Dakota. He left a wife and two children. I hope you catch the sonovabitch that did this. Anything I can do to help you, you just ask."

"When did you and the senator first meet?" Jake asked.

"Back in Desert Storm. Clayton was a Captain at that time. He was the platoon leader. I served under him. We should have finished the job over there the first time. If we had, we wouldn't be in the mess we're in now with over three thousand American deaths so far. Don't tell anyone I told you that or I'll be looking for a new job before my retirement in October."

"Yes sir, it's a different army today than it was twenty years ago," he added.

"So, you've been friends ever since?" Sully asked, trying to get back to the point of their meeting.

"Yes sir," the colonel replied, aware that he was getting off track. "The senator, Joe Preacher, he's the director, ah... Deputy Director of the CIA, and I've been friends ever since we served together in Iraq."

"Ever serve time?" he asked, standing and looking at a picture hanging on the wall. "It's amazing how close you get," he continued, not waiting for either of them to reply.

"No, I guess I kinda slipped between the cracks," Jake replied. "Viet Nam was over by the time I was old enough to get drafted and then the all volunteer service came in. I never took the opportunity to do any time in the service. Sometimes I regret that. I think the military is probably a good idea for most people. Makes a lot of em grow-up. I suppose you do get pretty close when your butt's on the line with someone shooting bullets at you from everywhere."

"Yea," he muttered.

"Tell me, Colonel, anyone you know of that might have had it in for the senator? Anything from your past that you can think of?" Jake asked.

"Nothing." I can't think of anybody that would harm Clayton Powell. The man was a pillar in the community. Top dog he was. One of the finest men you would ever want to meet."

"I understand you had lunch with the senator every Wednesday," Jake followed up.

"Yea, yea... We meet every Wednesday around noon. Well, we did anyway until this happened. The senator, Joe and I. We ate at the Hawk and Dove, a little joint not far from the Capitol. The senator liked to meet there because he could grab a quick lunch and be back before the afternoon session started."

"Did you meet for lunch the Wednesday before the senator was killed?"

"Yea, I'm sure we did," he replied, glancing down at his calendar. "Yea, it's marked here on my calendar."

"Did he seem bothered by anything? Did you talk about anything that would indicate that he was concerned or worried about something?"

"No, just the usual; what's happening in Washington, our families, the senator's weekly golf game. Things like that. Nothing out of the ordinary."

"Well, thank you, Colonel," Jake said rising from the chair. "We'll be in touch. If you think of anything, give us a call," he said handing his business card to the colonel. "Do we need an escort or can we see our way back downstairs?"

"I'll have the captain take you back down. This place is tighter than Fort Knox ever since we got hit by that plane in 2001. I don't think it will ever go back the way it was."

Jake and Sully left the Pentagon and walked toward the parking lot.

"So, what do you think?" Jake asked Sully, searching for the car keys.

"I got a funny feeling like he wasn't telling us the whole story," responded Sully.

"Yea," Jake said. "Something's missing. According to everyone we speak with, the senator walked on water. Somehow that doesn't jell with being a politician."

CHAPTER 15

On their way back to the office, Jake decided to call Deputy Director Preacher and see if he would meet them for lunch on Friday at the Hawk and Dove. Neither Jake nor Sully had ever eaten there but it sounded like a good place to get a nice lunch and Jake wanted to check the place out anyway.

Jake placed a call to the director and was put on hold several times before finally getting through to his secretary. After giving her his name and the fact that he was working on the senator's murder, she told him the director couldn't make lunch on Friday due to schedule conflicts but arranged a lunch meeting with them the following Tuesday at noon.

There was a message on Jake's desk when he returned to the office that morning. His boss, Director Avery, wanted an update on the investigation as soon as he arrived. Jake didn't look forward to the meeting but he also didn't envy the director his job. As Director of the FBI, Mike Avery was always under the watchful eye of the house and senate. As a political appointee, everything he did was scrutinized. The recent forced resignation of the attorney general caused every appointee in the current administration to second guess their every move.

Jake asked Lynn to gather the files they had made on the investigation and meet him and Sully in one of the small conference rooms. Jake wanted to make sure that he had reviewed everything they had on the investigation prior to his meeting with the director. Together, they went through in chronological sequence the interviews, meetings, phone calls, and follow-ups including their meeting with Colonel Hatcher earlier that morning. To that, Jake added a log of the evidence that they had stored in the evidence room. After refreshing his memory for twenty minutes, Jake called the director's assistant. The director was in a meeting that had just started but his assistant agreed to call Jake as soon as he was out.

CHAPTER 16

Saturday, May 3

The weekend rolled in accompanied by severe thunderstorms. Jake awoke Saturday morning to a loud clap of thunder directly over the townhouse and lightning flickering in the sky like the fourth of July. The rain pelted down in sheets flooding the streets and driveways. The storm drains couldn't keep up with the volume of water that came rushing down the streets causing the excess water to jump the curbs and settle in pools six inches deep on the front lawns. Strong winds that accompanied the rain filled the umbrella on the deck causing it to topple, knocking over plants and scattering chairs across the deck. Jake was disappointed when he woke to the sound of the rain and the gray skies. For years he had talked about buying a Harley-Davidson motorcycle and had gotten a good deal at the end of the 2007 season on a Low Ryder. He had taken the Harley New Rider Course in November and only got to ride it twice before putting it up for the winter with less than one hundred miles on the odometer. He had been thinking about riding it for weeks when the weather started to break but something always came up at the last moment. With the dew rag he wore under his helmet, black leather jacket and motorcycle specs to keep the bugs out of his eyes, he fit the picture of the typical motorcycle badass. Sam had bought him a pair of leather chaps for his Birthday last month to complete his wardrobe. For the past week, he had been looking forward to a short trip to Annapolis, Maryland for the day.

At nine a.m. it was still dark enough outside to keep the street lights lit. The rain had subsided but the wind continued to blow. The neighbors had set their trash out the night before and the containers had blown over and had rolled down the street emptying their contents as they bounced along the curb.

Sam had decided to sleep in. They had planned on getting in a nine mile run but when the thunder woke her; she pulled the comforter over her head and welcomed the opportunity to catch a few more hours of sleep.

It started to sprinkle again as Jake darted out of the house to pick up the morning paper at the end of the driveway. Fortunately, the carrier had placed it in a plastic bag and only the outer edge was wet. He spent the remainder of the morning drinking coffee, snacking on granola bars and listening to CNN news while browsing through the Washington Post. Sam finally decided to join the land of the living around 11:30 a.m. Jake made fun of her for sleeping in but then decided to make a full breakfast. Within minutes after locating the eggs, bacon, cheese, mushrooms and a variety of garden vegetables, the kitchen was filled with the smell of bacon and onions.

"What are you making?" Sam said, coming into the kitchen with her pajamas still on.

"The Jake Hunter special omelet," he responded, flipping the omelet in the pan.

Sam laughed at him when the omelet landed half in the pan with the other half splashing across the stove top.

"Good thing you didn't decide to become a professional chef," she joked. "I don't think you could afford to cover the cost of the food that would never make it to the table."

"Just set the table and make the toast, little lady. I may be a little rusty, but I you just wait until you bite into this little baby."

"Looks like that little trip you planned on your big boy toy is gonna have to wait," she said looking at the rain running down the outside of the slider. "I don't think you want to venture out on that today. It's pretty gray out there. Doesn't look like it has any plans to let up for awhile."

After a fun filled breakfast with more jokes being directed at him, they decided to clean up and walk over to the Lakeland shopping center for some groceries. Jake learned a long time ago to shop for groceries on a full stomach. They cut through the rear of the development and braved the four lanes of traffic on Lakeside Drive before running across the street to the Giant Eagle.

CHAPTER 17

Tuesday, May 6

Jake and Sully arrived at the Hawk and Dove on Tuesday around 11:30 a.m. Jake wanted to spend a little time talking with the waitresses and owner before Director Preacher showed up for their scheduled lunch. They were just opening for business when the two agents walked in. A beautiful hand carved bar made of solid cherry ran the entire length of the north wall in the main dining room. The interior was decorated with large paintings of Washington scenes. Huge ceiling fans with lights hung from chains anchored to the exposed beams in the high ceilings. The brick floor with its weathered grout gave added character to the old establishment. Booths lined the walls with tables occupying the center of the room. Jake requested the table usually occupied by Senator Powell and his company when they lunched there on Wednesdays.

"No problem sir. As the first person here, you can have your pick of tables," the young waitress said, ushering them to an outside table.

"The senator usually sat right here," she said. "It's really sad what happened to him, isn't it?" she followed up.

"Tell me," Jake started. "Did you know Senator Powell?"

"I knew who he was. I didn't know him personally but he ate lunch here quite frequently. He was always friendly and left a nice tip."

"Did he eat with anyone in particular?" Jake asked.

"I don't work every day but I do work Monday through Thursday and sometimes on the weekend if someone calls off sick. I used to see the senator here on Wednesdays. He usually sat with an Army Colonel and another gentleman that was always dressed in a suit. I don't know who he was but they all seemed to be pretty good friends. They always took this table when the weather was nice."

"Here he comes now," she finished as Director Preacher joined them. After exchanging pleasantries with Jake and Sully, he took a seat across from Jake. The hostess nodded in recognition and took their drink orders while she passed out menus.

"I'll be back with your drinks in a minute and tell you the specials," she said, leaving them to look over the menus.

"So, tell me Director, did you ever play golf with Senator Powell?" Jake asked, before the waitress returned for their lunch order.

"No, I never took up the game. My father was not a golfer. We were raised as hunters. My dad took us out deer hunting when we were ten years old. I grew up with three other brothers. Deer season was a big deal for us. I still try to get back to upstate New York in November to hunt. My father is getting up there in age but he still manages to get out with us for a few hours a day. He got frost bite in Korea and his fingers go numb when its cold. How about you?"

"I'm a hacker on the golf course," Jake replied. "I enjoy the game but I'm not much competition. I don't get much time to play."

"I could never hit the ball straight," Sully added. "I spent more time looking for lost balls. Hell on my salary, I can't afford two dollars a ball," he laughed.

The waitress arrived at the table with their drinks and recited the Daily Specials. Sully decided to order the Wednesday Special of Beef on Kummelwick while Jake and the director stuck to a healthier meal of soup and a side salad.

"Thanks for meeting with us, Director," Jake began. "I know you've got a busy schedule, but we really want to get this investigation going. Anything you can tell us that would help us out is surely appreciated. I understand that you've been acquainted with Senator Powell for some time now?" he asked.

"Ever since West Point," replied the director.

That was news to Jake. He shot a glance at Sully to see if he had picked up on this. If he had, he didn't give me any indication. Colonel Hatcher never mentioned West Point in their prior discussion.

"So, you met Senator Powell at West Point?" Jake continued.

"Yes. He was two years ahead of John and I."

"By John, I take it you mean, Colonel Hatcher?"

"Yes. Colonel Hatcher and I graduated in 1987."

"So, you've been friends for quite a while."

"Yea, we ended up serving together during the first Gulf War. Senator Powell was the commander of our unit. Both John and I were lieutenants at the time."

"After the War, Clayton's four years were up; he went back to North Dakota, got married and went into politics. John liked the Army and decided to make a career out of it. He's planning on retiring later on this year. I spent my last two years stateside and then went back to grad school. We kept in contact over the years and when we all ended up in Washington several years ago, we decided to try to meet for lunch once a week."

"Any reason to think that the senator's murder is related in any way to terrorist activity?" Sully chimed in.

"I wouldn't think so," he replied. "In my experience, if the senator's murder was terrorist related, some group would have come forward by now and taken credit for it. And…They would not have hesitated in killing the men he was golfing with. Terrorists aren't picky like a professional hit man. They tend to take out anyone who's around. I had discussions with Homeland Security right after the shooting and they don't think there's any connection. The senator wasn't involved in any intelligence gathering with us or Homeland Security."

"Has the senator ever confided to you either as Director of the CIA or personally that he had any concerns regarding his safety?" Jake asked.

"Never. I was totally shocked when I heard that Clayton had been killed."

Just then, the food arrived and they ate mostly in silence. Sully's lunch special was enough to feed two people and he commented that he was going to need a nap if he finished it all.

By the time they had finished eating, the place was crowded with lunch patrons and the line of patrons waiting for an empty table extended halfway down the block.

"Director, before we part ways, is there anything you can think of in your past relationship with Senator Powell that you think is important for me to know? Anything at all that comes to mind?" Jake asked, laying his fork down and wiping his mouth with the napkin.

"Not really. Nothing comes to mind," he said, standing and extending his hand.

"Gentlemen, I must get back to the office. If I think of anything, I'll be sure to give you a call. And, thanks for lunch."

Jake handed his credit card to the waitress and waited for Sully to finish before leaving the tip on the table. They left the restaurant walking toward the Capitol Building on Pennsylvania Avenue. Jake couldn't help but think that there was more to their military relationship.

"Why would Colonel Hatcher not mention anything about their being at West Point at the same time?" he asked Sully.

"I dunno. It could have just been an oversight but you might be on to something."

CHAPTER 18

Saturday, August 16

It had been four months since the senator's murder and Washington was sweltering in the August heat and humidity. Algae had claimed ownership of the pond behind the townhome and the outdoor flowers had wilted, now looking more like a dried flower arrangement. The townhouse section where Jake and Sam lived looked like a ghost town. With the oppressive heat, everyone chose to stay inside and run their air conditioners full time. It was so hot that people weren't even going to the community pool. The only time anyone moved was to and from their cars for work or grocery shopping. The Alexandria City Council had placed a ban on water usage. No grass watering or car washing. Records indicated that this was the hottest summer in the past ten years. The heat index was well over one hundred five for the past four days. Even at six a.m. when Jake started his morning run, the air was heavy. By the time he finished his first mile, he was drenched with perspiration. Jake had gone to shaving his head the past two years due to his fast receding hairline and thinning hair. For a brief moment, he had thought about a comb-over but just couldn't get himself to do it. Sam joked that with his chiseled chin and bald head he resembled Bruce Willis in the current movie hit, "Live Free or Die Hard".

"If I only had his checkbook," he'd respond.

Jake didn't let on but he had been thinking a lot lately about Jillian Harris. There was no doubt that he was immediately attracted to her when he first saw her but he hadn't really dated anyone since losing Rachel. He wasn't sure even how to approach her. Since Rachel's death, Jake had thrown himself into his work and didn't allow for any personal time. Somehow, he couldn't see himself with another woman. Rachel had been everything to him. They had planned on having this great family and settling down in the South after retirement to enjoy their grandchildren. Her sudden death totally devastated him. Outside of work,

51

he had become somewhat of a recluse, choosing to read or watch old movies. Sam had been telling him for the past five years that he needed to go on with his life. In one of their heart to heart talks, she confided that she wished that he had found another wife after the death of her mother. She said that no one could ever replace her mother but that she missed having another female to talk to when girl things came up.

CHAPTER 19

Wednesday, August 20

Jake awoke Wednesday morning with a four Excedrin headache. He had been bothered for years with sinus headaches when storms were approaching but this one was a real doozy. He felt like he had been walloped in the back of his head with a baseball bat. The nightly news had predicted a change in weather patterns over the next couple of days with thunder storms and flood conditions in low lying areas. The rain would be a welcome change in Washington after the blistering August heat. He walked out on the deck with a cup of coffee and a bottle of Excedrin Migraines to ease the throbbing in his head. The wind was blowing briskly and the leaves on the maples were turned upside down. He snickered as he thought about his mother. She had a saying that when the leaves turned upside down it meant that a storm was on the way. The sky in the west was a mixture of gray, orange and shades of pink. Heat lightening was visible off in the distance over the horizon. It started to sprinkle as he picked up a couple of empty Corona bottles he and Sam had left out on the table last light.

It started to come down pretty heavy just as he got back inside and closed the door. Jake didn't have any appointments in the morning so he had decided to work at home for a couple of hours before heading into the office. After firing off an email to Lynn letting her know he'd be in around 11 a.m., he browsed through the Washington Post on line and then sat back in the Lay Z Boy and closed his eyes for a couple of minutes. An hour later, his cell phone rang waking him out of a nice dream. It was Lynn. She had been sending him emails for the past hour but since he had not replied, she was worried. She said that she was ready to send Sully over to the house if she couldn't get a hold of him. Jake assured her that he was fine and that he'd be in the office shortly. After making a couple of notes, he grabbed a quick shower, dressed and ate a couple of hard boiled eggs with rye toast for breakfast. Sam was in Richmond for a couple of days so he left the dishes in the sink with the intention of cleaning up when he got back home.

As he strapped on his shoulder holster and packed up the laptop, last nights telephone discussion with Sam came to mind.

"Dad, if you don't call her, you're never going to go out with her."

With a fair amount of trepidation, he picked up the phone and called Dr. Harris' office. Jake had spoken to her several times since the murder but it had been all business. It had been so long since he had asked a woman out that he wasn't even sure how to ask for a date but Sam suggested a quiet lunch meeting to get the jitters out of the way.

"Somewhere not too romantic where there are other people around," was her suggestion. *"Make it a lunch date and you'll both have an excuse to get back to work if it starts getting uncomfortable".*

Sometimes he thought Sam was the adult and he the child.

Dr. Harris' assistant answered the phone and put him on hold. Nervous and feeling lost for words; he almost hung up the phone when she picked up.

He got through the awkward first moments and finally stammered out, "Dr. Harris…"

"Please call me Jillian," she said.

"I would like to meet you for lunch sometime. I mean, if you're not too busy. If that would be all right?"

"Business or personal?" she quipped.

"Ah…, ah personal…"

"I would love to," she replied, letting him off the hook. "What did you have in mind?"

"Are you available for lunch on Friday?" he asked, feeling like a little school boy.

"That would be great. I've got a couple of appointments in the morning but I should be done by eleven…eleven thirty. How about if I meet you at Brews Cafe just around the corner from my office at noon?"

"Great. See you then," he said and hung up the phone. He realized as he shut the door behind him on the way out that he was beaming from head to toe. He was just glad Sam wasn't there to witness his debut.

CHAPTER 20

Jake was still looking like a Cheshire cat when he walked into the office. Sully gave him one of those looks like he knew he was up to something but he wasn't quite sure what.

"What?" Jake said, looking across the room at him.

"Nothing," Sully snickered. "What are you smiling about? You look like you just got caught with your hand in the cookie jar. You better get that shit eating grin off your face before someone thinks you're nuts!"

"What are you working on?" Jake asked, trying to ignore Sully's stare as he poured a cup of coffee. "Want one?" he said, holding up the pot and nodding in Sully's direction.

"Nah, I've already been to the bathroom half a dozen times this morning already. Christ, I feel like my old man. The first thing he says every time I call him is, "Hey... How's your prostate? Hell, that's before he even says hello."

"On another note, you know, I've been wracking my brain on this case all morning. It's been over five months since the senator was shot. No group's taken credit for the murder. We don't really have any witnesses and no suspects. I'm thinking this case is getting pretty cold. I don't know if this is going to go anywhere unless someone comes forth either claiming the shooting or the shooter starts shooting his mouth off, someone hears him and give us a call."

"I'm not ready to throw in the towel yet," Jake replied. "Let's go back out to the golf course and speak to the maintenance crew again."

"Yea, okay," he said, grabbing his shoulder holster from the back of his chair as he followed Jake out the door.

"I don't know what good that's going to do us but it beats hanging around here. I don't want to be in here twiddling my fingers if the director comes in. At least if we're out of the office when he calls, we have some time to come up with something for him."

"You got that right," Jake said, jotting down a quick note letting Lynn know they'd be in Bethesda for most of the afternoon.

"Hey, I'm starved," Sully said, as he slammed the car door shut. "Think you can go through the Wendy's window on the corner before we jump on the freeway?"

"Anything for you," Jake laughed, pulling out of the parking garage. Sully had a thing for Wendy's Quarter-Pounder Combo and Jake guessed he ate there at least three times a week.

CHAPTER 21

The maintenance crews were working on the greens when Jake pulled into the parking lot outside the clubhouse. The course had been closed for two days while the grounds crew aerated and prepared the course for a weekend tournament. Even though the course was closed, the pro-shop and restaurant were still open and it looked like they had a pretty good lunch business based on the number of cars in the parking lot. Jake slipped the Infiniti into a spot between a BMW Five Series and a Mercedes convertible.

"Must be nice," remarked Sully, stopping to look into the interior of the Mercedes before catching up with Jake who was already entering the Pro Shop to ask for directions to the maintenance department. The head golf pro walked out onto the deck with them and pointed out the direction of the maintenance barn, handing them a key for a cart.

"Take any cart. They're all charged up for a tournament this weekend. Just throw the key on the desk when you come back if I'm not here."

They drove in the rough along the fairway on hole number one and crossed over the fairway to the lane leading to the maintenance barn. There wasn't anyone standing around but the doublewide doors of the barn were opened so they walked into the barn looking for anyone that could help them.

"Hello," Jake hollered. "Is anyone here?"

"Hell, I could start a hardware store with the equipment in this barn alone," Sully said, as he walked along the power tools lined up along the wall.

"Look at them damn mowers over here. They got to be worth ten grand a piece. I'd like to have one of these babies just for shits and giggles. There's enough chainsaws hanging on that wall to take down a forest in no time."

"Money talks, big boy," Jake said. "When you charge a hundred grand initiation fee and monthly fees whether you use the place or not, you have the money to do anything you want."

"What? Are you kidding me?" Sully said. "You gotta pay whether you use the place or not?"

"From what I understand, that's the way it works. But hey, I heard that senators get about a hundred fifty a year on their pension even if they only serve one term. Can you imagine that? That's what our taxes go to pay. They don't put into social security either from what I hear."

"Lousy bastards!" Sully responded. "That's why they don't give a shit whether Social Security goes down the tubes or not. Hell… We don't even get our parking covered."

"Relax, big boy. Don't get your dander up."

Just then, a truck pulled up and parked outside. As they walked towards the door, two men in blue coveralls entered the barn.

"Can I help you gentlemen?" the older man asked.

"Yes sir," Jake replied. "I'm Agent Jake Hunter from the FBI and this is my partner, Sully Gilmore. We're investigating the murder of Senator Powell."

"Yea, you still haven't caught that guy, huh?" the younger man said.

"Haven't caught anyone yet…but, we will… It's just a matter of time"

"Were you two guys working that Saturday?" Sully asked.

"I was here," said the older man. "I'm John Berger. I'm the maintenance supervisor. I'm here every Monday through Saturday. Stevie here is new. He's only summer help and didn't start with us until June. He'll be going back to college in another week."

"Mr. Berger. I spoke with a Toby Daniels the day of the murder," Jake said, referring to his notes. "He still around?"

"Yea. He's still here. He's been working the aerator the last couple of days. He was at lunch but should be back by now. Last I saw, he was on the back nine working up around hole number fifteen. Come on, follow me. I'll take you up that way."

Jumping into the cart, they followed the maintenance supervisor through the course, winding their way around sand traps and water hazards until they came to the fifteenth green. Toby Daniels was operating the aerator, punching holes in the green and throwing little rolls of dirt behind him that looked like tootsie rolls. Berger motioned for him to shut the machine down and come over. Toby wiped his sweaty forehead with an already dirty rag and joined them.

"Do you remember me?" Jake asked.

"Sure. You're the guy from the FBI. How ya doing?"

"We'd be better if we could find the guy that killed the senator a few months ago," Sully blurted out before Jake could respond.

"Sorry," Jake said. "This is my partner Agent Gilmore."

"Mr. Daniels," Jake started, opening his notebook. "I'd like to go over that morning again with you, if you don't mind?"

"No problem. Shoot, Oops, bad choice of words," he said, leaning against the maintenance cart and lighting a cigarette.

Jake ignored the bad joke. "I'd like to go over what you saw that morning. Why don't you start from the beginning when you first got to work that morning."

"Sure. I punched in around six that morning, same as usual. I had bunker duty. That means I had to rake the sand traps. I always start on hole number one and work my way through the whole course. That way, I get to all the bunkers before the first golfers get there and I can pull out any tree branches that blow down during the night. Takes me bout three hours total if I don't have to keep jumping off the machine to pick up trash and other stuff that people throw in the traps"

"Specifically, that morning according to your earlier statement, you saw someone walking in a sand trap or bunker as you call it up around the fifth green. Is that right?"

"No, the guy was walking at the edge of the trees on five. I thought he was looking for a lost ball. I didn't really pay that much attention. This is a tough course. People lose balls all the time."

"Were you close enough to see what the person was wearing or could you tell me what he looked like?"

"I remember a light colored hat. I was raking the bunker up in front of the green when I saw him. He was probably at least a hundred yards away. I didn't see him there when I came up the fairway to the green but he could have been in the trees. If I recall, he didn't look very big but from that distance who knows?"

"So you didn't see anything strange or out of place?"

"You know I didn't think about it then but now, it didn't really make a lot of sense. All the players here are required to use golf carts but this guy was carrying his bag. It just didn't dawn on me at the time. He was in and out of the tree line. Almost like he didn't want anyone to see him."

Jake made a couple of additional notes in his notebook before thanking him and climbing back into the cart. Daniels went back to the aerator while Jake and Sully headed back in the golf cart in the direction of the Pro Shop.

After parking the cart back in line and leaving the key on the counter, Jake and Sully left the golf course feeling that they were onto something. There shouldn't have been any golfer on the fifth fairway at that time the senator was shot, especially someone carrying their own bag. Toby Daniels saw the shooter; he just didn't know it at the time.

CHAPTER 22

Friday, August 22

"Looking a little dapper aren't we?" joked Sully when Jake got to the office Friday morning.

Sam had picked out his outfit for the day. They had discussed his lunch with Dr. Harris over breakfast and Sam said that he should change from his usual "crummy cop wardrobe".

"This is a special occasion and you don't want to look like a "Fed", she said. "Put a little color in your outfit. Business conservative with a colorful tie is nice. She'll like that."

Sam chose a conservative dark gray plaid suit with a pale buttoned down blue shirt and scarlet and gray striped tie.

"I have a lunch appointment today," Jake responded to Sully, trying to slough off his wise remark.

"Oh, sounds like our boy is in love," he kidded as Lynn brought Jake a cup of coffee. Thankfully, she only gave him a casual glance and didn't ask any questions.

Jake and Sully spent the morning reviewing notes from their interviews and discussions earlier in the week. It sounded like there may be something to Toby Daniel's remarks on seeing that lone golfer the morning of the shooting. They had spoken with every golfer that was on the course the morning of the shooting and no one admitted to being in that area or wearing a light colored golf cap that morning. Fortunately, in addition to the senator's foursome there were only eight other golfers on the course.

At eleven, Jake decided to drive up to Bethesda for his lunch with Dr. Harris. He didn't want to get stuck in traffic and show up late for his first social call. He wasn't sure how much time she had reserved on her calendar, but he wanted to spend as much time with her as he could.

Dr. Harris arrived at the restaurant ten minutes early and requested a quiet corner booth in the rear, out of the main traffic pattern. It had been five years since her divorce and she hadn't officially dated since that time. She left word with the girl seating tables that she was expecting another guest and gave her a description of Jake.

Traffic wasn't bad. Jake shot up The George Washington Parkway and arrived at the restaurant just before noon. As soon as he entered, the hostess asked him if he was meeting Dr. Harris and showed him to the table. As he sat down, he recognized the slight hint of "White Linen". It was his favorite perfume. He had bought Rachel a small cachet to carry in her purse years ago.

"So, what did you tell the girl at the front? Be on the lookout for an old bald guy?" he quipped, his feeble attempt to make small talk.

"I did no such thing. But, I must have described you to a tee," she laughed. Jake noticed for the first time the cute little dimples that formed at the corners of her mouth when she smiled.

"So, how have you been?" he responded, trying to quickly change the subject.

"Good. I've been good and how about yourself?"

"Other than pulling my hair out, so to speak, over the senator's shooting at the golf course, I'm doing well, thank you."

"Have you eaten here before?" she asked.

"No, never had the opportunity. Looks like a pretty good selection," he said, glancing at the menu the waitress had just handed to him.

"If you like sandwiches, they make a killer Reuben. There's also a great selection of salads. I'm partial to their Chicken Salad. They serve it in a carved out tomato with lettuce, grapes and walnuts and bits of pineapple. Like a friend of mine says, "It's to die for"

"That sounds like a winner to me. I'm trying to get my weight down a few more pounds. I'm running the Marine Corp Marathon with my daughter in Washington in a couple of weeks and I don't need to be lugging anymore weight than I have to."

The waitress returned and after placing their orders, Dr. Harris asked Jake about Sam. He told her all about Sam and his moving in with her when he relocated from New York. She hadn't asked about a wife but Jake told her about Rachel's passing when Sam was only thirteen.

"Must have been pretty rough on her," she said. "I remember when I was thirteen and all the things teenage girls go through. That can be a pretty tough time for a girl. You must be quite the dad."

"I wish I could say that but unfortunately, I spent a lot of time at work and let Sam ferret out some of her own issues. We are now much closer. Since I've moved down here and taken over her lower level, we've had some pretty deep discussions. I think she's quite mature and turned out pretty good despite my shortcomings."

"You sound like a proud papa," she said. "Your face lights up when you talk about your daughter."

"I suppose I am. She's been good for me. Forces me to look at the brighter side of life."

"How about you?" Jake asked, trying to get the subject off of him. "Any children?"

"No, I put myself through school and then dove pretty deep into my medical practice, putting my personal life on the backburner. I was married for a short while but that didn't work out. Neither one of us were ready. We were two different people going down different paths. We're still friends but we get along much better as friends than we ever did as husband and wife. Sometimes when I see how happy other women are when they're shopping with their daughters, I get a little jealous. Oh well, I suppose what's meant to be is meant to be."

Their lunches arrived and they continued to talk while they ate. Jake realized that he was really enjoying her company. It had been a long time since he had a real conversation outside of his work with another female other than Sam.

"So, tell me what you can about the case. How is the investigation going on the senator's murder?"

Jake told her that they still didn't have any suspects but were following up several leads.

They finished lunch and ordered coffees while they continued to chat. She owned a home in Bethesda just around the corner from her office. She was an avid outdoor person and loved to ride horses. They had skiing in common and she hunted deer with her father when she was still living at home. She was raised in Lake Placid, New York, and went to some of the events at the 1978 Winter Olympics. Jake was there also during that time. He was stationed at Hancock Air Base outside Syracuse and his crew volunteered to help out with the parking in exchange for tickets to some of the events.

After an hour and a half which seemed like minutes, she glanced at her watch.

"Oops! I gotta get going. I have a two o'clock that I still need to prepare a little for."

"My treat," she said when the waitress brought the bill.

"Nope, I got it," said Jake, reaching for the bill. "I haven't had the luxury of sharing a meal with such a beautiful woman in a long time." He blushed when he realized what he had just said.

Jake paid the tab as they left the building and walked to the parking lot.

"Thank you for lunch," she smiled, extending her hand when she reached her car.

"You're most welcome," he said, grasping her hand for a gentle shake.

"Can I call on you again?" Jake asked as he opened the car door for her.

"I would like that. Thanks again," she said as she smiled and pulled away.

Jake kicked a stone across the gravel lot as he walked to his car with a cocky smirk on his face. *The old boy still has it, he thought!*

CHAPTER 23

Sunday, October 26

The alarm went off on the cell phone at 4:30 a.m. and Jake quickly shut it off, deciding to lie there for another fifteen minutes. Sam had come home late last night from Los Angeles and he wanted to give her another half hour of sleep. After strolling down the driveway for the newspaper, he started the coffee, quickly read the headlines in the morning paper and ate a couple of granola bars while he waited for Sam to get up. Today was race day and he was getting nervous as the starting time of 7 a.m. slowly approached. He had trained pretty hard but was still concerned that he would be able to make the entire twenty six miles. They had decided to take the Metro from the Springfield-Franconia Station to avoid the heavy traffic. Fortunately, they had pre-registered and could leave at five thirty and have plenty of time to get to the starting point at the Arlington Memorial Bridge in Arlington, VA.

Jake woke Sam at five and they quickly packed their running gear and headed out for the Metro.

There were several other runners on the train with them and they quickly made introductions and small talk about the race. It was early and the train was only half full. They arrived at the race start at 6:30 a.m. Sam and Jake decided use the restroom facilities that had been placed along the starting line before finding the nine mile marker. Organizers of good quality races always have mile marker designations. Runners fall in behind the mile marker that designates the finish time or mile pace that they intend to run. That allows for runners to run with other runners that maintain the same mile pace.

"Settle down, dad. You'll do fine," Sam said, trying to calm his nerves that must have been obvious from the look of concern on his face. Sam had run a couple of marathons in the past and knew what to expect. But Jake, a novice, was scared to death. Jake's goal was to just finish the race. The announcements were made regarding first aid and the various water stations along the route. It was a comfortable fifty four degrees for an October morning when Jake finally settled down for the start of the race. He was amazed at the thousands of people that had lined up to put their bodies through twenty six miles of torture. At 7 a.m. sharp, the gun went off and the crowd slowly inched its way forward. With the number of runners in front of them, it was a couple of minutes before they even made it to the starting line. Jake suddenly realized what cattle must have felt like when they were herded to the market back in the cowboy days. Fortunately, the computer chip attached to his shoelace didn't start to register the time until he crossed the starting line.

As the crowd began to spread out, they settled into a nice pace and Jake found himself enjoying the run. He had completed a couple of twenty mile runs during his training and he knew that he would be able to make it that far. *Another six miles, would be a walk in the park.*

Sam and Jake had brought their own water packs and energy bars that they carried in fanny packs around their waists. Jake kept his pager and backup piece, a Springfield Armory EMP 9mm weighing only 26 ounces in the pack as well. He reached for an energy bar around the eight mile marker to stop the gnawing in his stomach. After washing it down with six ounces of water, he felt pretty good. Some of the runners who had started out at faster paces were now walking along the side of the road. Sam who had experience in running marathons warned him of the urge to start out fast and cautioned him to keep the pace down.

At the ten mile point, Sam could tell that he was getting frustrated by the number of runners that seemed to be passing by them at a pretty good speed.

"You'll feel like you should be going faster when the crowd starts to go by you but eventually, you'll see most of them walking or even stopping when they hit the wall. They're all pumped up at the beginning but haven't trained right and they won't be able to endure the hills and distance."

The wall. That's something he hadn't paid much attention to. He had never run twenty six miles and heard time and time again about the wall. The wall was when long distance runners reached a point of utter exhaustion, when muscles and minds conflict causing hallucinations and blackouts. He quickly put it out of his mind. He was feeling good and actually enjoying the challenge. *Suck it up, he thought. You're almost half way there.*

CHAPTER 24

Stryker sat quietly, relaxing on the rooftop over the U.S. Postal Service at 1750 Crystal Drive watching the runners below make the turn on Crystal City Drive at the 22nd mile marker. The first runners had passed under him over an hour ago. Fortunately for Stryker, the course designers had provided him with ample opportunity to spot his target. As the runners crossed the Arland D. Williams Jr. Memorial Bridge, they took a right turn, running south along Crystal Drive directly below him. At 20th Street, they doubled back, running in front of him again as they approached the twenty-third mile marker. There was only one number he needed to see and he knew that it would be another ten or fifteen minutes before he'd have it in sight, proudly displayed on the bib across the chest of the runner. He re-checked the rings on the scope, making sure that the scope was tightly secured to the rifle. He had sighted it in earlier in the week but didn't want to take the risk that the scope had loosened during transport.

At 9:30 a.m., he picked up the Nikon ATB 10X56 Binoculars he had purchased from Cabella's in Wheeling, West Virginia on his way to Washington just for the occasion. From his perch he could see a good half mile in either direction. Over the past several months, he had watched his target train, timing his runs. He knew that his target would be running at around an 8 minute pace and should be approaching the prime target area shortly after ten a.m. As long as the target remained on track and didn't have to drop out of the race for an injury, he'd be ready for him. It was a nice day and Stryker was enjoying the sun that filtered through the clouds, warming his back. Over the past three weeks, he had stood on several rooftops along the race course before choosing this location. He had selected this site because it provided good visibility, would have the sun to his back, was hidden from view by anyone on the street below and provided plenty of escape routes. During the past week, he had sat in this exact spot with his spotting scope to make sure that he would have a clear shot without trees, wires or overhangs blocking his view of the street below. He had calculated the precise angle and location of his shot. With the range finder, he had measured a two hundred yard shot. Now it was up to the target to be there.

Glancing at his watch, he calculated that he had about fifteen more minutes before he needed to get ready for action. He settled back and enjoyed the sun shining on his face while he chewed on a Hershey bar and watched the runners below. At 9:45a.m., he poised for action. He needed to be ready in case the target was making better time than he had anticipated. When 9:55 came and went and there was no sign of the target, he started to worry. Then he spotted the target as it came into view in the wide angle binoculars. He watched as the runner took the turn south directly below him on his way to the turnaround. Reaching for the rifle that lay next to him, Stryker placed it between the shooting sticks he brought to steady the rifle and waited for the target to move back into range. He turned the bill of his cap to the rear so that it wouldn't interfere with his view. Even in this cool October morning, tiny beads of perspiration broke out along his forehead in anticipation. Clicking the safety into the off position, he placed his finger over the trigger and peered through the scope, placing the crosshairs right in the center of the numbers. Just as he had planned for weeks, when the target filled the scope, he gently squeezed the trigger. In a matter of milliseconds, his wait was over and the target dropped to the ground, never knowing that this was the last race he would ever run.

As the target lay in the center of Crystal Drive with a gaping hole in his chest, Stryker pocketed the bullet casing and quickly broke the rifle down, packing it beneath some folders in a leather briefcase. He knew it would only be a matter of time before the area would be swarming with police officers. Turning the ball cap back around to cover his face and putting on a pair of dark sunglasses to shield his eyes, he descended the fire stairs leading from the rooftop to the floor below, stopping at the bottom of the stairwell before entering the hallway. He didn't expect to see anyone in the top floor offices on a Sunday morning but didn't want to take any unnecessary chances. Opening the door just enough to see, Stryker slipped into the hallway and headed to the elevator that would take him to the Mall level. He pushed the button for the elevator and waited. With the briefcase in hand, he wanted to appear like any businessman, catching up on a little weekend work. After what seemed like a long time, the elevator finally opened and he stepped in. When the doors opened, he stepped into the Mall area and slowly walked along the store fronts toward the Metro. The Mall was busy with shoppers so he didn't have any difficulty losing himself in the crowd. After stopping briefly at a newsstand to pick up the current edition of the Washington Post and a bottle of water, he approached the escalator that would take him down to the platform where he'd pick up the Blueline.

After a five minute wait, which seemed more like fifteen, the Blueline entered the station and stopped, opening the doors directly in front of him. After waiting for the passengers to get off of the train, Stryker settled into a window seat in the front of the train. Smiling to himself, he set the briefcase on the seat next to him and opened the newspaper. He had a short ride that would take him to the rented car he left at the Van Dorn Station earlier that morning.

After an uneventful twenty minute ride, the train pulled into the Van Dorn Station. Stryker picked up the briefcase, folded up his newspaper, sticking it under his arm and headed for the parking lot. When he knew he was clear of the other passengers, he pulled slowly on the moustache beneath his nose causing it to release from the glue that held it there. Smiling at his success, he reached into his pocket and retrieved the shiny brass casing, dropping it into a trash container on his way to his car.

CHAPTER 25

Sam and Jake had just passed the twenty mile marker when his pager went off. They were on the Arland D. Williams Jr. Memorial Bridge heading towards the Pentagon when his pager started to beep in his fanny pack. Jake slowed to look at the message that was displayed in the view window and suddenly felt his stomach tighten. There had been a shooting up ahead and the D.C. Metro Police had stopped all runners from proceeding past the twenty three mile marker. Fortunately, the course took a turn south on Crystal Drive just over the bridge on 20ᵗʰ Street and Crystal before winding back again on Crystal Drive to the twenty-third maker point which was just ahead to the right. Police cruisers suddenly appeared from behind them with their lights flashing and sirens blaring, trying to get past the runners on the bridge. Jake flashed his badge at a car as it was moving by and the driver, recognizing the federal shield, slowed.

"Hop in," he said. "There's been a fatal shooting up ahead and that's all I know for now."

Jake hollered to Sam who looked like she had just seen a ghost that he'd call her later and jumped in beside the driver. With the number of people that filled the streets and sidewalks ahead, it took them another five minutes to get to the location of the shooting. There were already several police cruisers on the scene directly in front of the Crystal City Shopping area but no ambulances had arrived. Several of the police officers were holding spectators back while a couple more were already stretching the barrier tape across the road to preserve the scene and protect any evidence from being compromised. A lone runner lay in the middle of the road. A pool of blood had already formed around the lifeless form of what was until a couple of minutes ago a marathon runner three miles from the finish line of a gruesome 26.2 mile race.

"Anyone know who this is?" a policeman hollered at the crowds gathering around to gawk at the lifeless form. "Was anyone running with him?" he continued, without waiting for an answer to his first question. When no one responded, Jake walked over to the body that lay in the middle of the road and looked down into the gunmetal gray steely cold eyes that were staring directly at him.

"I know who he is," he responded. "This is Colonel John Hatcher. He worked at the Pentagon."

CHAPTER 26

It was a long morning for Jake already when the shooting happened. He knew that he was in for an equally long night. Sam and Jake had brought a change of clothes with them to the race. They had expected to spend the afternoon after the race enjoying the warm fall weather together and catch dinner somewhere around the Capitol. Now, still in his running clothes, Jake started to get cold as his body temperature lowered with his heart rate and his damp clothes clung to him.

The killing had taken place within the jurisdiction of the D.C. police but caused a major stir within Homeland Security as well. Not knowing whether this was the start of a terrorism threat, both the CIA and Homeland Security had been alerted. The FBI was already involved since Jake was asked to assist the DC Metro Police when he recognized the victim and related that he was already working on another homicide that could be linked. The body of Colonel Hatcher had been moved to the D.C. morgue and was currently being autopsied. Jake had called Sully to meet him at the office. Jake was just changing after a hot shower in the locker room at the FBI headquarters in the Hoover building when Sully showed up with a Subway sandwich he had picked up for him on his way in. After eating candy bars from the vending machines all afternoon, the sub hit the spot. They were awaiting word from the medical examiner and reviewing their notes on Senator Powell's shooting when Sam called. She knew that he would get involved in the case and forget to eat. After assuring her that Sully had provided him with dinner, she told him that there had been a message on the home phone from Jillian Harris when she got back home. Jake wanted to call Jillian but decided that he'd follow up with her in the morning. He knew Chuck Embers would not be in the office at Quantico on a Sunday night but decided to leave a voicemail message asking him to call him in the morning when he got to the office. Jake knew that it would be at least another day before the D.C. ballistics expert had a chance to look at the markings on the bullet that had killed

Colonel Hatcher. He wanted Chuck to compare the ballistics of the bullet that had killed Senator Powell with the one that was discovered embedded in the asphalt after exiting Colonel Hatcher's chest.

CHAPTER 27

After the shooting, Stryker decided to lay low and stay in the motel room for a while before leaving for Ohio later that night. After all the activity in the city, he knew that additional troopers would be called in to monitor the heavy traffic during the daylight hours. Up to this point, everything had been going according to his plan so he didn't see the need to risk being stopped for a minor traffic violation.

He spent the better part of the afternoon leafing through the Sunday edition of the Washington Post and searching the cable stations for updates on the shooting. The police were pretty tight lipped about the shooting and weren't making any comments to the press. The six o'clock evening news ran a short story with the newscaster interviewing runners on the scene of the fatal shooting. She ended the broadcast by saying that no suspects had been arrested. Stryker had paid for the room through Monday morning but decided to get out of Washington and beat the morning rush hour traffic. Facing a seven hour drive to Ohio, Stryker packed what few clothes and toilet articles he had in his backpack, turned off the light and closed the door behind him. It was almost 8 p.m. when he left the motel, walked across the parking lot to the Nissan and headed out of town. He had called his uncle earlier in the day and told him that he was coming through town. Uncle John, his mother's younger brother and only sibling, now lived alone on the family farm, having lost his wife to cancer several years earlier. Stryker hadn't been back to Coshocton, Ohio, population twenty thousand, give or take, in almost a year. He was really looking forward to getting back to the farm and spending time with Uncle John. Coshocton was blue collar, second and third generation factory workers. Real Estate offices were still owned and operated by mom and pop teams, agents who grew up there and whose children played little league for the local Kiwanis teams. The big city names of ReMax and Keller Williams hadn't taken over the town with college educated agents driving Lexis or BMW all wheel drives. He really missed the small town atmosphere. When his mother Katherine died, he was left alone at the age of thirteen without a legal guardian. If it hadn't been for his Uncle John, the courts would have made him a ward of the state and he would have ended up in the county home for children. His uncle and aunt didn't have any children of their own and had petitioned the court for guardianship. He got along good with his uncle and was grateful that they had taken him in. Katherine had gone into a severe depression after Tommy died and was never quite the same. She died of a heart attack shortly after they buried Tommy. He was always close to Tommy. Tommy was ten years older than Stryker and it was Tommy that taught him how to shoot. They set up targets and shot twenty two caliber rimfire rifles for hours until Stryker could put every shot within a three inch spread at seventy-five yards. During deer season, Tommy taught him how to stalk a deer. Tommy was the one who was with him when he shot his first buck, a two hundred pound ten point. Tommy taught him how to field dress the deer and it was Tommy who sent the picture of the two of them with the deer to the local newspaper, the same picture that he carried in his wallet for the last twenty years. This was the last picture ever taken of Tommy and him. He really missed Tommy and thought of him often.

Traffic was light on the beltway at that time of night as Stryker drove north toward I-70 passing the Rockville, Maryland exit. He had only counted three state troopers since he got on the north beltway and two of them were headed in the opposite direction. He was making good time and figured that he'd make the Ohio border by two a.m. The 2003 Nissan Altima he had borrowed from the used car lot around the corner from the motel handled nicely. With a Virginia license plate he pulled from a car in a nearby Wal-Mart parking lot he'd be safe as long as he kept his speed within the limits and wasn't stopped by any troopers. He'd exchange the Virginia plate for an Ohio plate when he got to Ohio. Traffic was traveling at seventy two mph so he felt comfortable setting the cruise at 70 mph and settling in between two eighteen wheelers.

At ten thirty p.m., the gas gauge measured less than half and he was getting hungry and a little drowsy. He needed to get a cup of coffee and had to take a leak. He had gone one hundred twenty miles since leaving D.C. He was almost a third of the way there. Since it was already dark, he had decided to take the Pennsylvania Turnpike and stay on I-70W instead of the more scenic route through Cumberland on I-68. In another fifteen miles, he'd be getting off the turnpike at Breezewood. There were plenty of truck stops and fast food restaurants to get a sandwich and a cup of coffee.

CHAPTER 28

Monday, October 27

"Morning dad," Sam said, as she waltzed into the kitchen while Jake was eating a grapefruit, planting a kiss on the top of his head. "What time did you get home last night?"

"I don't know. Sometime after midnight. Sully dropped me off. There wasn't much else we could do last night."

"The place went pretty crazy yesterday," she continued. "After you got picked up in that police car, the cops appeared from everywhere. The race was stopped and I couldn't go any farther north on Crystal Drive so I just went over to the Metro at Crystal City and came back home. I listened to the news on CNN last night. I can't believe someone shot a runner. What was that all about anyway?"

"Don't know," Jake said. "We're still trying to figure it out. I think it may be linked to that shooting of that senator up in Bethesda earlier this year."

"Oh, before I forget, did you get a chance to call Dr. Harris?" she said with a flair of sarcasm.

"No, I figured I'd call her this morning," Jake responded. "There was just too much going on and I didn't have any time to call her. I'm not going to the office until later this morning anyway."

"Well," she said. "I know your propensity to stall. I'm going to take a long hot bath so...no time like the present." With that said she tapped him on the top of his head with the morning paper and danced off with her cup of coffee in hand.

Jake decided to read the headlines in the morning paper before placing his call to Dr. Harris. The Post ran a front page spread showing the chaos on the street in front of the shops. He had barely escaped yesterday from getting sandwiched by a couple of reporters as he left the scene. Fortunately for him, he got a ride from one of the D.C. police cruisers over to his office in the Hoover Building.

As Jake read through the articles regarding the shooting, he couldn't help but think that there had to me a link between the two killings. How coincidental could it be that both Senator Powell and now Colonel Hatcher had both been killed by different assassins? He couldn't wait to talk with Chuck Embers when he got into the office.

CHAPTER 29

"Jillian, Jake Hunter," he said when she answered the phone.

"Sorry I didn't get back to you yesterday. Things got pretty hectic down at the office and I got pretty involved with that shooting. It was pretty late when I got out of there."

"I didn't want to bother you," she said. "But, I knew you were in that race and I got worried when I heard about the shooting. Did you get a chance to finish or were you behind the victim? I heard once the shooting started that they stopped the race and didn't let anyone finish."

"Well, unfortunately, all my hard work was for naught. Sam and I were just crossing the bridge at the twenty-one mile marker when it all happened. I ended up identifying the victim and Sam caught the Metro back home."

"You knew the victim?" she asked, surprised.

Jake spent the next ten minutes telling Dr. Harris about the shooting. He told her who the victim was and the connection he thought there may be to the earlier killing of Senator Powell.

"Wow, that's a little frightening," she said when Jake had finished.

"Jake, it's been a while since we had lunch together and I was wondering if you'd like to come over for dinner tonight. That is, if you don't already have plans. I've actually got the day off so I feel like cooking a big meal and I don't have anyone to share it with. I know its short notice, so I'll understand if you can't."

"Dinner tonight?" he said, eyeing Sam coming around the corner, drying her hair with a towel.

Sam had caught the last part of their discussion and motioned for him to go all the while mouthing, "go, go!"

"I'll bring the wine," he said.

"Fine," she agreed. "See you about six then. Oh, by the way, my address is 26 Fennel Drive in Bethesda. You can't miss it. It's just around the corner from my office."

Hanging up the phone he could hear Sam singing in the other room, "Jake and Jillian, sitting in a tree..."

CHAPTER 30

The morning was almost gone when Stryker rolled out of bed. He had run head on into a major thunderstorm during the night. By the time he reached Wheeling, West Virginia, traffic had slowed to a steady crawl. Traveling was treacherous and visibility was near zero. Any minute, he feared that he would be hit from behind by a tractor trailer that would send him through a guardrail and careening down the mountainside. When the rain started, he turned on the wipers. The wiper on the driver's side needed to be replaced. The frayed rubber skipped across the window smearing the dead bugs that had found their final resting place on a pane of glass. The driving rain forced cars and trucks to pull off the road or into rest stops to wait out the storm. Stryker decided to continue on, making the best of a bad situation. With the defroster on high, he leaned forward in the seat, staring through the window, fixating on the road ahead. Both hands gripping the steering wheel, he fought to keep the wind from blowing the car sideways. After squinting through the scraping wiper blades for the next three hours as they swept the water across the windshield, he finally turned into the private drive leading to the family farm at 4:30 a.m. The road was dirt and gravel but with the heavy rains he thought for sure he'd get stuck in the deep ruts, now filled with mud, before he made it to the house. It was late October. In prior years, they'd had snow as early as the first week of September. If the temperature dropped another ten degrees, the rain might turn to snow. Stryker almost wished for that to happen. The farm was always prettier, cleaner with a blanket of snow.

Uncle John was an early riser and was usually in bed by ten every night. He'd take a sleeping pill, read a little and then fall asleep with his glasses still propped on the bridge of his nose. Uncle John still maintained a small beef herd, arising by five every morning to feed the cows before leaving for his factory job in nearby Conesville. Uncle John had worked at the Conesville Power Plant ever since he was a senior in high school. He never was much of a student, didn't see the real need for any additional education and figured he made pretty good money, earning close to thirty five thousand a year. Besides, the house was paid for and the truck ran pretty good. He had put a little money away in the local bank for a rainy day and didn't eat out in restaurants more than once a month. He was not one to leave home. He never traveled more than a couple hundred miles from the farm since he took the school trip to Niagara Falls during his senior year in high school. Stryker had found the key under the mat where it lay hidden for the past fifteen years. Even Fritz, Uncle John's ten year old black lab that had his run of the land hadn't stirred from his bed near the wood burner when Stryker let himself in. The place would have been perfect for a home invasion sitting out in the country as it did. The problem was there wasn't anything valuable in it. As it was, the whole place would have sold for under a hundred thousand at any farm auction and that included the contents and all farm equipment to boot. Stryker made himself a cup of hot chocolate before making his way up the stairs to the bedroom he had shared with Tommy. Within five minutes of laying his head on the feather pillow, he was sound asleep.

It was almost noon when Stryker pulled his jeans on, grabbed his sweater out of his backpack and walked down the backstairs leading to the large farm kitchen. The old farmhouse was built in the late eighteen hundreds and had been remodeled several times over the past forty years. For convenience, Uncle John had kept the two stairwells. The one in the front of the house was the larger of the two, leading from the first floor gathering room to the upstairs front hallway. The second stairwell, being much narrower, connected Uncle John's bedroom at the back of the house to the kitchen below.

Even before reaching the bottom of the stairwell, he could smell the wood smoke and feel the warmth from the wood burner as the heat worked its way up the narrow stairwell. Fritz, now wide awake, met him at the kitchen door with his tail wagging, striking the door frame like a wooden club.

"Hey old boy, remember me?" said Stryker, rubbing the dog behind the ears. "How you been?"

The heavy rain that fell during the night had slowed to a light drizzle by late morning leaving large puddles of water in the backyard where the downspouts emptied. Uncle John had left hours earlier for work at the factory but left a note for Stryker on the table. His message said that he'd be home by five and would like to take Stryker to dinner at the Rusty Nail, a local hangout serving the best fish n' chips in Coshocton County. People came from as far away as Newark, Ohio, thirty miles west, to eat the specials.

Stryker looked around the large farm kitchen. The wallpaper was gray with smoke and soot from the wood burner. The dry heat caused the seams in the wallpaper to separate from the cracked plaster. Stryker remembered the day his mother and Uncle John hung the paper over twenty years ago. There were still some pencil marks and scribbling on the door frame where Stryker's mother had written in the date she measured their height at various times during the year. The white and gray linoleum floor was now a dull shade of yellow, brittle and cracked. A well worn path lead from the back door to the wood box next to the wood burner.

On a shelf above the stove, Stryker found a mismatch of cups and saucers. Grabbing a mug from the shelf, he poured himself a cup of coffee from the pot that Uncle John had made six hours earlier.

"Whew…tastes like oil," said Stryker making his way to the sink where he poured the thick, oily substance down the drain.

"That'll grow hair on your chest," he remarked to the dog that had found his way back to his bed near the wood burner.

His stomach grumbled and he realized that he hadn't eaten anything since he stopped in Breezewood at the twenty four hour McDonalds and had a couple of greasy cheeseburgers and fries. Rummaging through the refrigerator, he settled on a hard boiled egg and a bowl of oatmeal.

Just as he took his first bite of egg, the phone on the wall behind him rang, causing him to jump. Reaching up to grab the handset, he laughed when he saw the old dial phone. Uncle John wasn't one to keep up with new technology.

"Hello," he answered, trying to talk around a mouthful of food.

"Yo, Uncle John," he said, recognizing the party on the other end.

"Got in early this morning. Yea, I ran into some heavy rain in West Virginia and some crazy drivers. Yes. I did see your note. Rusty Bucket sounds great!"

After a brief conversation, he hung up the phone and made himself a cup of tea. Uncle John told him he had left a box of pictures in the den for him to go through.

He finished his breakfast and took his tea to the den where he found the box of pictures on top of the sewing table. Plopping down on the floor, he leafed through the albums and loose pictures for the next hour. After a while, he realized that he was smiling as he sifted through the pictures…pictures of Tommy and him. He found a picture of the two of them standing in front of the barn, Tommy with a plaster caste covering his arm. He remembered the day that Tommy fell from the hayloft and broke his arm. They were swinging on a rope from an old beam when the rope broke and Tommy fell ten feet. He landed on his arm and broke it in two places. Tommy made Stryker promise to never tell their mother or Uncle John what they had been doing before the accident. Two years earlier, a neighbor boy had accidentally hung himself swinging from the rafters and died. From that day on, they were not allowed to swing on ropes in the barn.

After another hour of reminiscing at old photos, school awards and certificates, he needed to get away and decided to take a walk.

It was cool and overcast but the rain had stopped. He grabbed a jean jacket hanging by the back door and found a pair of rubber boots that almost fit. They were a little large but with a couple of pairs of thick socks, would keep his feet dry.

"Come on, Fritz," he said, opening the door for the dog to lead the way. He walked down to the barn where the cows were busy munching on hay Uncle John had left them before leaving for work. The cows glanced over at him as he approached the fence but then ignored him and continued eating. He and Tommy had been members of the Future Farmers Association when they were in school. Stryker showed a lamb while Tommy, being older and much stronger, showed a heifer at the county fair. Tommy had won reserve champion one year and sold his heifer for a thousand bucks. After much pleading with his mother, she finally relented and agreed to let him use some of the award money to buy a twelve gauge shotgun. That's the gun that Tommy and Stryker had used for years to hunt deer before Tommy left for Iraq. When Tommy didn't come back from the war, Stryker lost interest in hunting. It wasn't fun anymore. The year Tommy died, Stryker put the shotgun in the closet and never took it out again. He did, however, spend a lot of time shooting at cans and targets with the twenty two rifle, envisioning the faces of Iraqi soldiers when he slowly squeezed the trigger.

Opening the side door to the tack room in the barn, he ducked to miss the spider web stretched across the entrance. The smell of gear oil and insecticides pierced his nostrils. The tack room was a mess. When his mother was alive, they kept a couple of riding horses. She loved to ride and insisted that he and Tommy learn how to ride. Uncle John had cut trails through the woods with the Kubota and Bush hog so they could ride and play cowboys. His mother had kept the tack room broom clean, hanging the bridles on the wall above the saddles which sat on saw horses along the wall. After every use, the brushes, combs and buckets were cleaned and lined up on the shelf above. Now, the equipment was dusty from years of neglect. The fancy stamped silver cockles on the saddles were rusty and tarnished, the leather bridles moldy and mice had chewed holes in the saddle blankets piled in the corner, making nests for their newborn.

He left the tack room and walked into the main barn. The old combine was still parked in the back of the barn. Stryker walked over and pulled the license plate easily off the magnetic strip that connected it to the combine. Uncle John never registered the combine with the Department of Motor Vehicles. He figured that since he only drove it a couple of times a year on the highway between fields that he would save the fifty dollars registration fee and attach another plate from the pick up truck with the magnetic sheet. The magnet would come in handy now when Stryker needed to switch plates in D.C. The barn smelled of old horseshit and moldy hay. Seeing the ladder, he climbed to the hayloft and walked over to the sliding door that was used to load the hay bales. Pushing hard on the door, it squeaked as the rollers made their way along the rusty rail. He sat on a musty bale near the window and looked out over the fields and pastures behind the barn. Something moved to the right causing him look in the direction of the driveway leading to the house. Then it hit him. He was right here, looking out the same doorway on that cold November morning seventeen years ago when the blue sedan came up the driveway and parked, the government car with the two men in uniform who left the car and walked up on the porch. In his minds eye, he could hear the knock on the back door. Then, his mother's screams. He had watched enough movies. He knew that soldiers only came to visit for one reason. After the blue car drove back down the driveway, he had stayed up there crying until he couldn't cry anymore. Wiping his face on his sleeve, he had climbed down the ladder and made his way to the house. She was sitting in the rocking chair in the kitchen by the wood burner. She had been crying and her eyes were red and swollen. He rushed over to her and knelt by the chair. She hugged him close, sobbing. He could feel her tears as they made their way down her cheeks and landed softly on the top of his head. They never talked about it much after that. Shortly after Tommy died, she too passed away. She was only forty two when she died in her sleep during the night. The doctor said she suffered a major heart attack but Stryker knew better. Tommy's death was too much to bear. Stryker knew that she died from a broken heart. From that day on, it was only he and Uncle John.

Glancing around the room now at the musty broken hay bales, his mind fluttered with more memories…memories he had suppressed. He sat down on the floor and pulled the tattered letter and picture from his wallet. *Why Tommy, why, he thought, a tear rolling down his cheek before dropping his head in his hands. It wasn't supposed to be this way.*

CHAPTER 31

The Rusty Bucket was just as Stryker had remembered it. The tables were made of pine, gummy now with numerous coats of shellac. It had been awhile since he had stepped foot into the restaurant and bar but the place hadn't changed in twenty years. The night before Tommy had left for Iraq, Uncle John brought them here to celebrate. A Budweiser light hung low over the two pool tables in the back. An old jukebox that still took quarters and played old time country music stood against the far wall near the small wooden dance floor. Vinyl covered stools around the bar were occupied by men drinking whatever was on tap for the night. Everywhere you looked were Carhart jackets and John Deere hats. The locals all had cans of dip imprinted in the back of their jean pockets, a symbol that they had graduated from the local high school.

Stryker made his way to an empty table as Uncle John went to use the restroom.

"Hey, how's it goin?" asked a patron, slapping him on the back. Haven't seen you around lately. Still shooting up a storm?"

Stryker turned and recognized Derrick Masters, an old classmate from high school. The joke in school was that Derrick was always on dimmer switch.

"Yea, haven't been around," Stryker replied. "I've been working out of town."

"Whatcha been doin?" he asked.

"Oh, little of this, little of that…how bout yourself?" he quickly asked, trying to change the subject.

"Still farming some. Times ain't like they used to be. Last ten years have been pretty tough. Took a job with the highway department couple years ago. I've been working up on I-77 toward Dover for the past month. Got the road down to two lanes. Pissin lot of people off. Trying to finish up before the winter hits. Can't do any paving when the snow falls."

"I here ya," Stryker said, looking for a table out of the way. "See ya around," he finished, walking toward a table in the back. He didn't really feel like talking about what he'd been up to or where he'd been.

When Uncle John returned, a waitress with a Dolly Parton hairdo and ten dollars worth of Mary Kay products on her face followed him from the bar.

"Drinks?" she asked, while they looked over the menu.

Stryker decided to stick with water while Uncle John ordered a Bud draught.

"Things haven't changed much round here," Uncle John said, nodding toward the pool tables and bar.

"Yea, I see that," responded Stryker, pointing to the top of the table where he and Tommy had carved their names a long time ago.

"Foods good and the prices are right though," continued Uncle John.

"Gonna stick around more this time?" asked Uncle John, peering over the top of his menu.

After high school graduation, Stryker had tried college for a couple of years at the University of Akron, an hour and a half away. That's where Tommy had gone to college. Stryker had gotten a partial scholarship for his shooting ability and made first position in his freshmen year, scoring high enough to make it to the nationals two years in a row. The only thing that kept him in college was being able to shoot on the college rifle team. But after his sophomore year, he lost interest, couldn't keep his mind on his studies and decided to quit.

Stryker had stopped back here a year ago, taking a part-time job at the Wal-Mart store. That was when he had found the unopened letter in his mother's box of personal belongings that Uncle John had stored in the attic after her death. Shortly after that, he had packed a bag and left.

"Nothing really here for me, Uncle John," he said. "I stopped back for a short visit. Haven't seen you for a while and you're the only close family I got."

"You're welcome to stay as long as you want. I might be able to get you on at the plant, if you're wantin to stay for awhile."

"Thanks but I think I'll move on after a week or so. I just wanted to spend some time with you. Relax a little bit. I've still got something to do before I settle down."

"Suit yerself," he replied, nodding to the waitress to take their order. "You know, you're always welcome here."

"I know Uncle John. And I appreciate it."

They tried to make small talk while they waited for their order.

"So, I see you still have some cows," he started.

"Yea. Might as well let them chew the grass. The way I figure it, with them cows in there, I won't have to bush hog around the barn and pasture. Those seven head I have penned in will keep the grass trimmed pretty short. I've even been thinkin bout putting a bull in there for awhile. Neighbor down the road has a two year old that he says I can put in with the cows for a bit. They should be ripe come this time next month."

Stryker was glad to see the waitress coming with their order.

"Best fish n' chips I ever had," he said, chewing a mouthful of deep fried cod.

"Yea, ole Charlie has an old family recipe that he won't tell nobody about," replied Uncle John. "I don't know what they're gonna do if he ever passes on."

"So what've you been doin with yourself the past year?" Haven't heard from ya since you left here after Christmas. Thought you might find your way back here when the spring came. I left a cupla messages on your cell phone but you never got back with me."

"I'm sorry," replied Stryker. "Actually, I lost that cell phone some time ago. I've had a lot on my mind. I've been pretty busy traveling around. I pick up odd jobs here and there. Nothing permanent. I still don't know what I want to do."

They finished dinner in silence and headed back to the farm. Uncle John went down to the barn to feed grain to the cows while Stryker found a book in the bookcase in the living room and sat on the floor in front of the fireplace half-watching "CSI Miami" on the television. By the time the show was over, he was falling asleep and decided to go up to bed. He said goodnight to Uncle John who was sitting at the kitchen table writing out bills and nursing a glass of Wild Turkey.

CHAPTER 32

In his excitement, Jake had failed to ask Dr. Harris whether he should bring a red or white wine so he decided to stop at the World Market in the Kingstowne Shopping Center around the corner from the townhouse and get a bottle of each. What he didn't plan on was getting sideswiped by a fast moving red mustang as he turned into the parking lot. The driver, a young woman in her early twenties never looked in his direction before pulling out in front of him as he turned into the parking lot. After calling the local police and providing the necessary information for the accident report, he ran into the store and grabbed a Franciscan Merlot and a Sebastiani Pinot Grigio. Quickly swiping his Visa card across the register, he jumped back into his Silver Infiniti G37, now painted with a bright red swath that ran from the front passenger door to the rear panel, and headed for Bethesda. He had planned on taking the route through Arlington but decided to ditch the local traffic and make up lost time on the I-495 Capital Beltway North.

Approximately twenty minutes later, Jake pulled off the Bethesda Exit and took little time finding Fennel Drive, a quiet tree lined street of older single family homes in an established neighborhood, just around the corner from Jillian's office. The houses sat back off the sidewalk on half acre lots. The homes appeared to be well taken care of and he guessed by their architecture that they were probably built in the sixties. Dr. Harris' house was in the middle of the block. It was a stately Tudor two story with a driveway running along the east side of the house leading to a two car detached garage on the rear of the lot. He parked in the driveway and knocked on the side door. Dr. Harris answered on the second knock and Jake stepped into a softly lit hallway. Still wearing an apron with her hair tied up behind her head, she apologized for not being ready.

"Sorry, I'm running a little late. I got called over to the office after we spoke this afternoon. What started out as a ten minute favor for someone ended up taking almost two hours."

He immediately could detect the scent of cinnamon and apples.

"Something smells really good," he said, trying to mask his awkwardness as she led him into an adjoining room with a wood burning fireplace that crackled as the flames leapt and danced, warming the room.

"I took the liberty to bake an apple pie this afternoon," she said. "I hope you like apple. Here, let me take your coat."

"Apple's my favorite," he responded. "I don't remember when I last enjoyed a home baked apple pie."

"Oh here," he said, handing her the bottles of wine. "I didn't know whether to bring red or white so you can make your choice."

"I've cooked a prime rib so I guess we can have either."

"Would you care for a glass of wine now?" she asked. "Or, is there another drink you would prefer before dinner. I think I have some bourbon, and I know I have vodka and gin. If you're a scotch drinker, I've got a bottle of single malt that I received last Christmas from a friend of mine that I haven't even opened."

"If you've got a single malt, how can I resist?" he said, following her to a wet bar in the far corner of the room.

She handed him a bottle of 12 year old Glenlivet and a couple of glasses.

"Why don't you pour us a couple of drinks while I check on the dinner," she said. "There's ice in the container to the right of the sink. I'll take mine with a little water and a couple of ice cubes. I can't drink it straight. It burns too much going down."

"Lightweight...huh," he laughed, opening the bottle and sniffing the cork at the end of the bottle top. He poured two glasses and then glanced around the room. The room was nicely furnished with a Cognac leather couch, matching loveseat, chair and ottoman, all neatly arranged in front of a warm glowing fireplace. Two Cherry end tables that held antique brass lamps were centered perfectly between the couches and chair.

Jake was standing with his back to the door, looking at a picture that was framed over the fireplace when she returned. He hadn't heard her coming and she stood there for a couple of moments watching him before he realized she was there.

"That's a picture of my parents and me on a trip we took after I graduated from medical school. They thought I needed a break before going into practice. They took me on a vacation to Europe. We spent a week between Paris and London. "

"Never been to Europe," he said.

"Oh, you should go sometime. It's a different world over there. So much history."

Jake turned and handed her a glass of scotch. She had removed her apron and it was obvious that she had run a brush through her hair. *Boy, she's beautiful, he thought.*

Raising his glass to hers, he said, "To health, happiness and the pursuit of justice."

"Here, here," she responded and clinked her glass against his.

"Dinner will be ready in about half an hour. Why don't we have a seat and you can start telling me about the race and...well, everything that happened. It must have been pretty exciting. I watched the television yesterday afternoon and it looked like every one with a badge was in Washington."

They took seats next to each other on the couch and Jake began to explain the events that took place on Sunday.

"Actually, I'd say that in addition to the D.C. police, there were obviously some FBI, Secret Service, Homeland Security and who knows what else. There were some guarded dignitaries at the race so the Secret Service was there even before the shooting but once the shooting occurred, the SWAT teams from all organizations were called in."

After listening to Jake talk about the events of yesterday for another fifteen minutes, Jillian jumped up to check on the dinner and returned a couple of minutes later.

"Dinner is served," she announced. Jake followed her to the dining room adjacent to the kitchen. The table was elegantly set with two place settings with real linen napkins, glass china, real silver and ornate stemware. The table was a Cherry wood French Provincial with matching high back chairs. An antique hutch lined the far wall and a claw foot corner cupboard displayed a pewter coffee set with cups and saucers. Overhead, a crystal chandelier shone down on the elegantly set table.

Noticing Jake's expression, she said, "I don't get to use this stuff much. I don't really have any guests and I haven't thrown any parties for quite some time. I was fortunate during the divorce. My ex didn't really want any of the household goods. He asked for the boat, tools, sports gear and his freedom. What a deal for me huh?" she laughed.

"This is nice," he said. "Sam and I usually plop down in front of the tube with TV trays, a couple of paper plates and a roll of paper towels."

"Here, why don't you do the honors," she said, handing Jake the Merlot and a wine opener.

After fumbling for a minute trying to remove the cork, Jake poured them each a glass of wine as they took their seats opposite each other.

"Do you say grace before eating?" she asked. "I though I saw you whisper a few words when we had lunch."

"Would you like me to?" he asked.

"Please."

After saying a prayer, Jake raised his wine glass to hers.

"To an enjoyable evening," he said.

She smiled and sipped the wine looking at him over the rim of the glass.

CHAPTER 33

Tuesday, October 28

Morning found Stryker sitting on a cold concrete bench surrounded by markers and tombstones, some dating back to before the Civil War. The bench was conveniently situated, overlooking the family plot in the old county cemetery. He came here often after Tommy was buried just to talk. Tommy was always the one Stryker could go to when he had a question. Even after Tommy died, Stryker felt that Tommy was listening. He always felt better after sitting here and talking. He now had another reason for talking with Tommy. When Stryker was home for Christmas last year, he started going through some of his mother's things that Uncle John had stored away after she died. It was then that he found the letter, an unopened letter from Tommy that had been delayed in the mails. It didn't arrive until after his mother died. With all that was going on at the time, Uncle John had just put it with her things and stored them in the attic. In the letter, Tommy disclosed what they had done in Iraq. He was ashamed and said that he was planning on going to the authorities and owning up to his part. In the letter, he also told her that he feared for his life. Tommy said that when he told the others what he was going to do, they had threatened him to keep him quiet. After reading the letter, Stryker knew that Tommy had not taken his own life. He stopped by to tell Tommy that he would make it right.

A cold front had moved in from the Northwest during the night, dropping temperatures into the low thirties. Stryker had left the house an hour earlier with only a pair of Asics running shoes and a light jacket. He now felt the cold wind penetrating the cotton jacket and his feet were damp from the steady drizzle, turning to sleet in front of his eyes. Grandpa and Grandma Sullivan had been laid to rest over fifteen years ago, just two years after Tommy died. They died within a year of each other. Grandma was the first to go, suffering from Alzheimer's for the last three years before she died. They never told her about Tommy. She didn't even recognize grandpa for the last year. It about broke grandpa's heart. They had been married for over sixty years when her illness was diagnosed. Grandpa was suffering from prostrate cancer but said he needed to hold on to take care of her. Walking three miles a day kept his mind clear and his body strong and agile so that he could care for her. He wouldn't hear of putting her in a rest home. Always said that he took vows and the reason you took them vows was for the tough times, not the easy ones. Grandpa finally succumbed to the cancer the year after grandma died. Stryker moved a broken branch that had fallen from the large oak tree during the night and landed across the headstones of his mother and Tommy. Tears started to well up in Stryker's eyes as he gazed at the words engraved on the bronze plaque.

Thomas J. Warner, Lieutenant U.S. Army
December 30, 1968 –November 12, 1991
Rest in Peace

"I'm not finished yet," he said aloud, to no one other than Tommy, rising from the bench to leave.

"A little cold out here to be dressed like that, don't you think?" the man said, startling Stryker. He hadn't noticed the man in the long woolen coat, a knit hat on his head and a scarf covering the lower part of his face that had walked up from behind.

"Didn't mean to scare you," the man continued, noticing Stryker had jumped at the sound of his voice.

"That's all right," responded Stryker. "I didn't hear you coming. I guess I had my mind on other things."

"Pretty day, isn't it," the man continued, putting a dry flower arrangement on the top of Stryker's mother's grave."

"You knew my mother?" Stryker asked.

"Yea, long time ago," he answered. "Different time. Way before your time," he smiled.

"Did you know my brother also?" Stryker asked, not recognizing the man, who had removed his scarf, displaying a salt and pepper beard.

"Yes, I knew your brother, too. I wish now I got to know him better," he said.

"You're not from around here, are you?" Stryker asked.

"Not anymore," he answered. "Hey, you feel like getting a cup of coffee or a hot chocolate? I'll buy," he said, before Stryker could respond.

Stryker's knew it probably wasn't a good idea going off with this stranger but his curiosity got the best of him and decided to go along.

Walking back to his car to follow the man for a cup of coffee, Stryker noticed the fresh deer pellets that were lying around the gravestones. Tommy would be delighted, he thought. He couldn't have picked a better deer stand.

CHAPTER 34

"So, tell me all about it," chimed Sam as she waltzed into the kitchen, still in her pajamas. "Wait, don't start. I need to get my morning cup of coffee and I don't want to miss anything."

"What makes you think I'm the kind of guy that kisses and tells?"

"All right," she said, ignoring his comment and grabbing a chair, holding her coffee up in front of her with both hands. "I'm ready. Start at the beginning and don't leave anything out."

Jake told her about his evening from the first smell of homemade apple pie to cleaning up the dishes together. That's where he stopped.

"Sounds like you had a nice evening. You really like her don't you dad?" she asked.

"Yea," he replied. "She's nice. I enjoy our conversations. She's pretty. She's confident. She's not pushy and I feel real comfortable around her. You okay with that, Sam?"

"Dad, you know that my biggest wish for you is that you find someone to make you happy. I know how much you loved mom but it's been thirteen years now and it's time you had a life. Mom would want that."

"We'll see," he said jumping up and conveniently changing the conversation. "What have you got going today? Are you going into the office or is today your day to work from home?"

Before she could answer, his cell phone rang. It was Sully on his way into the Bureau.

"Hey what do you say we head down to Quantico?" he asked Jake.

Before Jake could answer, Sully added. "I called the office on my way in and Lynn says there's a message for you from Chuck Embers. Sounds like he got bored at home yesterday on his day off and went into the lab to catch up on some work. He heard your voicemail message. The DC lab boys already delivered the bullet that killed the colonel so he started working on the ballistics yesterday afternoon."

"Sounds good. Why don't you pick me up here at the house and we can catch I-95 off of Van Dorn."

Closing his phone, Jake hurried out of the room before Sam could continue her interrogation. He knew this discussion with her was not over but he needed time to put some perspective on the issues.

CHAPTER 35

Traffic on I-95 South was light for that time of day and they made good time, arriving at the exit for the Marine Base and FBI Training Center in Quantico in less than an hour after leaving the townhouse. They easily found a parking space next to the ballistics building and made their way down the corridor, passing by the test range on their way to the lab. The red light outside the range door was red indicating someone was using the range. Even through the concrete, steel reinforced walls, they could hear the muffled sounds of weapons being fired.

"You guys are keeping me gainfully employed and for that I thank you," joked Chuck Embers, bowing to them when they walked into his office at the end of the hall. Chuck was dressed in a white lab coat and had been peering through a microscope before they entered.

"Don't mention it," said Sully. "We seem to keep plenty of people employed nowadays."

"Have you been able to make a match yet?" asked Jake, plopping down in a chair alongside Chuck.

"Not yet but I'm almost there," he said looking back through the microscope in front of him. "I was just starting to match the bullets when I heard you guys coming down the hall. Did you catch the shooter?"

"No. Shooter got away but we believe we have the location where the shot came from. Picked up a couple of candy wrappers and a Blackjack gum wrapper from a rooftop overlooking the crime scene. We think the shooter might have been up there for some time waiting for the perfect opportunity. We don't have anything concrete yet. Wrappers coulda been left by anyone working up on the roof the last couple of days. I understand that they were having some problems with the HVAC system the early part of the week and there were some workers checking on the system Friday morning.

"Here, take a look," said Chuck, pushing himself away from the microscope so that Jake could view what he had been looking at.

"See those striations along the right edge? Shooter must have used a silencer. Those marks you see are caused by the silencer as the bullet leaves the barrel. The bullet on the top is the one that they dug out of the asphalt on Sunday. The lower one is the one they recovered in the dirt after it took the back of the senator's head off in April. There's no doubt based on at least three matching points that I've highlighted that you're looking at the same gun."

"Let me take a look," said Sully, as Jake backed away from the microscope, giving him room.

"I don't suppose the shooter was kind enough to leave the gun this time?" asked Chuck.

"You would be right on that one," said Sully.

"You didn't find any casings at the scene either, I suppose?"

"No, shooter's not stupid…policed his brass before he left the scene," said Jake, sliding over to look through the microscope again. "Well, on the bright side, I'd say we're looking at a common shooter," he continued.

"Same gun at least," cautioned Chuck.

"Yea, well, at least we finally caught a break," responded Jake. "There's a definite link between these two shootings. With this evidence, I think we owe Director Preacher another visit. I don't think we've been told everything," he added.

"I'd say they've been covering something up and someone's out to clean the slate," said Sully.

"Chuck you've been a big help again," said Jake, shaking Chuck's hand. Appreciate your jumping on this so fast… Come on Sully. Let's head back to toward D.C. I want to shake up the director a little bit on our way back to the office."

"How bout we stop for lunch on our way. I didn't get a chance to eat breakfast this morning."

"Always thinking about food," said Jake, waving to Chuck on his way out the door.

CHAPTER 36

On their way back to Washington, Jake and Sully discussed how they were going to approach Director Preacher. Things were starting to add up. Somewhere, somehow, these two killings had a common theme and they were sure that Director Preacher knew more than he was letting on.

Jake called Lynn to check his messages and let her know that they'd be in after their meeting at Langley. They didn't have an appointment with the director but decided to make a surprise visit. No sense in giving him time to come up with a story.

After stopping for lunch at a Burger King, they arrived at Langley, home of the Central Intelligence Agency, the world's largest clandestine spy operations near McLean, Virginia. It was shortly after noon when they stopped at the checkpoint leading into Langley. Unfortunately, they couldn't make a surprise visit on the director, giving him ample time to prepare for their visit. After providing their shields and ID's to the guard, they were told to wait in the car until he called ahead for clearance. After five long minutes he returned and provided them with visitor passes, directing them to the director's office. They waited until the gate was lifted before proceeding through the checkpoint.

"This place gives me the creeps," said Sully. "I never did feel very comfortable around places like this. Who knows what all goes on inside these gates? They probably have listening devices hanging in the trees. For all we know, they could be watching us right now, listening to our conversation."

"You watch too many movies," Jake laughed. "I'm sure they have more important things to do than listen in on our conversation."

Jake found the main administration building and parked in the visitor parking area. On their way in, he noticed a car parked in Deputy Director Preacher's reserved spot. Upon entering and providing their visitor badges and ID's to the receptionist, they were told to have a seat while she called upstairs.

"I've spoken with the director's assistant. She'll be with you shortly," she said, returning to them. "Can I get you a drink while you're waiting? I'm sure it will only be a few minutes."

"I think we're fine," said Jake. "We'll just wait, if you don't mind."

Within a couple of minutes, a tall, attractive blond in her late twenties or early thirties exited the elevator and made her way over to them. Sully couldn't take his eyes off of her.

"Agent Hunter?" she asked.

"That would be me," Jake responded, standing to shake her hand. "This is Agent Gilmore," he said, nodding to Sully.

"Hello. My name is Lisa. I'm Deputy Director Preacher's assistant. If you'll follow me, I'll take you upstairs where you'll be meeting with Deputy Director Preacher," she said, walking over and pushing the elevator button.

They followed her to the elevator. Jake, who stood at an even six feet noticed that she was quite tall in her three inch heels. She had stunning features with high cheekbones and bright blue eyes. She was wearing red lipstick that matched her mid thigh seductively cut suit and earrings that dangled from her ear lobes. Jake detected just a scent of perfume that reminded him of fresh lavender. It was obvious that she was aware of the impression she was making on them. As they followed her to the elevator, Jake noticed that she was not wearing a wedding band or engagement ring. Entering the elevator, he looked over at Sully. Sully had been watching him and smiled. *He doesn't miss a beat, does he, thought Jake.*

CHAPTER 37

They rode the elevator to the third floor in silence, all eyes glued to the overhead floor indicator light as it blinked on then off as the elevator rose upward. When the elevator stopped on the third floor, the doors parted and they stepped into a carpeted hallway. She turned right out of the elevator and led them down the brightly lit hallway past offices with closed doors to the end of the hall where they entered through a set of double doors into the director's outer office, a large sitting area at least twenty feet wide by twenty feet deep, directly outside the director's private office.

"Gentlemen, if you'll have a seat, please," she said, motioning for them to sit in one of the chairs surrounding a table scattered with magazines. "Director Preacher's finishing up a conference call. He'll be with you shortly."

She disappeared into the director's office.

"She's quite the looker, don't you think?" said Sully, when she had closed the door behind her.

"Yea, she knows it too," responded Jake.

Jake had just picked up a copy of the New York Times and started reading the headlines on the front page when she reappeared and ushered them into Director Preacher's office.

On entering the room, Jake noticed that the director was seated behind a large wooden desk scribbling on a legal pad. Bookcases with leather-bound volumes lined the wall to his left. At the other end of the room was a sitting area with a leather couch and matching wing chairs.

"Director Preacher," said Jake on entering the director's office.

"Gentlemen. Welcome," he said, looking up and closing the legal pad. He arose and extended his hand to Jake, who took it and shook it firmly. Then, he offered his hand to Sully who shook it briefly.

"It's nice to see you again. Please, let's take a seat over here," he said, gesturing toward the couch and chairs.

Jake waited for the director to take a seat in one of the chairs before choosing a seat opposite him on the couch. Sully took a seat on the other end of the couch facing the director.

"Would either of you care for something to drink before we begin?" asked the director. The director had a bottle of Dasani water that he had carried from his desk.

"Thank you but no," replied Jake. Sully just shook his head "no".

On their way up from Quantico Jake and Sully had discussed at length how they wanted to approach the director with their new found evidence. They had agreed that Jake would take the lead on the discussion and Sully would pay attention to the director's body language and see if he could discern any sense that the director was covering something up.

"So. What's this all about?" asked the director, relaxing in his seat and taking a drink from his bottle of water.

Sully looked over at Jake to begin.

"Director, I'm sure you're aware that Colonel Hatcher was killed over the weekend? That he was shot during the Marine Corp Marathon on Saturday morning," he said, more like a statement than a question.

"Yes, I'm aware of that," he responded. "Terrible thing."

"Well," Jake continued. "We have just come from the ballistics lab at Quantico and have some information regarding the murder of Colonel Hatcher on Sunday."

"Oh," said the director. "Such as?"

"Well to start with," began Jake. "Our ballistics expert has concluded that the bullet that killed Colonel Hatcher was fired from the same weapon that killed Senator Powell in April."

Jake hesitated momentarily for the director to respond before going on.

When the director made no comment, Jake continued.

"Based on this information, Director, in your vast experience, wouldn't you presume that the chances are highly likely that we are talking about one shooter?"

This time, Jake waited for the director to respond. After an awkward ten seconds, the director finally responded.

"Well, I can see where you're going with this Agent Hunter but is there anything in addition to the ballistics report that would tend to indicate one shooter?"

"I don't know Director. You tell me. First, your friend Senator Powell gets shot during a weekend golf game, a game that he plays every Saturday during the golf season when he's in town. Then, six months later, your good friend, Colonel Hatcher gets taken out during a marathon race. Both men are killed by bullets that are fired from the same weapon. Correct me if I'm wrong but the three of you went to West Point Military Academy at the same time and served together in the Gulf during the first Gulf War. Do you really think that this is just coincidental?"

"Well, I dunno," he stammered, starting to look a little pasty around the gills. "I don't know what our being at West Point at the same time and serving in Iraq together has anything at all to do with this. I think you're barking up the wrong tree."

"Director," I have to ask you. Just where were you on Sunday morning around ten in the morning?" Jake continued.

"Well, you don't think I had anything to do with killing my friends, do you?" snapped the director, now becoming defensive.

"Director. We don't have our shooter yet and at this time, you're the only tie we have to both victims. You know I had to ask that question. If you're not the shooter, there's a good chance that you know who is?"

"Well, gentlemen, I can assure you that I am not the shooter. I didn't kill either Senator Powell or Colonel Hatcher. We were close friends. You get close when you spend time with other guys in combat. We've been friends ever since. And I have no idea who would have killed either one of them," he snapped, raising from his chair and walking back behind his desk.

Jake rose from his seat and followed the director back to his desk.

"Director, I'm not accusing you at this time of killing either man. What I am telling you is that there's someone out there that used the same weapon to kill two men on two separate occasions that were both good friends of yours. I find it extremely unlikely that this was a random act. Somehow, these two murders are linked and I don't mean just with the same weapon. Do you know how many people live in D.C. and the surrounding area? What do you think the odds are that two men who know each other like Senator Powell and Colonel Hatcher just happen to be in the wrong place at the wrong time? Director, aren't you just the slightest bit afraid that you may be the next target?"

"That's just ludicrous," he bellowed at Jake, his eyes filled with rage.

"We'll find our own way out," said Jake, leaving the director sitting in his chair as he and Sully closed the door behind them.

CHAPTER 38

"He knows something he's not saying," said Sully, first looking around to make sure that they were out of earshot of anyone else as they walked out of the building.

"There is no doubt in my mind that he's covering something up," replied Jake. "Just what, I don't know but he was way too uncomfortable in there. I think I hit a nerve and he knows he's in danger."

"I'd just like to bitch slap the sonovabitch," responded Sully.

"Let's get back to the office and see what records we can pull on their time together in the military," said Jake, laughing at Sully's last remark.

While Sully drove, Jake called Lynn on their way to the Hoover building to let her know that they were on their way in and to check for messages. Director Avery had been down looking for them. He instructed her to have them meet with him as soon as they got back.

Thirty minutes later, they were pulling into the parking garage.

"As soon as we finish our meeting with Mike," Jake said. "I want to start looking into their military records. I think we should start at West Point. Since Colonel Hatcher never even brought it up that they were there at the same time, I think that is a good place to start. Then we'll move on to their time over in the Gulf."

Lynn was on the phone when they came into the office but she handed Jake a stack of messages she had retrieved from voicemail overnight. He quickly glanced at them on his way to his desk. Not recognizing any of the callers, he threw them on top of the other eight unreturned messages still lying on his desk from last Friday.

"We'll be with the director," he mouthed to Lynn and pointed up to the ceiling as they passed by her desk on their way to the elevator. She was still talking on the phone but nodded her head in acknowledgement. In their busy office, they frequently communicated by nods of their heads or hand movements.

"How much to we want to tell him right now?" asked Sully, jumping in the elevator as the door closed.

"At this point, let's tell him everything we've got. We might need him to work his charm on getting us the school records. Without a warrant, it might be difficult getting West Point to let us get a peek at their records."

Mike Avery was on the phone when they walked into the outer office leading to his door. He saw them coming and motioned for them to come in and take a seat while he finished up his call.

Mike was a twenty two year veteran of the FBI. He had started his career right out of the Navy. Having served four years as a Naval Intelligence Officer, he resigned his commission to join the FBI as an analyst, attending night school to earn his law degree before transferring to the operations group. Married with two grown children, he was easy going most of the time but could be tough when necessary. Jake had worked a couple of joint cases with him when Jake was attached to the New York office and Mike was working on a case involving the transportation of illegal weapons across state lines. Jake considered Mike a good guy who would do what was right and not because it was politically correct.

"You guys must have caused quite a ruckus over at Langley earlier today," he said, hanging up the phone.

"How so?" asked Jake.

"Well, that was Director Edwards on the phone just now. He said that you two had gone in there and accused Deputy Director Preacher of holding out on you."

"You must have had a pretty good reason to stir that bee's nest," he said, raising his eyebrows in the form of a question.

For the past five years, Mike Avery had been working hard to mend relations with the CIA. His predecessor, Ramsey Solomon, let his political ambitions cloud his judgment and had caused a major riff between the two agencies. Whereas the FBI's primary role was to guard against illegal activities within the United States border, the CIA was tasked with providing intelligence on national security issues to government policymakers. That meant putting operatives in foreign lands to recruit spies from other countries. Spies were used to collect, interpret and disseminate information that could lead to potential harm to the United States or any of its citizens in foreign or domestic lands. In his zeal to make a name for himself, Director Solomon had leaked information that compromised secret activities, putting the lives of numerous agents in foreign countries at risk.

"I don't want to lose the goodwill that Director Edwards and I have built up over the past five years," he said. "You had better be one hundred percent sure of yourself before we go down that road."

"We didn't accuse Deputy Director Preacher of anything." Jake said. We asked some pointed questions and well. . . Let's just say that the director was not so forthcoming. We think he's holding out on us. He knows something and he's not talking. For all we know, he may know who the killer is."

After discussing the ballistics report that they had obtained from Chuck Embers with the director, Jake stopped.

"So, where do we go from here?" asked the director.

"We'd like to drive up to West Point Military Academy and look at their school records. There may be something in their past at the academy that will give us a clue."

"Let me make a call up there before you go," volunteered the director. "I don't want you to make a wasted trip. I've got some brownie points build up with the Commandant, General Davis. Just don't go in there like a couple of bulls in a china shop. A smile and a little courtesy go a long way."

"Now, get back to work," he said, shooing them out of the room.

"That wasn't so bad," said Sully, as they punched the elevator to go back downstairs.

CHAPTER 39

Jake didn't want to get stuck in the early morning traffic and figured that if they left by five a.m. that they'd be far enough north of the city before the slowdown occurred. He was sitting in the front of Sully's condominium before five the following morning, nursing a cup of black coffee. Sully rented a two bedroom on the sixth floor in a rent controlled apartment complex in Anacostia, part of a major gentrification project started two years earlier. Having tried the marriage life style twice, Sully was now a confirmed bachelor. Jake didn't know if that was by choice or the fact that Sully was paying a hefty amount each month for child support to both wives. He had a son, Jonathan, now fourteen with his first wife. Their divorce up was on less than amicable circumstances, Sully having found her one night with another man. She blamed it on the fact that he was never home, always working, or didn't pay any attention to her. His relationship with his son was tenuous at best. Sully tried to be a father to him but it was difficult only getting to spend time with him two weekends a month. They had split up when the boy was only four so he never really knew Sully as the father he wanted. On the rebound, less than a year later, he married his second wife and had a young daughter, Amanda, two years later. That marriage only lasted five years but Sully tried hard to stay in his daughter life. He tried to call her on the phone at least a couple of times a week and see her on the odd weekends.

Not wanting to find a parking spot and leave the warmth of the car, Jake called him on his cell phone to let him know he was waiting out front with hot coffee. On his way over to Sully's, Jake had gone through a McDonald's drive thru and had picked up coffee and a breakfast sandwich for each of them.

Five minutes after the call, Sully came bounding out the front door carrying his jacket and looking like he had slept in his clothes.

"Sorry you had to wait," he stammered, throwing his jacket over the front seat, landing on the floor behind. "I got in a pissing contest with Sally last night," he said, taking a gulp from the hot coffee. "She's got her panties in a knot again because my child support was a day late. Now she's threatening to have me pay it through the court. Says she's not going to let me talk with Amanda on the phone except for my weekends. I tell you, I can't win with that woman."

They picked up I-95 and headed north for the five hour drive to the Academy. Their appointment was at noon but Jake didn't want to risk getting stuck in traffic. He added an extra hour for any unexpected traffic problems. West Point was an hour north of the city overlooking the banks of the Hudson. He had only been there one other time, years ago, when he was based out of the New York Bureau. A neighbor boy from Queens graduated from the academy and he and Rachael had been invited to the celebration. He remembered all the hats flying in the air as the cadets threw them overhead at the end of the graduation ceremony.

Director Avery had left Jake a voicemail message the night before indicating that he had discussed their visit with the Commandant, General Stone Davis. The general had been apprised of the purpose of their visit by Director Avery and had agreed to make the school records available to them. General Davis was a highly decorated combat war veteran. Avery had forewarned them before scheduling the appointment that the general was a no-nonsense guy and they needed to be straight with him from the get go.

They rode in silence most of the way, Jake could see that Sully was still upset over the phone call from his ex-wife the night before.

"So, do you really think we're going to find something?" Sully asked, finally breaking the silence."

"Dunno, but we'll never know if we don't stick our noses out a bit. If we don't find something in their school records, I say we need to dig deeper into the time they spent together in Iraq."

"Sounds like a plan to me," Sully said, slouching down in the seat. "Okay if I take a snooze?" he asked. Not waiting for a reply, he added "I think I'm gonna lay my head back for a bit. Wake me up when we get to the City. In forty years, I've never been to New York. I hear it's a hell of a place to party".

Five minutes later, Jake could hear Sully breathing heavy in the seat beside him. He didn't mind the quiet. It gave him an opportunity to think. When he was alone in the car, he never played the radio. He could drive for hours in silence, letting his mind go wherever it may. It was a great day for a drive. The temperature hung in the high fifties and there wasn't a cloud in the sky. He could see forever and traffic was traveling nicely at a steady eighty miles an hour. His mind drifted to thoughts of the evening he spent with Jillian. It had been a long time since he felt that comfortable. There was something special about her. He enjoyed being with her and decided that he would call her again when they got back to D.C. Maybe Sam was right. Maybe it was time for him to put someone else in his life.

It was not until they were crossing the George Washington Bridge over the Hudson River, linking Fort Lee, New Jersey with Upper Manhattan that Jake woke Sully.

"That my friend is the big apple and don't ask me why they call it that," Jake said, nodding in the direction of the huge buildings that seemed to touch the sky.

"It was a much more impressive site when the towers were there," he said. "Boy, I'll never forget that day. I still can't get over the sight of those buildings coming down the way they did. It was like watching a movie. One minute they were there, the next; there was nothing but dust and smoke. People went crazy. Panic and chaos took over the city. Fire trucks and emergency vehicles were everywhere, trying to get around all the cars that were just left in the middle of the streets. People actually jumped out of their cars, leaving them running as they ran for cover."

An hour later, they were entering the Thayer Gate at Highland Falls, home to the United States Military Academy at West Point.

"Good morning," Jake said to the guard who approached their car from the guardhouse, dressed in full military uniform.

"We're here to see General Davis. He's expecting us."

The guard took their ID's and asked them to remain in the car while he called ahead for clearance. Two minutes later, he returned to the car, handed their ID's back through the window and provided them with visitor passes, directions to the Commandant's office and a map of the grounds.

"Take a right out of the gate, pass the parade grounds, and take your second left on Patton Place. Can't miss it, there's a big Bradley tank just before the turn."

Returning to the guard house, he pushed the button for the gate to rise and saluted them as they drove through.

"This place is wrapped pretty tight," remarked Sully.

Driving through the gate, they took an immediate right turn on McArthur Blvd., passing several of the classroom buildings and the parade grounds. Cadets in full dress uniform marched in cadence to the "Jodi" call led by the cadet leading the group.

Sully rolled the window down to hear what he was saying.

"Once knew a girl in New York City," the cadet belted out.

In unison the entire squad repeated, "Once knew a girl in New York City."

"Had the sweetest pair of titties," he continued.

Jake and Sully laughed as the squad repeated line for line.

"Makes you want to be twenty again, doesn't it?" joked Sully.

"Not me my friend," said Jake. "I'd be happy to stay in my forties."

They passed building after building of brick and stucco, some built in the early eighteen hundreds. The grounds were immaculately manicured.

"Did you know Patton graduated from West Point?" asked Sully.

"Yea, but did you know he was last in his class?" responded Jake.

"There's the tank," pointed Sully. "Man, that's a helluva lot of steel," he continued.

They found the Commandant's office without any problems and pulled into a visitor spot in the parking lot adjacent to the building.

"Let's go do er," Sully said, reaching behind him to pick his jacket off the floor.

"Remember what Mike said," cautioned Jake, as they walked up the concrete steps leading to the Georgian style office building. "This guy's been around the block a few times and doesn't mix words. We need him on our side. We don't need him holding back anything on us. Let's just approach this from the angle that we just want to look at old school records to see if there's anything in their past here at the academy that might shed some light on what's going on."

"Don't worry. I'll follow your lead. I don't feel much like fighting with anyone today anyway," responded Sully.

They entered through a heavy glass door and were standing in a wide carpeted hallway with offices in both directions. Directly in front of them was a set of double glass doors with the general's name prominently displayed in big letters.

"Looks like we're in the right spot," responded Sully.

Opening the door, Jake walked to the receptionist sitting behind a wooden desk working on a computer screen. A set of earphones connected to an IPOD hung from her ears. She stopped what she was doing and took the earphones out as they approached her desk.

"Good morning gentlemen. How may I help you?" she asked, coming from behind her desk to greet them.

Jake guessed her to be about fifty years old. She was quite petite standing next to his six foot frame. She wore little makeup but was naturally attractive. Her auburn hair was cut shoulder length and had recently been colored. Jake looked down into her green eyes and extended his hand.

"Hello," he said. I'm Agent Jake Hunter and this is Agent Gilmore. We have an appointment with General Davis at noon."

"Yes, I have it here on my calendar. He has a couple of cadets with him right now but I'm sure he'll be with you shortly." Can I get you something to drink while you're waiting?"

"Water would be great," Sully answered before Jake could say a word.

"Water's fine with me as well," said Jake.

While she was gone for the water, Jake looked around the reception area. On the left wall hung art prints of soldiers in uniforms. All had general's stars on their epaulets with rows of medals pinned to their front left pocket. Beneath the pictures were bronze plates engraved with names and dates. Jake guessed that they may be prints of predecessors to the general. On the right wall hung prints of battle scenes. Jake recognized some of these from his days as a political science major at Syracuse University in the eighties. A bronze bust of Stonewall Jackson astride his horse with sword in hand sat on an end table.

The door to the general's immediate office opened before she returned. Two cadets came out and walked to the door without speaking a word. The somber look on their faces indicated that they had just received a pretty good ass chewing.

"Martha", came a deep voice from the room the two cadets had just vacated.

"Martha are you out there?" came the voice again, sounding somewhat agitated.

Before there was time for any response, he appeared in the doorway, looking directly at Jake and Sully.

"Gentlemen," he said. "I didn't realize anyone was out here. I must have sounded pretty gruff, didn't I?"

"I'm General Davis, Commandant here at the academy," he said, walking toward them with an extended arm.

Before they could answer, he continued. "You must be the FBI agents from Washington. I'm sorry for keeping you waiting. Come on in," he motioned for them to enter and closed the door behind them. Jake noticed that he had an extraordinary firm handshake.

They followed him into a large office where he directed them to a couple of chairs in front of his desk. Behind him to his right at the corner of a large mahogany credenza was a United States flag. On the other corner, Jake recognized the flag of the Army Special Forces.

The general was dressed in desert fatigues, starched like they could stand up on their own. His black beret sat on the corner of his desk. Jake recognized the Ranger patch on his uniform. Jake knew that he was almost sixty, having looked him up on the internet before coming. With his crew cut and obviously physically fit body, he could easily have passed for forty five or fifty. Jake was glad he had looked him up before their trip. He didn't expect to see a Black Commandant of West Point but was quite impressed with the general's background, having served two tours in Viet Nam, one in Kosovo, one in the first Gulf War in 1990 and then two tours in Iraq since the initial invasion in March of 2003.

"Let's not waste each others time gentlemen," he started. "I understand that you're here to look at some records of a couple of graduates. I don't know what you expect to get out of a bunch of old school records but pursuant to Director Avery's request, I had them pulled out of storage this morning for you. But to be honest, I didn't look at them. I've got enough on my plate trying to make good soldiers out of cadets like the two that just walked out of here with their tails between their legs. They arrive here in September still wet behind the ears and four years later we're sending them to Iraq as second lieutenants in command of a platoon of men their same age. Don't get me wrong," he continued. "We train them well but they're still so damn young."

Realizing he had been ranting, the general concluded, "I'm sorry gentlemen. Sometimes I get carried away. Hell, my wife gave me a wrapped soap box last year for Christmas. Sometimes I just get to rattling on."

"I've had Martha set up a place in one of the conference rooms where you can work until we close the doors at six tonight if you want. I think you may be grasping for straws but have at it."

"Before we get to the records General, I wondered if you'd answer a couple of questions for us?" queried Jake.

"Shoot," he said, crossing his hands before him on the desk. "Ask away. I've got about fifteen minutes before I've got to be over at the parade grounds but I'll answer any another question or two if I can."

"Did you know either Senator Clayton Powell or Colonel Hatcher?" started Jake.

"Didn't know either of them personally. I knew who they were only because

I met them about a year ago in Washington. I was asked to meet with the Senate Arms Committee on a couple of issues. Senator Powell was the Chairman of that Committee. Colonel Hatcher was also at that meeting. If I recall, he was attached to the Pentagon. That's the only time I ever met either one of them."

"How about Deputy Director Preacher of the CIA? Have you ever met him?" asked Sully.

"No. Can't say I ever met the man. What else?"

Not waiting for Jake or Sully to respond, he rose from his chair and came around his desk.

"Well gentlemen, if you'll excuse me, I must get to the parade grounds. I'll have Martha show you to the conference room. I should be back in an hour or so and will have some time at the end of the day to answer any additional questions you might have for me."

When the general had left and Martha closed the door behind them to provide them some privacy, Sully looked over at Jake.

"Why didn't you tell me he was black?"

"Who?" Jake responded.

"Don't give me any of that shit," said Sully.

"I didn't think it made any difference," responded Jake, smiling. "Actually, I wanted to surprise you. I wanted to see the expression on your face."

"Well, I'll be damned. I about hit the floor when he came out of his office. That's about the last place I'd expect to see a black man. Nice to see that a brother made it to the top of the rock," replied Sully.

After spending the better part of two hours reviewing the school records for all three of the graduates, two now dead and Director Preacher the sole survivor, Jake turned to Sully.

"I don't see anything in here that tells me why any of these guys might be the target for a bullet. I wouldn't guess that any one of them was General material, but other than a couple of disciplinary measures, they seem to be average college students."

"Yea. I don't see anything here either," responded Sully. Maybe were looking for a needle in the haystack. Or...maybe, it was just coincidental after all."

They found Martha tidying up in the general's office.

"Martha, appreciate all your help," Jake said. "Thank the general for us. We'll find our own way out," he continued, handing her back the three files.

CHAPTER 40

By three thirty, they were back on the highway. Jake wanted to get south of the city before stopping for something to eat.

"If we get stuck in traffic," he commented, "it'll be midnight before we get home."

"I think my stomach has started to eat itself," complained Sully.

They made good time for the first hour but then got stuck in bumper to bumper traffic just as they hit the northern corporate limits of New York City.

"Damn," said Jake, coming to a complete stop behind a Mayflower moving van. "I knew it was too good to be true. We were making good time. At this rate, we'd be better jumping off somewhere and catching a bite to eat. By the time we eat and check in with the office, the traffic should be moving along pretty good."

"Well, if we're going to be sitting like this for the next hour, my vote's finding a nice greasy hole in the wall where we can get some cheap burgers and some big ole French fries," replied Sully. "Besides, I gotta piss like a racehorse."

Jake checked the rear view mirror, downshifted the five speed and gunned the gas pedal sending all 330 horsepower into a frenzy as he slipped the Silver 2008 G37 Infiniti Coupe into a hole between two cars in the right lane.

"Whoa doggie," screamed Sully, slipping down into the passenger seat next to him to avoid the car horns and four letter expletives exploding from the vehicles around them.

Jake steered the car down the next off ramp and made a sharp right turn at the stop sign at the bottom of the ramp.

"There," he said, pointing to a half lit neon sign displaying "Mannies" across the large window.

"Looks like just the kind of place we're looking for," he said, pulling into the adjacent parking lot.

"Yea, I spose good as any," replied Sully.

They entered the restaurant just as two men holding hands were leaving. Sully looked over to Jake to see if he had noticed the two but Jake had already stepped into the dimly lit room.

"Grab a seat honey," a waitress clearing tables hollered over to them. "I'll be with ya in a jiff soon's I git this table cleared," she said. With her broad shoulders and raspy cigarette voice she reminded Jake more of an on the road truck driver than a waitress.

Jake grabbed a table on the far wall opposite the bar while Sully ran for the restroom. Over the bar, blue smoke hung thick like a dense fog with a mixture of cigarettes and cigars. The ashtray on their table overflowed with gray ashes looking like it hadn't been emptied all day. Jake hated the smell of cigarette smoke, having given up the habit twenty years earlier. Shaking his head with disgust at the overflowing ashtray, he picked it up and placed it on the table behind him, wiping his hands on a napkin. Sully noticed Jake's look of disdain on returning to the table.

"Not used to these fancy digs huh?" joked Sully. "Betcha the foods outa this world. These are the kinda places where the atmosphere isn't the greatest but the helping's are big and the prices are right." Jake just looked around the room and smiled. The tables were just like the one he remembered in his family's kitchen forty years ago. The chairs were metal with cracked red vinyl seats that were wrapped with gray duct tape to hold the stuffing in place.

They had just decided on their order when the waitress arrived at the table.

"Sorry, we're out of the special," she informed them, pulling a pencil out of her bleached blond hair. "Had a pretty good run during the lunch hour. Didn't think it'd go that fast but folks just scarffed it up."

"So, what can I do ya for?"

"How's your burgers?" asked Sully.

"Best in town. Big'n juicy if ya don't get them cooked like shoe leather."

"I'll take two of em, medium...and a large order of fries," responded Sully.

Jake ordered a fried Haddock sandwich with coleslaw. They added a couple of Miller draughts to their order and she left the table, sticking the pencil back in her hair. Before she was three feet from their table, she hollered the order across the room to the man standing in front of the grill. There was no mistaking him as the fry cook with a pack of cigarettes rolled up in the sleeve of his grungy tee shirt that looked like it had been used for target practice.

Within ten minutes, she was back with their order, reaching across the table to lay Sully's plate down. Jake noticed that she hadn't shaved her armpits for sometime as her arm stretched in front of his face.

"So, where you boys from? You don't look like you're from round here."

"D.C.," Sully responded with a mouthful of hamburger. "We're from Washington."

"You here for business or pleasure?" she asked.

"Business," replied Jake before Sully could respond.

"You wouldn't happen to have any tartar sauce, would you?" asked Jake, trying to change the subject.

"Yea, sure we do. Back in a minute," she said, leaving them for the kitchen.

Forty-five minutes later, they were back on the road. Traffic was lighter and they quickly got up to seventy five mph, leaving the congestion of the big apple behind them as they headed south on Interstate 95 to Washington.

CHAPTER 41

Thursday, October 30

Jake and Sully were in Director Avery's office by eight the following morning.

"So, what did you find out?" he asked, looking up from the stack of papers he was signing piled high on the top of his desk.

"Nada, zilch" replied Jake. "We spent the better part of the afternoon looking through files. Other than a couple of minor disciplinary actions for your typical college pranks, there wasn't anything that seemed out of order."

"They all graduated in the top half of their class. Senator Powell graduated in 86 and both Colonel Hatcher and Director Preacher graduated the following year," added Sully.

"No run-ins with the law or anything like that while they were up there?" asked Director Avery.

"Didn't see anything," said Jake. "If there was, it didn't make it into their school records."

"What did you think about General Stone? Quite the soldier isn't he?"

"I was impressed," said Sully.

"He doesn't waste time," added Jake. "He was all fact, no bullshit."

"Could he add anything to the picture?" asked the director. "What did he say about the three of them?"

"He didn't really know them personally," responded Jake. "He had met the senator and Colonel Hatcher sometime last year when he was asked to testify in front of the Senate Arms Committee but he had never met Preacher."

"So... We're right back to square one on this, huh?" said the director.

"I wouldn't quite say that, sir," replied Jake. "I still think that there's a link somewhere. We're just gonna have to broaden our search. Look for something else. I mean, I just don't go along with the thought that this was just coincidental. Two men, friends for over twenty years, both shot by the same gun within six months of each other. I don't think so. I think there's a definite connection. We just haven't found it."

"What do you think about spending a little more time with Director Preacher? See if you can shake him. If he's hiding something, he's got to be running scared. Two of his closest buddies have been killed by a sniper and he's not shaken? I don't buy it."

"I understand security on the director has been increased since the colonel was killed?" queried Sully.

"Yea, he's under pretty tight protection right now. The D.C. police have security around the clock at his residence and I assigned a couple of additional agents to cover him to and from Langley. From what I hear, he doesn't go to the bathroom without an escort."

"Glad I'm not important," responded Sully, on his way out the door. "I like my private time when I'm on the porcelain throne."

Lynn handed a note to Jake as he walked by her desk on his way to his office. Dr. Harris was calling to schedule a lunch date. He smiled as he walked toward his desk. *He had been thinking a lot about her lately.*

CHAPTER 42

Friday, October 31

By Friday, Stryker was getting restless. He'd been sitting around the house for almost a week and was getting antsy. Until he had fulfilled his promise to Tommy, he couldn't get on with his own life. The Coshocton Gazette, the local paper was limited in its coverage, more social in nature than newsworthy. Uncle John had an old Apple Computer that he used for writing letters and keeping track of farm expenses but without internet access, Stryker couldn't check the activity on the colonel's shooting. Stryker had listened to the NBC National News every evening hoping to hear something but anchorman Brian Williams never mentioned the shooting in Washington. He didn't feel comfortable going into town. Coshocton was a small town and it was difficult going anywhere without running into someone who knew you or knew your family. He just didn't feel like answering any more questions about what he'd been doing or where he'd been.

When he awoke at eight that morning, a light snow was falling and the bedroom was cold. The wood burning stove in the kitchen was the only heat source other than the old oil furnace that Uncle John only fired up when it was really cold. Uncle John was from the old school and he couldn't see heating the entire house when he was only home to sleep and eat. Any even then, he spent the majority of his time in the kitchen. The heat from the stove kept the lower level toasty but Stryker had kept the bedroom door closed, shutting out any heat that rose in the stairwell. He could see his breath when he stuck his head out from under the down quilt.

He jumped out of bed and dressed quickly before he climbed down the back stairs to be greeted by Fritz, his tail wagging. Uncle John had left for work a couple of hours earlier, filling the wood burner before he left the house. Stryker opened the door to the wood burner, the hot embers glowing. He threw a couple of logs in from the wood box next to the stove and stood in front of the opening. Within seconds, the cooler room air was pulled into the stove, causing the flame to rise and the wood to pop as the moisture fizzled on the ends of the logs.

"Wanna go outside boy?" he asked the dog who was pacing wildly back and forth in front of the back door. After letting the dog out, he found a mug drying on the washboard and poured himself a cup of coffee. On his way to the table, he pulled the box of Cheerios off the shelf and grabbed the milk from the refrigerator. While eating, he decided that he'd head back to D.C. the following morning. He didn't want to disappoint Uncle John but he knew he'd understand. Uncle John was never one to stand in his way.

After a quick breakfast, he decided to go for a last walk in the woods. Uncle John didn't have a dishwasher so he rinsed the dishes and put them in the left side of the sink. He'd wash the dishes and clean up before Uncle John returned from work. Remembering how cold he was last weekend at the cemetery, he grabbed a hooded Carhart jacket from the hall closet, found winter gloves, a woolen cap and a pair of insulated boots before heading out the door. Fritz was rolling in a fresh cowpie next to the barn when he closed the door behind him and hurried to catch up with him.

"Geez dog, you smell like shit," he laughed, throwing a snowball at the dog as he ran past him.

Stryker walked down the tractor path behind the barn and into the woods where he and Tommy had filled many a deer tag over the years. The path wound through the woods just above the creek to an open field that had previously been planted with corn over the years. With fewer cows now, Uncle John had left it fallow the last several years, Osage orange briars now sticking up at all angles to catch your ankles. Stryker worked his way through the briars and crossed the creek back into the woods at the rear of the property. He stopped to watch a big gray squirrel gather hickory nuts from the ground around the base of a big tree, fill its pouches and scamper up the tree. After depositing the nuts in its nest, the squirrel ran back down the tree to repeat the ritual. After watching the squirrel for a couple of minutes, Stryker found an old used path and walked along it until he came to an open area. Here there was an old fifty five gallon barrel standing up on end. The old burn barrel. This was base camp. A "hooch" as they called it was covered with old tarps, an opening facing a ridgeline across a small creek. This was grandpa's hunting blind. A couple of old lawn chairs were still leaning against the back of the hooch. Stryker pulled one of the chairs out of the hooch and set it down by the barrel. He gathered up some dry kindling and pulled a plastic bag from the hooch filled with pine needles. Inside the bag he also found an old rusty quart of charcoal lighter fluid. Within five minutes, he had a roaring fire blazing in the barrel, flames reaching three feet out over the top of the rim. During deer season, this was the place that he, Tommy, Uncle John, and uncles from Dayton, Ohio and Dallas, Texas would meet after sitting in their deer stands for the first couple of hours each morning. They'd meet here to warm up, dry their gloves and woolen caps, exchange stories, grill deer burgers over the flame and drink coffee and hot chocolate. Those were the days. He really missed them. Other than for Uncle John, he hadn't spoken to his other uncles for over a year. He decided that after he finished what he needed to do, he'd look them up. They were the only other family he had and he didn't want to let that go. The fire was hot and the heat from the metal barrel felt good as he leaned back in the chair and closed his eyes. Within a few minutes, he had drifted off to sleep. Fritz too, enjoyed the warmth of the fire, lying down at the base of the barrel in front of Stryker's feet.

CHAPTER 43

Jake left the office early Friday afternoon. He had called Jillian Harris on his way home Wednesday and they made plans to see a movie and catch dinner Friday evening. Things were slow and Jillian had taken Friday off and was going to be doing some shopping at the National Mall on I-95, just south of Jake's townhouse and suggested that she stop by to pick him up around six p.m. They could eat dinner at the Macaroni Grill in Kingstowne and catch a movie at the AMC Theatre. Jillian was looking forward to meeting Sam. To mark her words:

"We've been seeing each other for a couple of months and it's about time I met your daughter."

Jake started getting nervous around four thirty. He had changed outfits twice, finally settling on a striped blue and white golf shirt with a pair of Polo khaki's and his favorite Sperry boat shoes. At forty four, he felt odd having to introduce his date to his daughter. He knew that Sam would like Jillian but that didn't stop his nervousness.

At six p.m., Jake found himself pacing in front of the television, looking out the window periodically for her car to come into view.

"Geez dad, relax," chided Sam. "You're acting like a boy on his first date. I'm sure she's a very nice person. We'll get along nicely… Hey, why don't you pour us a couple of glasses of wine?"

Jake knew that was her way of trying to calm him down. But what the heck, that sounded good.

He found a bottle of Merlot that Sam had put in the refrigerator earlier and had just poured them a couple of glasses when she drove into the driveway.

"And I suppose you chilled this just in case I needed to have a drink, huh?" he asked, handing her a glass on his way to the door.

"Oh, I don't know. I wasn't thinking of anything in particular. I just thought it might be nice to have a glass of wine later," she replied, looking up from her book with a sarcastic smile.

"Don't go running off either. Invite her in for a drink so that I can check her out," she joked, putting her book down and following him to the door.

It had been a nice day with temperatures in the low seventies. Jillian wore a salmon colored blouse, khaki Capri's with a pair of tan shoes with the higher, flatter heels women are wearing nowadays. Her hair was down, curled under, just barely touching her collar. She had just the right amount of lipstick and eye shadow.

"Hi, I'm Jillian", she said extending her hand to Sam.

Sam shook her hand and raising her glass with her other hand remarked, "You're just in time for a glass of wine. Dad and I just opened a new bottle. Won't you have a glass before you two trot off to do whatever you have planned for the evening?"

"I'd like that," responded Jillian, following Sam into the townhouse with Jake trailing behind.

Jake poured Jillian a glass of wine while Sam chatted away with Jillian on the couch.

After a bit of small talk, Sam inquired, "So, what movie are you two going to see? I hear the "Bucket List" is a hoot. I just love Jack Nicholson and Morgan Freeman. I can't wait to see it myself."

"Why don't you join us?" asked Jillian, looking at Jake for approval.

"Fine with me," replied Jake, nodding his head and raising his shoulders toward Sam.

"Nah. You two go and enjoy yourselves. I want to finish this thriller novel I started earlier today. I'm right at the good part and want to see how it ends."

Sam had always been an avid reader. Jake remembered that during the summer between her tenth and eleventh grades, she finished over a hundred books. He thought that she would make a great teacher but after college, Sam couldn't see herself spending any more time in a classroom.

After a finishing their glass of wine, Jake turned to Jillian: "Well, Macaroni's doesn't take reservations so if we're going to get a table in time to catch the movie, we'd better get moving."

Jillian and Sam exchanged goodbyes and Jake held the door open for her looking back at Sam now seated back on the couch. She gave him the thumbs up sign and smiled.

"Have a nice time tonight and don't forget your curfew," she kidded him.

"She's really nice," Jillian said handing Jake the keys to her car when they reached the bottom of the concrete steps. "Here, you drive."

"Yea, I think I'll keep her," he replied. "She'll do in a pinch."

CHAPTER 44

Saturday, November 1

Stryker started back to Washington early Saturday morning after waking to the smell of fried bacon and hash browns wafting up the stairwell. It was still dark outside and the crows hadn't even started to caw when he jumped out of bed and made his way down the back stairwell into the kitchen. Uncle John was standing in front of the stove with a spatula in one hand and a cup of steaming coffee in the other.

"I can't send you on your way on an empty stomach," he said. "Coffee's hot. Help yourself to a cup. Breakfast will be ready in a jiff."

Three minutes later, Stryker sat down to a breakfast of farm fresh eggs, bacon, hash browns and wheat toast. Uncle John was a great short order cook and it was always his appointed job to make breakfast every morning during hunting season. Stryker remembered the sourdough pancakes with Ohio maple syrup loaded with butter and whipped cream. Uncle John said that in order to stay warm and spend the day in the woods you needed to eat something that would "stick to your bones". Stryker had second thoughts about leaving but had finally broken the news to Uncle John over dinner the night before. He didn't know how Uncle John would respond but felt relieved when he just nodded in understanding without asking any questions.

Traffic on I-70 East was light at 6:00 a.m. and the only vehicles Stryker had seen since leaving the house were eighteen wheelers trying to make time before the old ladies hit the highway. After settling in between two semi-trailers, he set the cruise at 70 mph, turned the radio to a local talk show station and adjusted the lumbar in his seat. He enjoyed the way the little Nissan handled but was sure that the police would be looking for it by now. He'd have to leave the car somewhere in Maryland or Northern Virginia when he got back after removing the Ohio plates that could lead back to him. An hour and a half after saying goodbye to

Uncle John, Stryker crossed into West Virginia and was approaching the Cabella Drive Exit. He decided to stop and get some shells for the rifle. The store was closed but there were men with camouflage hats sitting in pickups in the parking lot sipping coffee. Must be turkey hunters he thought. That thought brought back more memories of gobbling up turkeys with Tommy in the autumn woods. The sign on the door indicated that the store opened at 8:00 a.m. so with a half hour to wait, Stryker drove to the McDonalds across the street from the Cabella parking lot for a cup of coffee.

It looked like everyone else had the same idea. After standing in line for ten minutes, he ordered a large coffee. By the time he got back into the car, the parking lot had begun to fill up with shoppers. The doors were just opening and people were rushing for the doors to spend their paychecks. He took the coffee with him. He had no problem locating the 7.62 caliber shells he needed and was back in the car within fifteen minutes. Stryker didn't have any time schedule to meet so he decided to take the southern route through West Virginia, taking I-68 East through the mountains along the more scenic route passing through Cumberland, Maryland. Glancing at his watch, he figured that with one gas stop in Hagerstown, Maryland, he'd be rolling into Alexandria by two-thirty in the afternoon. Traffic was still light at 9:30 a.m. when he reached Morgantown, West Virginia, changing from I-79S to I-68E that would take him east through the mountains, connecting back to I-70E at Hancock. He was only forty miles east of Morgantown when he ran into a thick fog, decreasing visibility to only fifty feet and slowing traffic to a crawl. After squinting his eyes and straining his neck to see for fifteen minutes, he regretted his decision to take the southern route. He glanced at his watch to recalculate his time and looked back through the windshield just in time to see bright red brake lights directly in front of him. He hit the brakes and steered the car to the right onto the berm, just barely missing the truck before coming to a stop. *That was close,* he thought…*way too close.* He couldn't risk an accident. Once they ran the Ohio plates and compared it with the VIN number on the Nissan, it would all be over for him. He'd be cuffed and hauled off to jail to stand trial for stealing the Nissan. Not something he wanted to do. He decided to pay closer attention to his driving. For the next twenty minutes, it was touch and go with both lanes starting and stopping, trying to make their way through the heavy fog. Stryker surfed the radio stations trying to find a local news station that would tell him what was slowing the traffic. After fumbling for a minute, he settled on WNTR 1230AM, a local station out of

Cumberland. The newscaster had just started reporting an accident just East of Exit 42 in the eastbound lane. A tractor trailer had jackknifed and overturned blocking both lanes while attempting to make the exit after missing the off ramp in the fog. By the time traffic came to a halt, five other vehicles had plowed into the overturned trailer causing numerous injuries. Both West Virginia and Maryland State Police had been on the scene for over an hour and were diverting traffic from the east bound lanes off onto Exit 40 and Braddock Road before getting back onto I-68 east of Cumberland. *Of all the fucking luck thought Stryker.*

CHAPTER 45

Stryker left the Nissan Altima in a Wal-Mart parking lot in Rockville, Maryland after removing the Ohio plates. The accident on I-68 had added almost two hours to his trip. He decided to grab a late lunch at a nearby Arby's before he called for a taxi to Dulles International. After a twenty minute cab ride, he paid the driver in cash and walked into the terminal with just an overnight bag before walking back through the turntable doors and crossing the street to the overnight parking garage. Stryker watched the long term parking lot for over an hour before selecting a 2007 White Chevy Tahoe that had just driven into the airport. Its occupants, a man and woman and three children with smiles on their faces appeared to be dressed for a vacation. Between them, they carried seven bags into the terminal. With that amount of luggage, he thought, they'd be gone for at least a week. Stryker followed them into the terminal and bought a cup of coffee at the Starbucks Kiosk. Better get his Starbucks now, he thought. From what he had read in the morning paper, Starbucks was expected to close six hundred stores. No wonder he thought. Last year, while traveling through Denver, he counted four Starbucks on all corners at a traffic light. He sipped on the coffee while watching them check in at the Delta Terminal. Within minutes, they had checked in their bags and were walking toward the security checkpoint. He followed at a safe distance, looking like any other person waiting on a passenger who was arriving on a plane. After showing their boarding passes and ID, they were cleared through security and on their way. Satisfied, he headed back to the long term garage.

Within five minutes of breaking into the SUV with his pocket tool, he was driving out of the long term garage and was back on the I-495 Beltway headed south for Washington. The attendant had given him a strange look when he handed her two dollars in cash and the long term ticket he found on the top of the center console. The SUV had been in the long term lot a total of forty minutes.

Stryker selected a Comfort Inn, just off the Van Dorn Exit in Alexandria. He pulled the Tahoe into the parking lot just after five thirty in the afternoon and parked in the rear of the lot next to the Waste Management dumpster. From here, it was only a five minute drive to the Van Dorn Metro Station, twenty minute drive into D.C. and easy access to head either south toward Richmond or east to Baltimore if he needed to get out of the area quickly.

CHAPTER 46

Monday, November 3

"So, where are we on these two murders?" Director Avery asked Jake and Sully on Monday morning, indicating for them to have a seat in his office after closing the door behind them.

Lynn had emailed Jake on his BlackBerry that Director Avery wanted to see them in his office at 10 a.m. He had spent the last hour putting his notes together while he waited for Sully. Sully finally arrived at 9:30 looking like he had slept in the rain on a park bench. His suit was wrinkled and his shirt was smudged with dirt.

"Geez, what happened to you?" Jake inquired when Sully finally came into the office.

"You really don't want to know," replied Sully, dropping into his chair behind his desk. "I feel like I've already put in a full day."

"Well, wake up. Go throw some water on your face. We've got to meet with Mike in a half hour and he's going to be looking for answers."

"Jesus Jake. Why don't you just meet him without me? I look like shit and I feel worse."

"The director specifically said that he wanted to see both of you," chirped Lynn before Jake could respond.

"Well, gimme fifteen minutes. I'll jump in the shower and I've got another suit in my locker," said Sully, heading off to the men's locker room.

"Don't be long," hollered Jake behind him. "I don't want to be late for our meeting."

Sully had returned fifteen minutes later looking like a new man.

"Boy, you actually can clean up can't you?" teased Jake. "Come on. I'll brief you on the way upstairs."

Now, Sully, his hair still wet from the shower, looked to Jake to respond to the director's question.

"Well Mike. We're not getting anywhere. We definitely believe that there's a common thread in these two shootings. According to Chuck Embers, ballistics tests support that the same weapon was used in both murders. Although we still don't have the actual weapon. The two victims were more than casual acquaintances. They have known each other for over twenty years, went to the academy together, served in the military together and have remained friends over the years."

"I know your trip to West Point didn't uncover anything," said the director.

"That's right. Nothing from the school records indicated anything," responded Jake.

"What about the military connection. Have you requisitioned their military records? Checked on their military assignments?" asked the director.

"We know that they were stationed together in the Gulf during Desert Storm. We got that the first time we spoke with both Colonel Hatcher and Director Preacher," replied Jake.

"Call the Pentagon. Get a copy of their military assignments. See what group they were assigned to and start making calls on some of the men they served with. I know its been a few years but somewhere out there someone knows something that could answer a lot of questions. If you get stonewalled at the Pentagon, gimme a call."

With that said, the director closed his file, raised his hand to wave them off and reached for his phone.

Jake and Sully took that as their clue that they were done. Closing their files, they hurried out of the office and headed back downstairs.

CHAPTER 47

Sam had left Sunday for a class in Baltimore. She'd be there for the next three weeks, getting home just before Thanksgiving. She was doing some training to upgrade her security clearance. Sam would come home on the weekends but that left Jake to fend for himself during the week. Without Sam waiting dinner for him, he worked late Monday and didn't leave the office until after 6:30 p.m. By the time he got home, it was seven thirty and he didn't feel much like cooking. He fed Pete, a four month old Jack Russell Terrier that Sam had bought in early summer and let him out the back door to run and do his business. After quickly thumbing though the mail, he grabbed a cold beer from the refrigerator and drank half of it while he ordered a pizza from Donatos. With a half hour before they'd deliver the pizza, Jake jumped into the shower. After letting the hot water pound on him for fifteen minutes, he shaved, using the fog free mirror that Sam had stuck on the shower wall for him. He toweled dry and while his head was still hot, lathered and used the new "blade" for bald guys he bought over the weekend to shave his head. By the time he had finished, the doorbell rang and he grabbed his robe on his way out of the bathroom. The doorbell rang again before he got to the door.

"Hold on a minute, be right there," he hollered, pulling his wallet out of his pants on his way to the door.

When he peered through the peephole in the door, the pizza delivery boy was standing there with a pissed off look on his face. Jake handed him a twenty for a fourteen dollar pizza and told him to keep the change. The pissed off look disappeared. Funny how that happens. Pushing the door closed with his foot, Jake grabbed another Corona from the fridge, dropped in his leather Lay Z Boy and turned on the widescreen to the Fox Network. Bill O'Riley, red faced and looking like a good case of high blood pressure was spewing political vomit from his soap box and berating the other news stations for their biased coverage of the presidential elections. O'Riley was an outspoken talk show host that was not afraid to call anyone on their actions.

Jake took a big swig on the Corona and dug into the pizza like a man who hadn't eaten in a week. He had skipped lunch and spent the better part of the afternoon on the phone trying to locate the military records for Senator Powell, Colonel Hatcher and Director Preacher. After playing phone tag for what seemed like hours and being passed from office to office at the Pentagon, he finally connected with someone who put in touch with the National Personnel Center for Military Records in St. Louis, Missouri. After fighting more bureaucracy and red tape for another hour regarding privacy issues, his contact at the Personnel Center finally conceded and agreed to release the records to him but only after receiving a direct call and a faxed letter from Mike Avery as Director of the FBI. For awhile, it appeared that Jake was going to need an Act of Congress. Privacy has its place, Jake thought, but it sure has been thrown up as a smokescreen more often than not. He and Sully had booked a flight to St. Louis for early in the morning. They couldn't get a direct flight. They were leaving out of Dulles at seven on U.S. Airways with a connection in Pittsburgh, arriving in St. Louis at 9:30 a.m. It was a two hour flight but the time change was in their favor. That was the good part. They made up for it on the return trip. Jake didn't want to stay overnight in St. Louis so he made the return flight for as late as possible, leaving St. Louis at seven in the evening. The catch was that there was no return to Washington. They were routed through Philadelphia with the final destination being Baltimore. If things went as scheduled, they'd get into Baltimore around midnight and have to take the train to D.C., arriving sometime after five Wednesday morning. *Oh well, he thought when he booked the flight, it's just par for the course.*

At nine, Jake realized he hadn't made arrangements for Pete and called Mrs. Hicks, the neighbor who lived next door. Usually, Sam came home during her lunch hour to let Pete out but with her gone for three weeks, Jake needed to make other arrangements. He apologized for the late call but Mrs. Hicks agreed to feed Pete and let him out a couple of times during the day. Mrs. Hicks was divorced and worked as a legal secretary for a real estate attorney. The office was five minutes away and she came home at noon for lunch. She had two boys, Mark and Jackson, ages ten and twelve. The boys loved Pete. During the summer, they had taught him to chase Frisbees. Pete really enjoyed the boys. He'd stand at the back door and whine when he saw them playing outside. Jake was happy when they knocked on the door to see if Pete could play. He'd run and chase the Frisbee until he was exhausted. Then, he'd take the Frisbee under a tree and lay down panting until he cooled down and caught his breath. After regaining his breath, he'd be up again and running for another round. After an hour of running back and forth, he'd come home exhausted, drink a bowl of water and sleep the rest of the evening.

CHAPTER 48

Tuesday, November 4

Few cars were on the road when Jake left for Dulles at 5 a.m. the next morning. Sully had agreed to meet him at the airport. It was less than an hour drive from the townhouse to Dulles but he'd rather arrive early, get a cup of coffee and read the Post than chance missing the flight because of traffic or car problems. Sully on the other hand was another story. Jake had been on enough trips with him to know that he'd arrive just in time to check in, clear security and run on the plane just before they closed the door. Pete hadn't even stirred from his bed when Jake got up, showered and headed out the door. Mrs. Hicks said that she would feed him and let him out before she left for work in the morning.

Dulles was quiet when Jake pulled into the short term parking garage. He parked on the fourth level and took the elevator two floors down to the terminal level. He was carrying his Sig Sauer .40 SW semi-automatic in his shoulder so he needed to check in with the desk to get a pass for boarding. The airlines didn't have any problem with law enforcement officers carrying weapons on board as long as they were notified in advance. Jake never had to use his weapon on board and it was a pain in the ass and a waste of time to put it with checked luggage. The airlines actually liked to have armed officers on board. Knowing that there was an armed trained officer on the plane gave the captain a sense of added security.

Jake stopped at the newsstand for a morning copy of the Washington Post before clearing through security and heading for the gate. Once through security, he found the Starbucks Kiosk and ordered a tall dark roast and a slice of lemon pound cake. He was glad Sam wasn't there to get on him about the pound cake. Jake found the gate and had just settled into to one of the seats when Sully arrived.

"What?" Sully asked, noticing that Jake had glanced at his watch. "Didn't you think I was going to make it?"

"No, I knew you'd make it. You always do. It's just that I was expecting you to make your standard grand entrance just as they were closing the door."

"Ah, bullshit!" he said, dropping his bag in the seat next to Jake. "Where'd you get the java?"

"Couple of gates back...on the right just before you get to the security gate."

"Don't let them leave without me," he hollered back to Jake as he headed for the men's room and the Starbucks.

CHAPTER 49

The plane they flew on was one of those small U.S. Airways commuter jets with two seats on one side of the aisle and a single on the other. The plane was only half full so once she checked her passenger list; she let them move around the cabin for additional space. They each took a seat on the side with two seats, raising the middle arm holder to give them more room to spread out. It was less than an hour flight to Pittsburgh but took a full hour, with the plane bucking a headwind the entire way. Jake checked his watch when they landed. With less than twenty minutes between flights, he had to find a men's room. The cup of coffee he had earlier had worked its way through his digestive system and filled his bladder. He felt like he was about to burst. Fortunately, the gate they arrived at and the departure gate to St. Louis were only three apart with a set of restrooms between them. Jake ducked into the men's room to relieve himself and was happy to see that there wasn't a line to the urinals. The plane to St. Louis was already boarding when they got to the gate. The plane departed the gate on schedule and taxied to the active runway waiting for clearance. Within minutes, they were cleared for takeoff and were picking up speed, bouncing down the runway. Jake was seated over the right wing. He watched as the pilot adjusted the flaps at the edge of the wings to catch the airflow and lift the plane into the sky. The plane made a final hop before leaving the runway and angling into the sky. Once airborne, the plane banked to the right to catch the heading for St. Louis and Jake looked back over his right shoulder at the airport. It reminded him of an ant hill. Baggage carts, fuel trucks, people scurrying everywhere. He was amazed at the number of planes that were parked at the gates and taxiing for position or holding for takeoff. *With this many flights coming and going every day out of all the airports across the nation, he thought, it's amazing that there aren't more casualties.* He was jarred to his senses when he heard the thud of the wheels retracting into the wheel wells. Within ten minutes of takeoff, the plane had reached its cruising altitude and had leveled off. The cabin bell rang twice and the overhead light went off indicating it was safe to move around the cabin. Jake unbuckled his seatbelt to relax. He pulled his briefcase from under the seat in front of him to review some of his notes before landing in St. Louis. The attendant was working her way up the aisle with her cart taking drink orders. Jake looked over at Sully, who sat across the aisle from him. His eyes were closed and he had leaned his seat back. Jake had no doubt Sully was already asleep or he'd be sleeping in five minutes. When the attendant got to Jake, he ordered a cup of coffee. She smiled when she reached in front of him to place the coffee and a napkin on the tray he had pulled out from the back of the seat in front of him. Jake noticed that she wore a wedding band on her left hand. It seemed like more and more attendants were either married women or men now. Jake finished his coffee and handed the paper cup back to the attendant just as the seat belt sign came on. They were within thirty minutes of landing and the captain made his final announcement thanking them for flying U.S. Airways before directing his full attention to landing the aircraft. The flight to St. Louis had been uneventful. They had cruised at twenty eight thousand feet, had little to no turbulence and would be arriving on schedule. Within fifteen minutes of landing, they had taxied to the gate and were walking off of the plane.

"Good sleep?" Jake kidded Sully as the walked through the gangway toward the terminal.

"Who slept?" he replied. "I was just resting my eyes."

"Yeah."

CHAPTER 50

Within fifteen minutes of landing, Jake and Sully had cleared the airport and hailed a taxi for their ride to 9700 Page Avenue, home of the National Personnel Center for Military Records. Jake didn't know what he expected to find searching old military archives but the only real lead they had in the murders of Senator Howell and Colonel Hatcher was a common link to their military backgrounds. Director Preacher hadn't given them anything to go on. He was pretty tight lipped and didn't allude to anything in their past that would cause someone to kill them. But, Jake was sure that he was hiding something. He was definitely running scared. Since the killing of Colonel Hatcher, the director never went anywhere without his bodyguards. He stopped driving himself, always taking the bulletproof SUV. There was something in their past that he was hiding. You could see it in his mannerisms. Jake hoped that this trip would give him and Sully the one hot lead they needed... Something in their records that would be a clue to open up this entire investigation.

It was a short ride from the airport to the Personnel Center. Passing by the Gateway Arch, Sully commented that he had only been in St. Louis once before and that was in 2005 when St. Louis hosted the final four in basketball. The driver turned left at the Spencer Avenue traffic light and into the entrance, stopping at the guard house for clearance. The guard directed them to the east end of Building 100, the Research Center. Jake paid the cabbie the fifty dollar fare, requesting a receipt. The place reminded Jake of the Pentagon, big official looking buildings of cement and concrete. The notice on the door indentified the building as the Research Center with the normal hours of 10 a.m. to 4 p.m. weekdays. Jake checked his watch. It was 10:20. Perfect Timing. They walked a flight of stairs and entered a set of double wide doors leading directly into the reception area. A large raised counter that appeared to be made of marble spanned the entire width of the room. Behind the counter sat fifteen to twenty administrative staff busy talking on telephones and flipping from screen to screen on computers. Jake figured this is where his call must have come into yesterday when he first called. From here, it was obviously routed to Marlo Jackson, someone with more clout. Jake had made arrangements to meet with Mrs. Jackson between 10 and 10:30.

"Can I help you?" asked a young brunette, jumping up from her computer and stepping to the other side of the counter. The room was filled with people and Jake didn't want to arouse any suspicions or bring any attention to himself so he quietly showed his ID badge and explained that they were there to meet with Mrs. Jackson.

"I'll let her know you're here," she said returning to her desk to make the phone call.

"Sir, she'll be with you in a minute," she said hanging up the phone. "Would you care to take a seat over there," she continued, directing them to the far corner of the room where there was a lounge area with magazines and newspapers.

They no sooner sat down when a rotund little lady in her late fifties with curly short gray hair appeared. Raising her eyebrows she looked at them and said: "Agent Hunter?"

"Yes," responded Jake, raising and shaking the hand she extended to him.

"Mrs. Jackson. This is Agent Gilmore," he said turning to Sully and stepping back for Sully to grasp her hand. "I want to thank you for your patience with me yesterday. I know I might have come across pretty rough."

"Not a problem, Agent Hunter. Believe me, I've had worse...lots worse."

"If you gentlemen will follow me," she said turning, "I'll take you to someplace more convenient. After we spoke yesterday, Agent Hunter, I thought you may want someplace to spread out. I took it upon myself to reserve a room for you that would be more private...someplace where you could work, make phone calls if necessary, and not be disturbed by anyone else. We don't usually make accommodations like this but after speaking with you regarding your particular situation; I thought it might be more appropriate."

"Mrs. Jackson, we really appreciate your help. I know it was on short notice but we're kinda in a hurry."

"Please, call me Marlo," she said, showing them into a wood paneled room.

"I've put a carafe of coffee and some cups on the table there for you," she said, indicating with a nod of her head, a table at the far corner of the room.

"I've arranged for two terminals for your use. As soon as you log on, there's a tutorial program that will instruct you on how to navigate the system and help you locate what you're looking for. If you get to a spot that requires a password, please come and get me. Some of the information contained in our files is confidential and on a need to know basis. I will have to use my password to get into that information. If there's anything else…or if you're having problems, please don't hesitate to let me know. My direct extension is 4456 if you want to write that down on something. I'm just down the hall and it won't be any problem at all for me. Oh…rest rooms are down the hall to your left and we have a cafeteria on the first floor that serves a great lunch. They open at eleven thirty."

"Thank you Mrs. Jackson…Marlo," said Sully, smiling at her, before she could correct him.

"Well, gentlemen, if there aren't any questions, I'll leave you two alone." With that, she left the room, pulling the door closed behind her.

CHAPTER 51

"So, whataya think?" asked Sully. "Want a cup of Joe before we get started?"

"Yea, pour me a cup," replied Jake. Why don't I take this terminal? I'll start with the senator. You get into Colonel Hatcher's file and let's start with the day they were commissioned at West Point. We'll track assignments, looking for common factors. I should've asked her about that printer over there. I don't know if these terminals are connected to it or not. We may need to make copies of some of this information. Once we get through the files on the senator and Colonel Hatcher, we'll bring up the director and do the same for him. Something tells me that what we're looking for is stored somewhere in these records. I don't want to go back to D.C. without a good lead. I think Mike is at the end of his rope on this. He said something to me yesterday before I left that he's had the patience of Job on this case but he wasn't sending us out here for shits and giggles. I know he's been taking a lot of heat from some of the cronies up on the hill."

"All right. I got your point," said Sully. "Here don't spill this on the computer or we'll really be in the shit," he said handing a cup of steaming coffee to Jake.

"Looks like we may need to log in with their Social Security Numbers," said Jake after two failed attempts to bring up anything using the senator's legal name. "I've tried first and last names and it's asking for identification numbers. I know my brother who enlisted after the end of the draft never got a Selective Service Number. He said they used his social to identify him on his dog tags. "Hand me that briefcase to your right", he continued, pointing to the floor next to Sully.

"I took the initiative to bring some background information with us. I didn't know just what to expect so I figured it would be better to be safe than sorry."

"Boy, aren't you the teacher's pet," teased Sully. "You get to sit in the front of the class."

"Hey, why'd they ever call them things dog tags anyway?" asked Sully. "What the hell do they have to do with dogs?"

"Good question. Look that up later. Maybe it'll help you win a trivia show someday. Okay…here we go. I got in using the senator's Social. Now let's see where this boy spent his time serving Uncle Sam."

"Okay, I'm in," said Sully. "Hey, how are you making notes so we can track for common activity?"

"I'm tracking his assignments with dates in the margin," replied Jake. "After that, we can compare the locations and dates and see where we have common ground. I'll be finished with the senator way before you finish on the colonel since he was still active right up to the date he was killed. When I finish here, I'll do the same for the good director. We know according to what they told us that the senator and director only served five years active duty."

"That sounds good to me. This shouldn't take us too long. These records seem to be in chronological order. The only problem is where do we go from here? I mean, so we have the dates that they spent wherever… What does that give us? The director already told us that they served together."

"Good point," replied Jake. "But once we know what group or division or platoon or whatever they call those things…hell, I never served, we'll get a list of the other soldiers that were with them and then we'll have to start interviewing some of them. Take down any information you find…address, phone numbers. We won't have email addresses. Email wasn't around back then."

"Gotcha," said Sully. "I guess this isn't going to be as easy as I thought."

"Hey, I gotta drain the main," said Jake, standing and taking a stretch. "I'm going to hit the men's room and then stop back at Mrs. Jackson's desk. There's got to be a shortcut to get the names and contact information for the other soldiers that were stationed with these guys."

"Yea, you'd think," muttered Sully, whose large size dwarfed the computer screen he was hunkered over.

"Hey, what say we check that cafeteria out, get some grub when you get back," he hollered to Jake as he left the room.

Ten minutes after leaving, Jake was back and smiling. "Hey, according to Mrs. Jackson, we're tied into the printer and can print off anything we need. The printer keeps track of our copies and we just have to pay at the front desk when we're ready to leave."

"Well that's easy enough. What did she say about a shortcut?"

"No problem. Once we know what we're looking for, we plug that name of the unit and the dates we're interested in. That should bring up everyone who is assigned to that unit during that time. Then, we click on the name and we're linked to a page giving us the next of kin and the serviceman's last known address and phone number."

"And, if they're no longer there?" asked Sully.

"Well at least we have something to start on. From there we would have to contact the authorities for the last known location and see if there is any forwarding information. If not, we need to knock on neighbors doors and see if anyone knows where they've moved."

"All right but that sounds like more work. Before we get into that, let's chow down. I'm starved."

"You're always hungry but all right. It's almost eleven thirty. If we go now, maybe we can beat the crowds."

They spent the rest of the afternoon comparing assignments among the three army officers. After attending West Point, Senator Powell attended advanced infantry training at Ft. Benning, Georgia before being assigned to the 24th Mechanized Infantry Division at Ft. Stewart, Georgia. Colonel Hatcher and Director Preacher were commissioned upon graduation at West Point and followed the senator a year later through infantry training then jump school at Ft. Benning, Georgia, before assignment to Fort Stewart. By the time Hatcher and Preacher arrived at Fort Stewart, Senator Powell had a command slot and the two junior officers were his direct reports. After two years at Fort Stewart, the 24th received orders for Iraq during the first Gulf War. By then, Senator Powell was Captain Powell and the Officer in Charge of a hundred soldiers. Jake and Sully made copies of the latest contact information for the men and women that served with the three before closing the files and exiting the system. On their way out of the building, they stopped by Mrs. Jackson's office to thank her for her help. After knocking on her door without any response, Jake scribbled a short thank you on a post-it note and stuck it on her door. After paying for the copies they made, Jake called for a cab. The rain was just starting to cover the asphalt when the cab arrived outside the building.

CHAPTER 52

By the time they arrived at the St. Louis airport, the wind was blowing the rain horizontally, soaking everything in its path. Jake and Sully arrived at the airport with plenty of time to make their evening flight from St. Louis to Baltimore only to find that it had been extended for two hours. Many of the flights from St. Louis had already been cancelled with passengers lined up in front of the customer service area and down the hall attempting to re-schedule flights on alternate routes that would get them to their final destinations. The gate boarding areas were full of passengers waiting patiently to hear an update on the status of their flights. All of the seats in the waiting area were occupied with disgruntled passengers. An overflow of passengers and carryon's stretched out along the walls and aisles. Some have been there as long as five hours. Jake noticed one poor woman with two infants, twins he thought, trying unsuccessfully to keep things under control.

"I don't know how anyone can travel like that," he said nodding toward the disheveled woman who looked like she was at her wits end.

"Yea," responded Sully. "And I'm worried about whether they're going to serve us snacks on the plane."

"Well, let's go down to the food court area," said Jake. "We can keep an eye on our flight from the monitors down there. We're not going to get a seat up here anyway."

They headed down to the food court just as an announcement was made indicating that the St. Louis airport was officially closed for weather. All inbound flights were being diverted to alternate airports and all outbound flights were temporarily delayed.

"Well, there you go," said Sully. "Maybe we should plan on spending another night. Doesn't look like we're going to be getting out of here anytime soon."

They decided to get something to eat and wait another hour to see if the storm would let up. Jake really didn't want to spend the night in St. Louis. He knew that Mrs. Hicks would have not problem taking care of Pete for another day but they hadn't planned on spending the night, didn't bring a change of clothes and he really didn't want to listen to Sully snore all night long.

CHAPTER 53

By nine o'clock the storm had passed through St. Louis and continued east. The Airport Authority opened for business giving priority to inbound flights that had been stacked outside the storm area by Air Traffic Control. Many of the planes were low on full and dangerously close to declaring emergency. Outbound flights remained on hold until further notice. Based on the local radar, this window of opportunity would not stay open long. Airlines were jostling for position attempting to get delayed flights scheduled for departure. Air Traffic Control was scrambling to put order back into the system. The local radar indicated that another thunderstorm was tracking due east and would hit St. Louis in less than an hour. At ten o'clock, the departure board indicated that Jake and Sully's plane was scheduled to depart in a half hour, just ahead of the next storm. Their plane was already boarding when they made it back to the gate. Sully stuffed an extra sandwich into his jacket pocket before showing his boarding pass and following Jake to the plane. You could still feel the wind blowing as it shook the causeway that connected the plane to the terminal.

They had no sooner placed their carryons in the overhead compartment and taken their seats when the captain announced that they had received their takeoff position, requesting all passengers to take their seats and secure their seat belts.

"We may be in for a pretty rough ride," said Sully, pulling his belt snug over his extended middle.

"Yea, I don't know if this is the right move to make or not," responded Jake, looking out the window at the foreboding rain that had started to bounce off the wing.

Within minutes, the cabin door was closed with the causeway retracting accordion like, locking them into the plane. Seconds later, the wheel chocks were removed and the Boeing 727 was being pushed away from the terminal. Jake noticed that the plane was only half full. He wondered what had happened to the remaining passengers.

"Excuse me, miss?" he said to a flight attendant walking briskly down the aisle to catch her own seat. "What happened to the other passengers?"

"The captain got his orders from the tower and decided to take off. We only have a short amount of time to takeoff before the next storm hits. Once we got our departure position, the captain had two minutes to get wheels rolling. He ordered doors closed. Those who left the gate area and didn't get back in time will have to book another flight."

"Lucky us... I think," said Sully, sinking back into his seat.

Jake looked intently out the window at the line of traffic in front of them as the plane taxied on the tarmac towards the active runway. When the plane made a ninety degree turn, he counted seven strobe lights on the silhouettes in front of them that quickly vanished as they received their wheels up order from the tower. Within seconds, the cabin lights were dimmed and they were rolling down the runway, leaving the busy terminal behind. Off in the distance and closing quickly, bolts of lightning announced the arrival of the next big storm.

CHAPTER 54

The pilot detoured around dangerous thunderstorms all the way to Minneapolis, attempting to find favorable winds at various altitudes before finally leveling off at thirty five thousand feet. The same storms that had pummeled St. Louis earlier in the evening were rapidly working their way East. Overhead, the seatbelt indicator lights in the main cabin remained lit the entire flight. The captain required the flight attendants to remain in their seats with the beverage cart strapped securely in the kitchen area. *No drinks on this flight.*

Sully sat quietly subdued with his eyes closed and his big hands gripping the armrests so tight that his knuckles cramped. Jake had flown on many rough flights in the past but this flight was taking its toll on him. He spoke little, concentrating on trying to quell the queasy feeling that rose from the pit of his stomach. Jake grew up in a strict Irish Catholic home, the oldest of seven children. His father worked two jobs during Jakes childhood to support the family of nine. He provided a good home and tried to be present at all of the school events, supporting his children. Jake attended St. Agnes Parish School for the first eight years of his formal education. The school was operated by the Sisters of Mercy but Jake didn't remember the nuns showing any mercy. In the early seventies, corporal punishment was still the norm in most school systems. His knuckles still bore the marks where the metal edged rulers left battle scars. Jake's mother was a homemaker who volunteered as a cafeteria monitor three days a week for reduced tuition. On Sundays, the family regularly attended the ten o'clock Mass service, occupying an entire pew. They were roused from their beds at eight so that all seven children could get in and out of the one bathroom they shared and be ready to leave for church by 9:30 promptly. Jake remembered fondly donut Sunday, the first Sunday of every month. After Mass, they'd rush to the parish hall where donuts were stacked three high, with coffee and juice. If they were good in church, dad would allow them to split an extra donut. By the time Jake was ten, he was an altar boy assisting Father Hurley, the parish pastor. Father

Hurley was a big boned ex wrestler with a deep voice that resonated through the halls when he laughed. Years later, when Jake first started dating Rachael, she was impressed with his devotion such that she accompanied him to Mass on numerous occasions. Jake was delighted when she told him that she was going to convert to Catholicism before they married. After Samantha was born, they attended church as a family but when Rachael died, Jake became angry and stopped attending. He blamed God for taking her from him and leaving Sam without a mother.

An hour from Minneapolis a bolt of lightning rocked the plane violently, the interior lights flickering before going out entirely. Without warning, the plane dropped suddenly as it fell into an air pocket. Passengers screamed. Jake found himself praying the rosary, something he hadn't done in over ten years. Sully made one of those promises you make to God when you find yourself in a situation beyond your control. After a few seconds that seemed like minutes, the plane leveled off with the captain apologizing over the loudspeaker for the turbulent weather even though it was beyond his control. The plane bounced along for the next half hour in and out of air pockets. The detours around the storms added an extra forty five minutes to their flight. Every once in a while Jake could barely make out a populated area as the cloud cover broke and lights could be seen far below. Fifty miles out of Minneapolis, the pilot steered the plane into a sharp bank to the right to begin his final approach into the Twin Cities. By the time they landed at Minneapolis St. Paul International, they had missed their connection to Detroit and were put on an alternate flight leaving for Detroit at 1:55 a.m. After the flight from hell, terra firma felt good under Jake's feet. They were not scheduled to arrive in Baltimore until 8:24 a.m. Jake wished that he had just decided to stay in St. Louis, get a good night sleep and leave the next morning on a direct flight into Dulles.

"Way to go, big guy," Sully, said when they realized they would not be picking up their cars at Dulles until noon the next day.

"Not much you can do about the weather," Jake said. "I suppose we should be happy to get back home in one piece."

"Always the eternal optimist," replied Sully. "Don't you ever look at the bad side of things?"

"What good does it do?" replied Jake.

CHAPTER 55

The storms that had wreaked havoc on the Midwest earlier in the week finally made their way to the east coast leaving in their wake, a sea of destruction. The winds that had accompanied the storms snapped trees like match sticks, bringing down power lines causing major outages. The severe flash flooding resulted in closed schools and washed out highways. Rain pelted the glass in the small window behind the closed drapes that separated Stryker from the outdoor elements. A small puddle of water had formed on the floor beneath the window where it leaked from the cracked putty that sealed the glass. It had been raining most of the night as the thunderstorms rolled through the area. The loud thunderclaps that followed the bolts of lightning across the black sky shook the walls of Stryker's little room at the end of the two story building, sending a full length mirror on the bathroom door crashing to the floor. A cold front that followed the storms had arrived during the early morning hours, plummeting temperatures to the low thirties, the rain changing to sleet. The loud thunder kept Stryker turning in his bed throughout most of the night causing him to sleep in. At nine, he couldn't sleep any longer and decided to get out of bed and make a pot of coffee while he waited for the rain to let up. He stayed in the room glancing at the local news channel while flipping through the morning paper. After his first cup of coffee, he had braved the elements and ran to the newspaper coin box outside the motel office, dodging raindrops and trying not to slip on the wet concrete. Nothing on the other stations other than the Maury Povich show playing the latest rendition of "Who's your Daddy?" When the rain stopped, he'd make his way over to the International House of Pancakes for breakfast. The IHOP was one of his favorite restaurants and within easy walking distance of the one bedroom efficiency he rented after leaving the Comfort Inn. The Comfort Inn was a little pricey and after spending one hundred twenty a night for two nights, he found the furnished efficiency for two hundred a week and paid cash getting a ten percent discount for paying two weeks in advance. Didn't have to pay a deposit or show any identification. The room included a small kitchen area on one end of the room with a microwave, stove and a small refrigerator. The little mom and pop motel was small, a two story concrete blockhouse with only twenty rooms but was just what Stryker needed. The motel was sheltered on a side street across from a neighborhood strip mall with a little grocery and less than a quarter mile from Interstate-95. Stryker walked over to the grocery last night after returning from a surveillance trip through the director's neighborhood. He purchased enough cold drinks, snacks and frozen dinners to last him a week. He'd eat dinner in, watching the local news but he enjoyed getting an early morning walk and stopping for breakfast while he browsed the local rag for any information on the shootings.

Stryker read the Post daily, searching for articles on the shooting. For the first few days after the latest killing, the paper ran numerous articles but it had been three weeks since the paper included any mention of either case. Stryker was especially interested in any articles mentioning Jake Hunter, the FBI Special Agent assigned to the case. Jake was the same Agent that was assigned to investigate the killing of Senator Powell earlier in the spring. Other than a general comment from Special Agent Hunter that they were following up on several leads, the information being released to the public was pretty sketchy.

Stryker had driven past the director's house twice within the past week and noticed that there appeared to be an unusual number of black SUV's parked along the road. He was sure that security covering the director had been beefed up after the killing of Colonel Hatcher.

By ten the rain had stopped and Stryker decided to venture out. Donning a rain jacket and cap, he crossed the street to the IHOP. The smell of worms filled the air causing Stryker to look down at the pavement and then choose his steps carefully. Night crawlers and mealworms were all over the highway. The heavy rain that fell during the night had saturated the ground, causing them to come to the surface in search of a mate. He reflected momentarily on earlier times.

CHAPTER 56

Jake didn't get home until 2:00 p.m., Wednesday afternoon. After picking up their cars at Dulles, he parted ways with Sully and jumped on the 495 Beltway which turned out to be a big mistake. The 495 was a parking lot with eastbound traffic stalled for miles. By the time he made it to the Van Dorn Exit, he had counted four fender benders, closing down one lane entirely. He had called Lynn when they landed in Baltimore, letting her know about their late arrival and informing her that he and Sully would not be in the office that day.

Jake parked in the driveway and checked the mailbox before climbing the steps to the townhouse. When he opened the front door, Pete greeted him with his tail wagging, anxious to take a walk.

"Not now", he said, reaching down to pat the top of his head. "We'll go out later after I get a little shut-eye."

Grabbing a bottle of water from the refrigerator, he glanced at yesterday's mail that Mrs. Hicks had left sorted in the middle of the kitchen table. She left a handwritten note on top that Jillian Harris had stopped by to say hello. Jake hadn't called her before his trip to St. Louis and he had been thinking about her quite a bit lately. He decided to call her after he got a couple hours of sleep and didn't feel like such a zombie. Pete followed him to the bedroom and lay down in his bed next to the closet where he'd remain until Jake woke up. He shed his clothes, throwing them into the laundry hamper on his way to the bathroom for a warm shower. The hot water felt good on his back after sitting in the plane for so long. After ten minutes, he shut off the water and toweled dry before closing the blinds and dropping onto his bed.

Jake slept soundly until six-thirty p.m. when the alarm clock on his cell phone woke him up with a startle. He had set the alarm to get him up before he got too much sleep and then be up most of the night. The light on the home phone sitting on the table next to the bed was flashing indicating he had missed a call. Jake had turned off the volume before going to sleep so that he would not be bothered by any telemarketers who seemed to call when he was in bed or just sitting down to dinner. He played back the message. It was Sam. She was just checking to see if he got home. When Pete saw that Jake was awake, he came running to the side of the bed whining; one of those whines he made when he was ready to eat.

"Okay," he said, climbing out of bed and putting on a tee shirt and a pair of sweatpants. After feeding Pete and letting him out the back door into the fenced yard, Jake mixed a bowl of cheerios with a handful of granola and topped it off with skim milk. He took it to the living room to watch the NBC evening news with Brian Matthews, his favorite anchor. He finished eating and watching the news before calling Jillian. They spoke for over an hour, catching up on what's been happening in their worlds for the past week. Jillian told Jake about a two day medical conference in downtown D.C. that she would be attending next weekend. The conference was being held at the Ritz Carlton in D.C. and started at 9:00 am Saturday morning. On Saturday evening, there was going to be an Awards Banquet followed by a formal dance. Jillian asked Jake to be her escort for the Banquet at the Ritz. It would be a black tie affair. He hadn't worn a tuxedo in ten years. Without hesitation, he accepted her invitation and agreed to be at her Hotel door at 5:30. They chatted for another ten minutes before saying goodbye. Before Jillian hung up, she suggested that he pack an overnight bag for Saturday night just in case it was late and he had too much to drink. With the thought of Saturday night still fresh in his mind, Jake reached for the leash hanging by the back door and called for Pete.

"C'mon boy. Let's take that walk I promised you."

CHAPTER 57

Saturday, November 8

Jake had been anxious all day, watching the clock. He wasn't supposed to meet Jillian at the hotel for another five hours but he had been looking forward to this evening since the day he returned from St. Louis. With schedule conflicts, they hadn't been able to spend any time together for almost a month.

He had gotten out of bed at seven that morning and by nine o'clock had completed a six mile run with Sam, did one hundred sit-ups on the Ab-Lounger and fifty push-ups. After a healthy breakfast of an omelet made from Egg Beaters, a couple of slices of wheat toast and two cups of black coffee, he worked from home until noon on his laptop.

Lynn's computer skills and knowledge of the Excel Program proved invaluable after he and Sully had returned from the Personnel Center. They brought back folders full of information that they had copied with last contact information for all the servicemen and women that had served with Senator Powell, Colonel Hatcher and the director. They had over one hundred names to follow up on. A lot of the information that they had was dated. For servicemen who had left the military after their first enlistment obligation was completed, the information was over fifteen years old. There was no requirement to keep the personnel center updated so much of the information was useless. Lynn showed them how to "Google" a name which provided updates for some but for most, the information was stale. With the information they did have, Lynn created spreadsheets that were easy to follow, with names, phone numbers, addresses and next of kin. Jake and Sully had split these up and had started making phone calls earlier in the week. Unfortunately, most of the calls went unanswered or were picked up by an answering machine. They didn't want to leave a message fearing that any message left from the FBI would cause bigger problems for them than they already had. Jake had been successful in reaching the homes of two of the prior servicemen. He spoke to the wife of one who had died three years earlier from a farming accident. She met her husband ten years after he left the military. He never spoke about his time in the military or Iraq. She knew he was in Iraq but she never asked him any questions and had assumed that his serving in Iraq was something he preferred to forget. Jake spoke to the other serviceman for half an hour. He had been injured by a roadside explosive device during the first week he was over there and returned stateside for extensive reconstructive surgery and rehab at Walter Reed Hospital. He was released from his military obligation and was receiving one hundred percent disability. He remembered Senator Powell, then Captain Powell who was the Platoon Leader at that time but had no recollection of either Colonel Hatcher or Director Preacher.

Jake called Sully to see if he was having any better luck.

"Yo, what's up?" he said when he recognized Jake's number on the screen of his cell phone.

"Just checking to see if you've been any luckier than me on making these calls," Jake replied.

"Well, if you don't count wrong numbers or numbers no longer in service, I've been able to speak to a grand total of three people. Two of them were good contacts but neither one of them remembered anything out of the ordinary. One of them said that he didn't have anything good to say about any Army officer but didn't have anything specific to say. I got the distinct impression that he was just a fuck up and didn't like authority figures. The other one was in Colonel Hatcher's squad. The colonel was a first lieutenant then. There were about twenty guys in the squad. He didn't remember anything out of the ordinary. He said that Captain Powell was higher up in command and didn't have any direct contact with him. Their time in Desert Storm was pretty short. From what this guy says, the 24th Mechanized Infantry Division was in and out in a matter of months. He said they put up with more shit in the Philippines after they departed Iraq but didn't go into any details. According to this guy, there were over 5000 deaths attributed to mudslides and high waters. They spent a couple of weeks pulling bodies out of the mud. He remembers the stench like it was yesterday. Other than that, he doesn't remember too much more."

"What about the third one you got a hold of?"

"What third one?...Oh yea, well I didn't actually get to talk to the guy. I spoke with his ex wife. They're divorced now. She says that they've been divorced for over ten years now. He couldn't keep a job when he got back. Always had headaches, couldn't sleep. I guess he was on some kind of depression medicine but didn't take it all the time. She says that after putting up with it for seven years, she finally called it quits."

"Any kids?" Jake asked.

"Fortunately no. She says that was part of it too. Apparently, he wasn't interested in sex anymore. I guess he had a hard time... Excuse the pun... getting it up."

"She volunteered all that over the phone?" Jake asked.

"Well, yea. I mean, I didn't ask her about their sex life. But, she was more than willing to tell."

"She doesn't have any idea where he is now. She gave me a name of his sister who lives somewhere in Pennsylvania but she hasn't spoken to her since the divorce. I'll follow that one up on Monday."

"Hey, isn't tonight the big night?" You been practicing with a broomstick? I don't guess you been out dancing in quite a while. Just kidding. Have a good time. See you Monday unless I get a brainstorm between now and then."

CHAPTER 58

"Boy, don't you look handsome. Hey, if I wasn't your daughter, I'd make a play for you," joked Sam, looking over the top of the book she was reading. She was curled up on the couch with Pete in the den when Jake waltzed into the room in his tuxedo.

"Oh... Stop it," replied Jake to Sam's kidding. "Whatdaya think? Do I look presentable?"

"You look great dad. Really. I don't think I've ever seen you in a tux before. I guess this is a preview for my wedding in... Oh, I don't know maybe another five years or so."

"Yea, well, give me a few years warning before you make that jump," he said, leaning down to kiss the top of her head.

"Hey, what's with the overnight bag?" asked Sam, noticing he had placed his L.L. Bean bag by the front door.

"Let's just say that like the boy scouts motto: Be Prepared," he responded, as he reached for his keys in the basket by the phone. "Jillian asked me to bring an overnight bag just in case the dance goes longer than expected and we have a couple of drinks."

Sam smiled at him with one of her smirks without saying a word.

"And ah...Make sure you lock the door tonight and use the deadbolt."

"Way to go Romeo."

Traffic was busy on I-395 into downtown D.C. Jake arrived five minutes late and decided to leave the Infiniti with valet parking. He pulled under the rotunda in front of the Ritz Carlton, leaving the keys in the ignition and reaching into the back for his bag.

"Will you need your car at the end of the evening sir?" asked the attendant, handing Jake a parking stub while holding the door open for him.

"Not if I'm lucky," he responded, winking at the attendant while opening the back door to get his jacket that was hanging behind the driver's seat. Jake slipped on the jacket, pocketed the ticket in the breast pocket of his tuxedo and entered the hotel through the nine foot high double wide doors into the spacious lobby carrying his overnight bag with him.

The hotel lobby was bustling with activity. Men in tuxedos and women in elegant gowns paraded through the hotel like high school students on prom night. Rays of sunlight shone through the open atrium lobby where the glass enclosed elevators reached from the floor to the ceiling. Jake pushed the button and waited for the elevator to descend to the main floor. Within seconds, the doors opened, Jake stepped in and pushed the button for the twelfth floor. Jillian had called earlier in the day and told him that she was in room 1204. Jake entered the glass enclosed elevator and pushed the button for the twelfth floor. He looked out over the atrium at the open air restaurant and lounge area as the elevator rose to the twelfth floor. When the elevator doors stopped, he stepped into the hallway to the right, followed the door numbers until he stood in front of 1204 and knocked. Jillian looked through the peep hole before opening the door to let him into the room. Jake stepped into the room and dropped his bag at his feet.

"Wow", he said. "You look beautiful."

"Like it?" she asked, doing a twirl in front of him. Jillian was dressed in a black and silver strapless gown that reached to her mid-calf. The plunging neckline accentuated her long thin neck. On her feet she wore three inch open back high heels. Diamond earrings hung from her ear lobes and a diamond pendant necklace draped her slender neck. She had gotten her hair done and her nails manicured at the hotel spa after the afternoon session. She wore her hair down and curled under as it reached her shoulders. Her bright red lipstick matched her nails. Jake was awestruck. She was so beautiful. He knew after their last time together that he was developing strong feelings for her but as he looked at her now, he could feel his heartbeat pounding in his chest. *Could she be the one, he thought.*

CHAPTER 59

The band was playing soft dinner music when they entered the ballroom through the doors off the main lobby. Jillian had her arm draped through Jakes and he could feel the warmth of her body next to him as he escorted her through the room looking for their assigned table. Jake detected the faint scent of White Linen, his favorite perfume, rising from Jillian's neck.

As they made their way through the narrow openings between the tables, a waiter in a white silk dinner jacket approached them with a tray of hors d'oeuvres containing fresh prawns, mini lamb chops, stuffed mushrooms, roasted water chestnuts surrounded by bacon and sushi. Jake was a big sushi fan and could not pass up the opportunity. He took a napkin from the waiter and selected a three inch prawn, a stuffed mushroom and two of the sushi rolls from the waiter's tray. Jillian decided to pass and removed her grasp from Jake's arm so that he could eat.

"This is all right," he said, biting into a piece of raw tuna surrounded by rice. "This sushi is really good. Sure you won't try some," he asked, extending the napkin in her direction.

"No thanks. You enjoy it. I like my seafood a little more done. I think I'll just wait until dinner," she responded looking away from the raw delicacy Jake was thoroughly enjoying.

"Let me finish this and I'll get us a couple of drinks from the bar over there," he said tipping his head in the direction of the open bar in far corner of the room. The tables were all numbered with a small placard protruding from the live flower arrangement in the center of the table. They found their table number twenty in the middle of the room almost directly in front of the podium and speakers table. The round tables were covered in linen tablecloths and held silver place settings for eight guests. Four of the other six guests sharing their table were already seated. Jillian knew one of the other conference attendees, Doctor Jonathan Grabow, a pathologist from Baltimore, Maryland. They had worked on several cases together over the last two years. She introduced Jake to him and his wife. The other couple, Dr. Carl Sorman, a retired pathologist from Richmond, Virginia, now teaching at John Hopkins and his wife of forty years rose from their seats exchanged introductions just as the fourth couple arrived at their table. When introductions had been made around the table, Jake excused himself to get drinks for him and Jillian. He had offered to get drinks for anyone else but they had already stopped at the bar on their way to the table. Jake left Jillian talking with the other guests while he stood in line at the bar, striking up a conversation with the man behind him. When he finally made his way to the front of the line, he ordered a Bloody Mary for Jillian and a Glenlivet on the Rocks for himself. Jake had been partial to single malt scotch every since his first year at Syracuse University Law School. He found that single malt didn't give him headaches and he never woke up with a hangover. As he turned away from the bar with the drinks in his hand, he ran into Julius Lowenstein, the medical examiner from Manhattan, whom Jake had worked with for several years prior to moving to the D.C. area.

Dr. Lowenstein could be pretty long winded and it was fortunate for Jake that the program director for the evening was just beginning announcements of the evening events. Jake took the opportunity to excuse himself and make his way back to the table.

"Sorry it took me so long," he said to Jillian, handing her the Bloody Mary. "I ran into an old acquaintance of mine that I worked with in New York. I thought he was no longer practicing but I guess he still does consulting work from time to time."

"That wouldn't be Julius Lowenstein would it?" Jillian asked after taking a sip of her drink.

"You know Julius?" queried Jake.

"Yes," replied Jillian. "Actually Dr. Lowenstein was one of my professors at the University of Maryland. He taught one of my Medical Microbiology courses. I spoke with him earlier today during one of our breaks.

"Brilliant man," added Dr. Sorman. I've known him for over thirty years. He's written numerous treatises on various aspects of the human anatomy. He's considered by many to be one of the foremost experts on forensic anthropology. I know he testifies as an expert witness from time to time in high profile murder trials. The Smithsonian has been trying for years to bring him on board.

"Sounds like an interesting character," added Dr. Grabow, not wanting to be left out of the conversation.

"Ladies and Gentlemen," the program director began. "If you'll please all take your seats, we'll begin with a short invocation and then dinner will be served."

Other than a few guests still waiting at the bar, the remainder of the room took their seats and began to quiet down. A tall slender man in a dark suit with a preachers collar, appearing to be in his middle fifties rose from his seat on the speakers platform and made his way to the podium. He looked very distinguished with a full head of hair, now graying at the temples. Looking over a pair of Harry Potter tortoise colored glasses, he stood at the podium until the room was so quiet that you could hear a pin drop. In a deep booming voice that sounded like it should come from someone much bigger than he, he lifted his hands, bowed his head and recited a short non-denominational prayer thanking God for the food and the evening's festivities. When he finished and returned to his seat, the head waiter standing by the double doors leading into the kitchen opened the doors and waiters immediately began serving salads as the noise level in the room increased again as conversations resumed. Jake unfolded his linen napkin, placed it on his lap and looked down at the place setting in front of him. At home, he would usually eat with a fork and knife and an occasional spoon if he was having soup or a bowl of cereal. He wasn't sure what to do with the three forks, two spoons and two knives that lined either side of his plate. He noticed that Jillian had reached for the small fork to her farthest left and did the same. *I guess you eat from the outside in, he thought. I'm sure there's a book out there titled "Table Etiquette for Dummies."* After collecting the salad plates, the waiter returned to their table pushing a cart with plates individually covered with a stainless steel cover to keep the food warm.

"This looks fantastic," exclaimed Jake when the waiter set a dinner plate of prime rib, new potatoes and asparagus in front of him. Jake waited for the waiter to complete serving everyone at the table before cutting into the prime rib.

"Would anyone care for a glass of Cabernet or Pinot Grigio?" the wine steward asked when he reached their table.

Several of the guests chose the Pinot Grigio while Jake and Jillian decided on the Cabernet. Conversation around the table was light while they finished the meal. Jake hadn't eaten anything since early afternoon and didn't waste anytime time in devouring the prime rib.

"The prime rib was done just right," he declared, wiping the corners of his mouth with the silk napkin when he had finished eating.

"It was a very good meal," replied Dr. Grabow. "I am surprised that they were able to serve everyone as quickly as they did," he continued.

"I'm sure they do this so often that they've got it down to a science," added Dr. Sorman.

Mrs. Sorman, who was seated to the right of Jake then asked: "Jake, I don't believe you're in the medical field. What is it that you do?"

"I'm in law enforcement," he replied casually, not wanting to mention the FBI and hoping that the discussion would go elsewhere.

"Right here in D.C.?" asked Dr. Sorman.

"Actually, I'm with the F.B.I. assigned to the Washington Bureau," he relented, realizing that there was no sense in beating around the bush.

"That's how we met," quipped Jillian, trying to rescue Jake from further questions. "We were working a case together."

"Oh that's nice, said Mrs. Grabow. Is it one of those high profile cases like you see on Criminal Minds? I just love that show. I watch it every week. I think those profilers on that show are so smart. I especially like that young doctor...oh what's his name...Reed?"

"Well, actually, I can't discuss the case. It is still under investigation." Jake didn't have the heart to tell her that most of the shows on television are about as far from reality as you can get.

"Oh, I see... Then, I won't ask you anymore about it," she said, winking at Jake.

Jake was happy when the master of ceremonies took to the podium and announced the guest speaker for the evening. He didn't like talking about his job and felt uncomfortable trying in a nice way to tell someone that it was none of their business. Fortunately, the guest speaker was a well known pathologist from Boston with a great sense of humor. After fifteen minutes of serious discussion, he kept the audience laughing for forty five minutes with his stories and jokes. When the speaker concluded, there was a fifteen minute intermission while the band set up to finish the evening. Jake and Jillian took the opportunity to excuse themselves from the table and find the restrooms in the hallway.

"Boy, I thought we were going to be in for a long evening when he started out," Jake commented, referring to the speaker, as they made their way into the hallway. "But, once he got going, he was really on a roll. I found him quite entertaining." By the time they made their way through the room, there was already a line forming in the hallway directly opposite the restroom doors.

"I'll wait for you at the entrance to the ballroom," Jake said to Jillian, as he let her pass in front of him to the ladies line on the other side of the hallway. "It looks like your line is longer than mine anyway."

"Always is," she replied, looking over her shoulder.

Jake and Jillian stopped by the bar on their way back to the table. The band was playing "Moments", by Emerson Drive and people were starting to get up from their tables and move to the dance area, a portable wooden floor that had been set up directly in front of the band during the intermission.

"That's one of my favorite songs," said Jillian, whispering the words along with the singer and swaying her head back and forth to the rhythm of the song.

"Let's dance then," replied Jake, rising and pulling her chair back for her.

Jillian wrapped her arms around Jake's neck as he held her to him and slowly glided on the dance floor like they were the only two in the room.

"Thanks for coming with me," Jillian said, pulling her head away and looking up at him. "I was afraid that it would be very boring for you listening to forensic pathologists talk about dead people all evening."

"Actually, I'm really enjoying myself…Especially, now," he said, smiling down at her as she laid her head back on his chest. Jake closed his eyes and let his mind drift to another place. For the next couple of minutes, they held each other close and Jake could feel his heart beating against his chest. He wondered if Jillian could feel it also.

CHAPTER 60

Sunday, November 9

They slept in the next morning and didn't wake up until Jake's phone rang. He reached for it on the bed stand and saw that it was Sam.

"Good morning Sam," he said, flipping open the Razor cell phone and noticing that it was already 9:30 a.m.

"This is your late morning wake up call," she joked before Jake could respond. "Hey dad. I don't want to disturb you but since you didn't make it home last night, Well, I just wanted to make sure you were all right."

"I'm sorry. I guess I could have texted you or something. One of these days, you'll have to show me how to do that. I'll be home in a couple of hours. Any calls for me?"

"Just Sully. But, I told him you weren't home yet. He called you a dog…whatever that means…Say hello to Jillian and sorry for the intrusion."

"Get outa here," he snickered, closing the handset.

Jillian had slipped out of bed and gone to the restroom while he was on the phone with Sam and returned with a black colored silk robe over her matching nightgown.

"Out past curfew last night, huh?" she joked, sitting back on the bed.

"Yea, I guess I need to clear my staying out past midnight in the future," he replied, hitting her with a pillow.

"Hey, whataya say I order us some coffee while you get your shower," he said. Then, I'll shower and take you out for a scrumptious breakfast before we go our separate ways."

"That sounds good," she replied. Check-out isn't until noon anyway." We can get showered, dressed, and check out, and either eat in the hotel restaurant or somewhere else."

"Sure you don't want to share the shower with me?" she said, looking over her shoulder as she walked from the bed to the shower. "We can save the hotel a little water," she continued.

"Always the environmentalist," he replied, chasing her into the bathroom.

CHAPTER 61

Tuesday, November 25

Early Tuesday morning, a nor'easter pummeled the east coast from Maine to North Carolina with a vengeance, catching maintenance crews off guard. The unseasonable winter storm paralyzed Washington D.C. and northern Virginia with temperatures plummeting during the night to the low twenties. Almost a foot of the heavy white stuff blanketed the ground by seven a.m. in the Nations Capital and forecasts called for an additional four inches by noon. Gale force winds of seventy-five miles an hour piled snowdrifts as high as ten feet across major roads and bridges, burying cars and stranding motorists. Public transportation, schools and many businesses were closed. The heavy wet snow snapped tree limbs, knocked down power lines and shut off electricity to over half the city. It was early November and D.C. road crews weren't prepared to deal with the early snows. Salt reserves used to melt the snow and ice had not been replenished from last year. The mayor of D.C. as well as the governors of Virginia and Maryland declared a level three emergency restricting travel and requiring all unnecessary vehicles to stay off the roads and highways. All available maintenance personnel were called in to work. Disaster Preparedness crews were put into action rescuing stranded motorists and providing supplies to emergency personnel. Highway maintenance crews worked around the clock removing the snow from the major streets and parking lots with snowplows and dump trucks. Cars on side streets were buried in six foot high snow drifts. It would be several days before the crews could reach the side streets. Both Reagan National and Dulles cancelled hundreds of outbound flights while maintenance crews plowed the runways and taxiways, trying to keep up with the snow. Thanksgiving Holiday travelers remained stranded. Air Traffic Control at both airports diverted incoming air traffic to Richmond or Philadelphia. Only planes low on fuel or declaring emergencies were able to land at either Washington airport. By mid afternoon, the snow had let up providing a winter playground for the thousands of children who stayed home from school. Shouts of joy and children laughing could be heard as they busily went about building snowmen and tunnels through the deep drifts. People emerged from the shelter of their houses to observe the damage and destruction caused by the heavy snow. The sounds of chain saws could be heard everywhere as tree trimming companies cleared the roads of fallen trees and limbs that blocked the highways so that the snow plows could make their way through the deep snow.

Stryker tossed and turned during the night listening to the wind howl and shake the door and window of his corner room. Cold air seeped around the edges of the windowpanes where the sealing putty had cracked and fallen away, blowing puffs of snow around the room. Lights flickered several times and the clock on the table next to the bed blinked a steady twelve o'clock. The transformer on the pole in the parking lot behind the motel threw sparks in the air as the pole swayed back and forth in the wind. The old space heater under the window struggled to keep up with the falling outside temperature. It hissed, moaned and knocked reminding him of the fuel oil baseboard heating in the old farmhouse. Finally, after fighting a fierce battle with the wind and snow for hours, the transformer surrendered with a loud boom sending sparks and black smoke through the air before leaving the motel into total darkness. Stryker heard the explosion and recognized the aftermath. Pulling the blanket up around his neck, he settled into the musty smelling pillow and waited out the storm.

It didn't take long for the temperature in the room to drop. By nine a.m. when Stryker poked his head out from beneath the woolen blanket, he could see his breath. The power was still out and the room was cold and clammy. Without the noise of the heater, Stryker could hear his own thoughts. It was eerie and somewhat freaky. He really had to go to the bathroom but had to force himself to leave the warmth of the bed. Shivering, he pulled the blanket from the bed and draping it around his shoulders like a cape as he walked into the dark bathroom. Only the light that crept in around the dusty window curtain found its way to a corner of the bathroom. He undid his pants and froze when he sat down on the toilet seat. Memories immediately flashed to the two hole outhouse behind the family home before plumbing was installed in the late eighties.

After sitting in the room looking at the four corners for a half hour, Stryker was bored to death and decided to leave the room and venture outside. He pulled a heavy sweater out of his backpack to put on beneath one of Tommy's green army field jackets and pulled a knit hat down over his head to cover his ears. He couldn't find his gloves but then remembered that he had left them on the front seat of the car the night before. Reaching in his back pocket to make sure that his wallet was still there, he slid open the safety latch on the door, pulled on the handle and stepped outside. Snow immediately covered the tops of his shoes, rising midway on his pant leg. The snow that found its way under his pant leg was cold against his bare leg. There wasn't another soul in the parking lot. Everything was covered in white. The cars that were parked in the lot the night before looked like mounds of snow. He thought about getting his gloves on the front seat of the car but then decided that he wasn't going anywhere in the car today anyway. Pulling his collar up around his neck, he lowered his head, dug his hands in his pants pockets and started to walk.

CHAPTER 62

Jake tapped on his Jawbone wireless earpiece when his cell phone rang on the corner of his desk. He had stalled for months against getting one of those "fancy ear pieces" as he put it but found that it sure came in handy when he was driving and could keep both hands on the wheel.

"Yea Sully," he said, speaking into space when he recognized Sully's name appear on the screen on the front of the phone.

"Hey," Sully's voice answered. "Doesn't look like I'm gong to be able to get into the office today. Power's been out here since early this morning and doesn't look like they're going to be fixing it anytime soon. Us po folks not like the privileged, you know. I suppose we're probably last on the list as far as priorities go. I haven't even seen a power truck and the parking lot looks like we're snowed in anyway. It seems the only thing working is cell phones."

"I hear ya," responded Jake, stepping out onto the second story deck of the townhome to survey the Norman Rockwell scene painted by the winter storm. "Our power was restored an hour ago but it's gone off and on several times in the last ten minutes. I don't know if they're checking it or not. From what I hear on the weather radio, it's supposed to let up sometime early afternoon."

"You gonna try to make it in?" asked Sully.

"No, replied Jake, quickly. "Mayor's declared a state of emergency and I called down there a bit ago and spoke with Johnny. He said that he was about an hour late for shift change. He only lives about a mile from the office but it took him over an hour to get through the snow. He's quite the trooper for sixty-seven years old. The guard that he relieved was none too happy having to work an extra hour but what the hell, at least he showed up. Johnny said that things were pretty quiet. They were on emergency power most of the night but he said power was restored to most of the offices downtown by eight this morning. The director called in at seven and said that there wasn't any sense in anyone trying to make it in today. Public transportation is still down and most of the businesses are closed anyway. I've been going through some of these hard files we brought back with us. Now that our power is back on, I'm going to see if I can log into the network. I think we're getting close. We're going to find some answers soon. From one of my contacts in the CIA, the director's been under pretty tight security for the past several weeks. He doesn't shit without an armed escort. And from what my source tells me, that's his request. That tell's me he's scared. He knows something and he's just not talking. Sooner or later he will."

"Okay. I'm just going to hang around home. You find something you think is important in any of them files, give me a call."

CHAPTER 63

Thursday, November 27
Thanksgiving

Jake woke Thursday morning to the smell of celery and onion cooking. He immediately thought of Rachel. He didn't have to go downstairs to know that Sam was making homemade dressing for the turkey. She was using Rachael's recipe. Thanksgiving had always been one of Jake's favorite holidays. When Sam was little, Rachael set her up on the counter next to the sink while she prepared the turkey for the oven. Before filling the turkey with the dressing, Rachael would hold the bird up in the sink and sing and do a turkey dance, bouncing the turkey up and down while Sam laughed and kept saying "Do it again mommy, make the turkey dance again." After two or three dances, Rachael finally convinced Sam that if she didn't get the turkey in the oven, they wouldn't be eating any dinner that night.

Jake grabbed his robe from the back of the bathroom door and headed upstairs for the kitchen.

"Something smells awful good," he remarked, grabbing a piece of sausage and bread stuffing from the pan and putting it in his mouth before Sam good hit his hand with the wooden spoon she was using to mix the dressing.

"What time are you picking Jillian up?" she asked, using both hands to fill the turkey cavity with the dressing.

"She's expecting me around noon. I thought we'd watch the football game before dinner. What time do you think we'll be eating?"

"If I get the bird in by nine thirty, we should be eating by three-three thirty at the latest. How's that work for your plans?"

"Perfect. I bought some cheese and summer sausage the other day. We can have a couple of drinks and snack on cheese and crackers while we watch the game."

"I'm gonna make a pumpkin pie for desert," she said. "I found mom's old recipe."

Jake smiled at her. Jake had always said that Rachael made the best homemade pumpkin pie.

A two foot deep drift of snow blocked the entrance to Jake's driveway, piled up from the snowplow that had cleared the road in front of the townhouse during the night. He could have shoveled the snow out of the way, but thought the afternoon sun and warming temperature would melt most of it by evening. He backed out of the driveway and hit the pedal when he got to the snow pile at the end of the drive. The all wheel drive Infinity, backed through the snow like a four wheel SUV, the radial tires gripping and throwing snow out of the way. He took the I-495 beltway around the city to Bethesda, the beltway being one of the first highways the road crews cleared. Jake made the thirty mile trip in less than a half hour, the traffic light, with most of the holiday travelers already at their destination. Jillian's neighbor boy was just finishing her driveway with a snow blower when he pulled into her drive, stopping by the side door.

Jillian saw him coming before he had a chance to knock, opening the door and giving him a toothy grin.

"What's so funny?" he remarked, closing the door behind him.

"You are," she said, wrapping her arms around his neck and pulling him close, giving him a long kiss on the lips.

"Whoa, maybe, we'll just stay here and forget the turkey and dressing." Jake said, pulling her back for another kiss.

"Not on your life. I've been looking forward to spending the day with you and Sam since she called me last week," she said. "I wouldn't miss out on home cooked turkey with dressing for anything. I told Sam I'd bring the cranberry relish, rolls and a bottle of wine. I've got it all ready to go on the dining room table."

Jake followed her into the dining room and draped his arms around her from behind, squeezing her and kissing her ear. "This is your last chance," he whispered, blowing softly into her ear.

"Oh geez…" she said. "Don't do that to me… We'd better get out of here before we start something we can't finish." She turned quickly in his grasp, kissed him on the lips and said, "Come on, let's go. Sam is waiting on us."

"All right, we're off," he said helping her into her coat. Picking up the food and wine from the table, they left the house, locking the door on their way out.

Jake pulled into the driveway of the townhouse just before one in the afternoon. The snow at the end of the driveway hadn't melted much in the hour he was gone. He centered the car and drove back through the tire marks he made earlier and parked in front of the garage.

"I like the way you shovel snow," remarked Jillian, laughing.

"Actually, I thought it was going to warm up faster and I didn't want to give myself a heart attack," he responded sarcastically. "We still have five hours of sunlight. It should be pretty much melted by the time we leave."

"The eternal optimist," she concluded.

The rock salt he had placed on the stairwell leading to the front door before leaving for Jillian's had melted most of the snow and ice.

Grabbing the food and wine from the back seat, Jake led the way up the stairwell, opening the door for Jillian.

"Hello," hollered Jillian on entering the house. "Boy something really smells good," she said to Jake who had taken her coat and was hanging it up in the closet.

"That's Sam's homemade pumpkin pie," he said. "I could skip the meal and go right to the pumpkin pie with plenty of whipped cream."

"I'm gonna take the relish and rolls to Sam," said Jillian, heading to the kitchen. "Why don't you check out the game?"

"No argument from me," said Jake, reaching for the remote.

Sam was leaning over the stove, basting the turkey when Jillian entered the kitchen...

"Boy, Sam. That pumpkin pie smells delicious. And that turkey. It looks too good to eat."

"Thanks, Jillian. I'm so glad you could spend the day with us. It's really nice having another female around here. Sometimes when it's just dad and me...well, we're just both so set in our ways."

"You ladies aren't plotting against me, are you?" Jake said, coming up behind Jillian.

"No, why would we do that?" said Jillian, winking at Sam. "I was just telling Sam that I think Thanksgiving is my favorite holiday. It's the one day of the year when I don't care how much I eat. I've got the rest of the year to worry about losing weight."

"Well, you ladies can sit out here and chat but I'm going to watch the rest of the football game. The Tennessee Titans are beating the Detroit Lions 10 to 7. They're just starting the third quarter."

"Dad, why don't you open a bottle of wine and take the cheese tray into the family room. I'm almost done basting this bird. Everything should be ready to eat around three."

"I don't know if I'll last that long," said Jake, stuffing a piece of cheese and summer sausage in his mouth.

They spent the next hour watching the game. Jake was happy when the Titans won the game. He had a lunch bet with Sully who had taken the Detroit Lions on an even bet. Sully was born and raised in Detroit and maintained his allegiance to the home team.

At three, Sam announced that the turkey was done. While Jake carved the turkey with the electric knife, Sam and Jillian set the remainder of the meal on the dining room table. Taking their places around the table, they bowed their heads while Jake led the Thanksgiving prayer.

A half hour later, they were pushing away from the table. Jake could have eaten a second helping of everything but forced himself to leave some room for the pumpkin pie.

"Why don't you two go into the front room while I clean up and then we can have dessert," said Sam.

"No way. We're not sticking you with the clean-up," said Jillian. "If we all pitch in, we can be done in ten minutes."

With all three working together, the dishwasher was loaded, the pots and pans were scrubbed and the kitchen straightened in less than fifteen minutes.

"Wow, I don't know when I've seen that done that fast before," said Sam. "You'll have to come over more often," she said, smiling at Jillian.

"All right, I'm ready for some pie," exclaimed Jake. "I'll make a pot of coffee"

"I'll second that, but only a small piece for me, please. I've pretty much stuffed myself."

Taking their coffee and pie into the family room, Jake and Jillian took a seat on the couch while Sam opted for her favorite chair.

They played several hands of rummy, Jillian beating Jake soundly until the Bengals game on. The Cincinnati Bengals was Jake's favorite team even though they weren't performing very well this season. At seven, Jillian said that she was ready to go home.

"It's been a great afternoon," she said. "But, I do have an early day tomorrow, so I better get going."

Jake went to the closet to get Jillian's coat while she and Sam exchanged goodbyes.

"I'll be back in a bit," he said to Sam, pulling the door closed behind him, checking to ensure that it locked.

"See," Jake said, pointing at the slush in the driveway as they descended the stairs to the car. "You wait long enough and it will melt."

They spoke little on the way back to Jillian's. Jake drove in silence, his thoughts on the woman sitting next to him with her head resting back against the headrest, her eyes closed. After ten minutes without exchanging any words, he thought she might have been asleep until she startled him by saying, "You know... I could get used to this." For the first time in a long time, Jake was speechless.

Pulling his car into Jillian's driveway, he stopped at the side door, shutting off the ignition. She pulled her keys from her purse, opened the door and invited him in.

"I had a great time," exclaimed Jillian, throwing her coat over the chair. "And Sam's a fantastic cook. You're a pretty lucky guy to have her."

"Yea, I'll say," he responded, sticking out his stomach and patting it.

"Can you stay a little while? "I'll put on a fresh pot of coffee."

"Yea, I'm sure Sam isn't expecting me to pull into your driveway, hit the ejection button, sending you through the rooftop," he laughed, removing his coat, and laying it over the top of hers.

"Grab a seat and see if you can find the game we were watching. They should be in the fourth quarter by now. The remote is on the table next to the couch. I'll get that pot of coffee going."

Jake turned on the tube, scrolling through the channels until he found the Bengals playing on the ESPN channel. Settling into the couch to watch the game, he was almost asleep when he felt Jillian slide in beside him. After putting the coffee on, she had snuck upstairs and slipped into a nightgown and silk robe. She curled up next to him on the couch, her head beneath his chin. He detected the feint hint of perfume that she had dabbed behind her ear.

"Mmn," he said, breathing in heavy, his chest rising. "Boy, you smell good," he added, draping his arm around her and pulling her close to him.

She looked up at him, their eyes meeting. "I like this," she said.

"Yea, I could get used to this," he agreed, leaning down to kiss her.

Their lips pressed together momentarily before she thrust her tongue into his mouth, their breathing becoming heavier. Jake hadn't felt this way in a long time.

There was something special about Jillian. She stirred a passion within him that he had forgotten he had.

She reached up, pulling on the tie that held her robe together as she continued to kiss him passionately. Jake slipped his right hand beneath her robe. His hand cupped her breast caressing it, her nipple turning hard at the gentle touch of his fingers, causing her to moan and breathe in deeply. Jake felt himself becoming fully aroused, his maleness pressing against his pant leg.

"Oh Jake, I want you," she said, looking up into his eyes. "You don't know what you do to me."

"I think I do," he responded. "Because I'm feeling it too."

She reached back over her head, turning off the table lamp, the only light now coming from the television screen. He continued to fondle her breast, moving from one to the other, while kissing her passionately on the mouth. Their breathing became erratic, he kissing her on the neck while she lay back and let him tantalize her with his lips and tongue. She reached down and stroked his erect penis through his pants. Jake closed his eyes, and sighed.

"I'm falling in love with you, Jake Hunter, she whispered.

CHAPTER 64

Friday, November 28

By Friday morning the major streets were clear of the record snowfall that had besieged the city three days earlier. Maintenance crews even worked Thanksgiving Day trying to clear the roads before the weekend. After hauling hundreds of truckloads of snow outside the perimeter of the city, what remained was pushed to the edges of parking lots. It would take another two weeks of warm temperatures to melt the mounds of gray snow mixed with gravel and pieces of asphalt. The pristine white that had covered the city in a bed of white linen was gone, replaced by a dull grungy gray slush.

For several weeks before the storm, Stryker had been watching the director come and go from the big brick and stone mansion in the wealthy section of McLean. The home was a large Georgian style that occupied the better part of an entire city block. The property was surrounded by an eight foot tall wrought iron fence and a massive gate that operated with a remote control. Security cameras were strategically placed around the premises to pick up on any unwanted visitors. You didn't get in if you weren't invited. At seven a.m. Friday morning, Stryker was again sitting quietly around the corner parked between two cars with the Honda's engine running. With his binoculars on the seat next to him, he waited. He sipped on the coffee he had picked up at the carryout on the corner by the motel. He had changed his location frequently maintaining a safe distance from the security guards that seemed to be keeping a close guard on the director's house. Stryker knew the director's weekday schedule pretty well. One of the new FBI black armor plated Chevy Suburban Hybrids would arrive at the house between seven and seven thirty, pull into the circular drive in front of the brick mansion. Two Agents carrying MP-5 submachine guns would get out of the back seat and approach the front door while the driver and front seat passenger remained in the vehicle, the engine running. The front door to the house would open; two more armed men would appear in the doorway and escort the director to the car. The two men on the front porch would remain, holding their weapons on ready alert, until the director entered the vehicle, sitting between the two armed men. The SUV would then depart the director's residence and proceed to Langley, never going the same way on two consecutive days. The director would return to the residence anywhere between six thirty and eight o'clock at night under the same guarded protection. At seven fifteen, he saw the black SUV approaching his position. It passed by him and he watched it round the corner in his rear view mirror in the direction of the director's home. Ten minutes later, the SUV passed by him again headed in the direction of Langley. Stryker pulled out behind the SUV, keeping a distance so as not to alarm the driver. As the bulletproof SUV made its way through the streets of McLean toward Langley, the director looked past the FBI agent to his right at the beautiful mansions with Mercedes and Jaguars parked in their driveways. For over fifteen years things were quiet. He had served five years in the Army before leaving to join the top spy agency in the world. He had married his high school sweetheart; they had two children attending a private high school. He had risen through the organization on a fast track, working twelve hour days, finally securing the Deputy position. The SUV made a right turn at the next intersection and Stryker looked into his rear view mirror as he was turning on his right blinker. A police car with lights flashing and siren blaring was coming up fast on his rear. For a moment, he thought of hitting the gas pedal and trying to get away but then his better judgment took hold and he slowed and pulled to the right side of the road, expecting the police car to pull in behind him. The police car never slowed but continued by him, turning left at the intersection, opposite the direction of the SUV. Stryker remained parked for another minute, letting his pulse slow and catching his breath before pulling back into the street in the direction of the motel.

CHAPTER 65

Jake rolled over and fell back asleep after setting the snooze alarm for another fifteen minutes when his cell phone woke him at 6:00 a.m. He had gone to bed with the intention of getting up early, eating breakfast and being in his office by 7:30 a.m. Unfortunately, he tossed and turned all night long and didn't fall asleep until after 2:30 a.m. At one point, he had even gotten out of bed, went upstairs and sat in the Lay Z Boy reading a copy of "The Shack" by William P. Young that he had picked up earlier in the day at Barnes and Noble after reading a review in the New York Times. He thought that reading might make him tired but by the time he was fifty pages into the book, he was hooked. The book was a work of fiction that depicted a man who had met god, a black woman, after his young daughter was kidnapped and brutally murdered. At 1:30 a.m., Jake finally had to force himself to put the book down and close his eyes. Even then, visions of lost children flooded his mind, keeping him awake for another hour.

At six fifteen when the alarm sounded again, he turned it off and lay there for another ten minutes before forcing himself to get up. He threw a robe over his pajama bottoms and headed into the bathroom before going upstairs for a cup of coffee. Splashing some cold water on his face, he looked into the mirror at the image that stared back at him. Boy, he thought, you're starting to look pretty old, the crow's feet at the corners of his eyes, becoming more pronounced every day.

Sam was in the kitchen drinking a cup of coffee over the morning paper.

"Morning sunshine," he said leaning down to plant a kiss on the top of her head.

"How'd you sleep last night?" she inquired, looking over the top of the coffee cup she held with both hands while she sipped.

"Lousy," he replied, pouring himself a cup of coffee and sitting down across from her.

"I thought I heard you up a couple of times walking around," she said. "Were you not feeling well?"

"I dunno. I couldn't fall asleep. I think I ate too much turkey yesterday. What's that stuff in turkey that supposed to make you sleep? Tryptophan or something like that. I was real tired right after dinner but then I drank a couple of cups of coffee at Jillian's when I took her home and I think the caffeine kept me awake. I just tossed and turned and finally decided to come upstairs and read for a bit. I got a glass of milk and started reading this book I picked up a couple of days ago about a black female god. Before I knew it, it was already almost one thirty and I was still reading. The book is pretty good. Makes you think... Not that I have any problem thinking, mind you."

"Black, female god, huh? That's a good one. I suppose if god is going to be female, might as well be black also."

"Hey, how bout some waffles?" she said jumping up from the table and grabbing the waffle maker from the kitchen cupboard. "I'll even put some of the blueberries in that I picked up at the grocery."

"You're on," he said, reaching for the sports page.

CHAPTER 66

It was almost eight thirty when Jake walked into the office. Sully hadn't arrived yet and Lynn was away from her desk making copies. He grabbed his cup from his desk that was still half full of Wednesday's coffee. He poured it down the sink, rinsed the cup and poured himself a fresh cup before logging into his computer to check his emails. Twenty three new emails since he logged off before leaving the office Wednesday evening. Jake had a policy of only looking at emails where he recognized the sender or it was a reply to something he sent out. That eliminated all but seven of the messages remaining in his inbox. Jake was reading the last email when Sully walked in.

"Hey, what's shakin bacon?"

"Boy, that's a new one," responded Jake, not looking up from his computer screen. "You just hear that on the radio on your way in this morning?"

"What? You don't like my new vocabulary? I'm trying to…"

"Hold on a minute," Jake interrupted, listening to his voicemail. "I might be on to something. This voicemail is a response to a phone call I made Wednesday morning to a guy in Richmond. He say's that he might have something that we'd be interested in. Doesn't want to discuss it over the phone but says he'd meet us."

"Did he at least give you a clue what he's talking about?"

"No, just says that he was close friends with another soldier…an officer…and would like to talk. Gave me a cell phone number to call to set up a meeting but says he won't discuss it over the phone."

"Well, give it a call," said Sully, glancing at his watch on his way to the coffee machine. "We can be down in Richmond before noon if we leave right away."

Jake punched in the numbers on his cell, pressed send but went immediately into voicemail. He left a message and his personal cell number to call back.

"I'm gonna run up to Mike's office," he said to Sully, catching him on his way back from the break room with a cup of coffee and a glazed donut.

Jake decided to take the stairs up the two flights to the director's office. He was still on his exercise kick and had decided over a month ago to forego the luxury of using elevators whenever possible He pushed open the door at the end of the hall and bounded up the stairs, taking two at a time, trying to catch his breath before entering the director's outer office. Sandy, the director's executive assistant lifted her head from her computer screen when he entered the room.

"Hey Sandy," he greeted her. Is Mike available? I'd like to speak with him for a couple of minutes if I could. It's pretty important."

"He's on the phone right now," she said looking down at the green indicator light on the phone at the corner of her desk. "As soon as he's off, I'll give him a buzz. What did you do run up here? You sound like you're outta breath."

"Yea, well…I'm not as young as I used to be. I envy those new guys downstairs. Somehow I don't remember ever having as much energy as they do."

"Yea, but they're pretty wet behind the ears. I'd take someone with your background any day over those young guys. Oop, he's off," she said, when the green light went off, indicating the director had completed his call. "You better catch him before he makes another call."

She buzzed into the director's inner sanctum on the intercom letting him know that Jake was there. Within seconds, the door opened and Mike Avery invited Jake into his private office.

"Come on in Jake, he greeted him, extending his hand and gripping Jake's outstretched hand. "Have a seat," he said, closing the door behind Jake and walking to the other side of his desk to his well worn leather chair. "You saved me a call. I've been meaning to talk with you. I was going to give you a call this afternoon to see how things were going."

"That's why I stopped to see you," responded Jake. "Ever since we returned from St. Louis last week, we have been making calls. Hadn't really had much luck. Most of the information was dated and we've spent a lot of time trying to update the list. Those who left military service are not required to keep St. Louis updated. We weren't getting very far but I got a voicemail this morning from a phone call I made Wednesday. The guy said he wanted to meet, wouldn't talk over the phone. He now lives in Richmond. Might not be anything useful but I thought that Sully and I would take a trip down there today and see what he has to say. I left a message on his voicemail to call me. As soon as we connect, we'll head down that way."

The phone in Jake's pocket vibrated and he pulled it out looking at the number displayed on the screen.

"That's him now," he said, indicating to the director that he needed to take the call.

"Jake Hunter," he said, tapping the Bluetooth in his left ear to connect the call, and reaching for a pen and piece of paper from the director's desk.

"Mr. Hunter," the voice on the other end of the phone said. "This is Steve Jackson. I understand that you may be looking for some information regarding Captain Powell and Lieutenant Hatcher."

"That would be correct," replied Jake.

"Well, I might be able to help you with that," he said. "Can you meet with me? I don't feel comfortable talking over the phone."

"Mr. Jackson, my partner and I can be down there in three hours. Where can we meet you?"

"Not here. I don't want my wife to hear us talking. There's a restaurant right off Exit 84B where 95 meets 295. It's on the service road on the north side. It's called "Bark'n Dog". I can meet you there. It's a little after nine now. Can you be down here between 12:30 and 1?"

"We'll be there," replied Jake, scribbling the name of the restaurant and exit on the piece of paper.

"I'll grab a booth in the back. I'll be wearing a red ball cap."

"Do you have a cell phone in case we get delayed?" asked Jake.

"Don't have one. Don't worry. I'll be there. I don't have anyplace else to be."

Jake hung up and looked at the director.

"Sounds like you may be on to something. Check in with me after your meeting. Let me know what you find out."

With that, Jake stood and walked out of the room.

CHAPTER 67

Jake bounded down the two flights of stairs and found Lynn still standing by the copy machine.

"Sully and I are headed to Richmond," he said, slowing to tell her where they were going. "Call me on my cell if you need to get a hold of us. We should be back by five unless we run into traffic or something comes up. I'll call you if it looks like we're not going to make it before you leave."

Jake stopped by his desk to pull his back up piece out of the bottom drawer and slide it into the ankle holster on the inside of his right ankle. With the sixteen shot capability of the Springfield XD 9mm on his ankle and twelve bullets in the Sig Model 229 .40 Caliber he carried in his shoulder holster, Jake felt he had enough fire power to take care of himself and anyone else that depended on his quick reflexes.

"Come on Sully. Finish up. We're headed to Richmond. I'll tell you about it on the way."

Arising out of his chair, Sully gulped the last bit of coffee in his mug and downed the last donut hole in the box. "We need any files or anything to take with us?" he said, grabbing his jacket from the back of his chair.

"Nope. I've got a legal pad for notes and a digital recorder if we need it. We should be back by five."

Sully followed Jake out the door and over to the elevator. Jake knew that Sully wouldn't take the stairs and he wanted to fill him in on the conversation he had with Steve Jackson on the way to the parking garage. The door to the elevator opened with three other people inside. Jake decided to hold off on discussing the case until they were alone. They rode the elevator in silence down to the second level where Jake had parked his car. Backing out of the parking space, they exited the side entrance of the garage onto 9th Street, heading south to I-395 where they could pick up I-95 to Richmond. Once they reached I-95, they were going to be going opposite the traffic headed into D.C. so they shouldn't have any problem making it to the restaurant by 12:30.

"So, what's the scoop?" asked Sully, when they were out of the busy traffic. "What's this guy all so secretive about?"

"I'm not sure," Jake said. "But he was adamant about not talking over the phone. Say's he has some information that we might find interesting. Jake told Sully about the discussion he had with Jackson while he was in the director's office.

"Bark'n Dog huh?" Sully repeated when Jake told him where they'd be meeting Steve Jackson. "Sound's like someplace out of a Simpsons cartoon."

CHAPTER 68

Once they hit I-95, Jake set the cruise to seventy mph. Thirty minutes later they were passing the exit for Quantico.

"If we have the time, I'd like to stop off on our way back and see Chuck Embers. There are a couple of things I want to run by him."

All kinds of thoughts were running through Jake's head as he drove towards Richmond. What could be so important that he needed to meet in person? What was Steve Jackson afraid of? Jake hoped that this wouldn't just be a wild goose chase. He really needed something to crack this case wide open. Maybe, just maybe, he thought, he was finally going to get a real break.

At noon, they were just north of the exit to the service road and Jake decided to fill up the gas tank. He got twenty five miles a gallon highway mileage in the G37 but the tank was only twenty gallons and was less than half full when they left D.C.

"We made better time than I thought we would," he said, pulling off the exit into an Exxon station. "I don't know how long we're going to be talking with Jackson. I'm going to fill up now so that we can head back right away and see Chuck before he leaves for the day."

It didn't take Jake more than five minutes to fill the tank and slide his credit card under the secure window at the station to the attendant who was preoccupied reading a comic book.

"Four bucks a gallon. That's highway robbery," Jake said to the attendant who ignored him and ran his credit card through the machine, placed it back in the drawer and sent it back for Jake's signature.

Jake retrieved the receipt, signed the slip on the bottom and pulled the yellow copy from the back.

"You have a great day too," he hollered to the attendant as he walked toward the car. The attendant continued reading his comic book without ever looking up or acknowledging Jake's comment.

Sully was on his cell phone talking loudly to someone when Jake got back in the car. After a minute, he realized by the tone of the conversation that Sully was getting a pretty good reaming from Sally. *It was times like this, he thought, that it was nice to be single.*

CHAPTER 69

"There it is," Sully said, pointing ahead to the right. "The Bark'n Dog. Arff...arff. Looks like a pretty quiet place. Don't see many cars around. Maybe we're just early for the lunch crowd."

The restaurant was a converted gas station. The pumps and underground storage tanks had been removed as required by the EPA but the island that once held the pumps remained. The Shell emblem was still partly visible beneath the weathered sign that now advertised the daily specials and the nightly entertainment.

Jake pulled into the parking lot in front of the restaurant and tucked his car in between a couple of Harleys and an old Ford Fairlane. The doors on the car were painted with a gray primer coat, the muffler held up to the frame with baling wire. The convertible top was ripped with the back window held together with duct tape. He thought about the acronym FORD...Found on road dead.

"My guess if he's here...he drove the Ford," he said, getting out of the car and admiring the two bikes before walking toward the door.

"A 2007 Screaming Eagle Fatboy, Anniversary Addition," exclaimed Jake, sounding like a kid with a new toy. "That's my kinda bike," the envy obvious in his voice.

"Never had a bike," said Sully. "But I dated a motorcycle mamma once that could suck the chrome off a bumper."

"Ooooh," said Jake. "Come to papa."

Jake pulled open the front door, the handle almost coming apart in his hand. The glass in the door had been replaced by a sheet of plywood. *Probably a good bar fight*, he thought. Entering the restaurant, Jake stole a glace around the room, waiting for his eyes to adjust to the dim light. The place still had the ambience of a gas station with a pool table and dart board at the far end of the bar near the Hog and Sow restrooms. The room stank of stale beer from the night before. Two bikers in leather jackets and chaps with skull caps resting on their heads occupied two stools at the far end of a long bar smoking cigarettes and sucking down a couple of cold ones. The State of Virginia was one of the few states that still allowed smoking in public bars. By the thick blue smoke that curled in the air above the bar, these two had been smoking quite a few. Either that or the ventilation in the place wasn't working and the smoke from the night before still hung heavy in the air.

Damn, Jake thought. *He had just paid seven bucks to have the sport coat he was wearing dry cleaned and he could almost hear it sucking up the smoke in the place like a vacuum cleaner.*

The place was definitely a biker hangout with pictures of motorcycles, old license plates, worn leather vests and buckles from all across the country decorating the walls. There was even an old 1995 poster advertising the Harley Rally in Sturgis, South Dakota tacked on the wall by the restroom doors. A couple of flat screen TV's hung over the bar, tuned to the political coverage to give the place a little class. The Bark n' Dog wasn't anyplace you'd want to take a girl you were trying to impress for your first date.

Jake looked past the tables and chairs in the middle of the dance floor and spotted a man sitting in a booth by himself at the far end of the room. He motioned for Sully to follow him and started walking toward the man, crunching the peanut shells that littered the floor. The light was too dim to tell if he was wearing a red ball cap but when Jake was twenty feet away, the man looked up and motioned for them to join him.

"Steve Jackson?" Jake asked quietly.

"That'd be me," he responded, extending his hand.

"Agent Hunter," Jake replied, shaking his hand while sliding in the booth across from him. "This is Agent Gilmore."

He nodded to Sully without shaking his hand.

Jackson was thin with dark set eyes and a nose that looked like it had been broken a time or two. Greasy hair protruded from his cap, hanging over his ears and his face sported a week's growth of black and white whiskers. He was sipping on a cup of black coffee and twirling an unlit cigarette deciding whether to light up or not.

They had just sat down when a waitress with a bleached blond bees nest piled high on her head and bright red lipstick stopped at their booth to take their order. She was chomping on a mouthful of gum and Jake could see the wad rolling around her mouth when she spoke.

"Turkey Hash's the special today," she announced without missing a beat. "It'll go fast when the lunch crowd gets here'n minute."

"Just coffee for me please...black," said Jake.

"Make that a double but ah...put a little cream in mine," added Sully with a wink.

"How bout a big piece of pumpkin pie to go with that coffee?" she asked before leaving the table.

"I'd love to," said Sully, patting his stomach. "But, I think I'll just stick with the coffee."

"Suit yourself," she answered, leaving to get their coffee.

Jake wasted no time in getting to the heart of the matter, unloosening his tie and looking directly at Steve Jackson.

"Mr. Jackson, I understand that you might have some information that would help us with our investigation."

"Well, that would depend. I'm not sure exactly what you're looking for but your phone call sounded like you were trying to dig up some dirt on Captain Powell or Lieutenant Hatcher. I might be able to help you there." Jake had to lean into the table to hear what Jackson was saying, the inflection in his voice as monotone as the middle "C" on a piano keyboard.

"It's not really dirt I'm looking for," replied Jake. I'm not trying to ruin anyone's career. Those two are dead and gone. What I'm trying to do is find their killer and maybe stop another murder. If you think that you have some information that can help us, I want to hear it. Now, from what we gathered from the records in St. Louis, you were stationed with both the senator and Colonel Hatcher in Iraq during the first Gulf War. I don't know if you're aware of it or not but both the senator and Colonel Hatcher were killed within the last six months."

"Yea, I heard. Word gets around bout stuff like that. I read the papers. Back in Desert Storm, the senator was a Captain. He was in charge of our battalion. A real prick if you know what I mean. Lieutenant Hatcher...well, let's just say that he was pretty close to the captain. Mind if I smoke?" he asked, already having struck the match and holding it to the tip of the cigarette, the other end stuck in the hole between his two front teeth.

"What about Director, ah... Lieutenant Preacher? How well did you know him?"

He blew a smoke ring to the side before responding, without looking at either one of them.

"Preacher was my first squad leader but we never seen eye to eye. Guy was always on my ass. If you weren't an officer, he treated you like dog meat. I put in a transfer and got assigned to Lieutenant Warner's squad."

"I get the feeling you didn't have much time for Powell, Hatcher or Preacher?" asked Sully.

"We used to joke behind their backs and call them the three stooges," he replied, blowing another smoke ring. "Lieutenant Warner... He was one of us. What I mean is...Tom...er the lieutenant wasn't one of them West Point fuckwads who thought their shit didn't stink. He came up through the ranks."

"He was prior enlisted?" Sully asked.

"Yea, he enlisted before they sent his ass to college. I guess they thought he'd make a good officer. He was just a farm kid at heart. Went to school someplace in Ohio. But he never acted like the others. Everyone liked him. He wasn't much older than the rest of us but we respected the man."

"Mr. Jackson. What is it that you wanted to talk to us about?" asked Jake, looking directly into the face sitting across from him.

"Well, if you checked," he started to say, looking around to make sure that no one else in the bar was paying any attention... "They say that Lieutenant Warner committed suicide."

"Go on," said Jake, giving him the opportunity to finish his statement.

"Well, I for one don't believe it for a second. There's no way that he would have done that."

"What makes you say that?" asked Sully.

"I just know. He was always talking about home and couldn't wait to get back there. I think he was pretty close to his family. I know the guy loved to hunt and fish. He was always talking about the big deer that they had back there. Guy wouldn't be talking like that if he planned on offing himself."

"Suicide?" How'd he do it?" asked Jake.

"Well, when they found him... They said he swallowed the barrel of his service piece. The officers all carried 9mm. From what we heard, his nine was laying next to him. It had been fired and there was a round missing. The casing was on the floor by the body where it ejected."

"Anyone witness the shooting?" asked Sully.

"Shit no. No one heard anything either. When he didn't show for chow the next morning, they went looking for him. Found him in a shack on the edge of town."

"Any note or letter that would explain why he did it?" asked Jake.

"Nothing. That's why I know he would 'na done it. He was always writing letters to the family back home. He would have left some explanation. Wouldn't have left them in the dark like that."

"Can you prove any of what you're telling us?" asked Sully, knowing full well that the odds of winning the Mega Million Lottery was probably better than the odds of proving murder after seventeen years.

"Can't prove it but it sure got hushed up real quick like."

"Did you tell anyone else what you just told us?" asked Jake.

"Nah. Wouldn't have done any good. I mean with everything else that was going on, the way they found him with his own gun and all…well…they called it a suicide and it was wrapped up pretty quick."

"Where'd this happen?" asked Jake.

"Philippines."

"Philippines?" choked Sully.

"Yea, we was diverted on our way back from the desert. We were only in Iraq a couple of months, spent a few months in Kuwait and I guess the government didn't think we spent enough time in that hellhole so they made us stop on our way back. We were coming home when Typhoon Thelma hit the Philippines. They made us stop there and help with the rescue efforts. Was worse than Iraq… Mudslides and high water. There was fucking mud and shit everywhere. We dug bodies out twelve hours a day… Spent over a month in that damn place. Stench was enough to gag a maggot. That's a smell you don't forget."

"Who did the investigation?" asked Jake.

"Well, that's where it gets a little funny. There weren't any of them CSI guys around like you see on TV. When they found the lieutenant, they called the captain. He was the ranking officer and he went to the scene. Like I said before, all we were told was that the lieutenant had shot himself and his gun was lying next to him. Captain called it a suicide. They bagged the body just like they were bagging all the other bodies we were digging out of the shit over there. I guess they put him on a plane and shipped him home. It wasn't like they did any kinda investigation or anything like that."

"Did you see the body?" asked Sully, holding up his cup for a refill from the waitress that had come back around to check on them.

"You fellas gonna eat today?" she interrupted, emptying the remainder of the pot in Jake's cup.

"Thanks, no, just coffee," replied Jake, looking around the bar that had started to fill up with the lunch crowd while he waited to hear the answer to Sully's question.

Jackson waited for the waitress to leave the table before replying. "No. None of us did. I mean…other than the guys that found him."

"What happened after that?" asked Jake.

"Nothing. Business as usual. We stayed there on that island for another month before they shipped us back home."

"You never heard anything else about the lieutenant?" asked Sully, stirring cream into his refilled cup until it looked more like milk than coffee.

"No. About three months after we got back to the states, my enlistment was up. I got the hell out of there. To be honest with you…I never thought much about it until I got your phone call the other day. I guess that's a part of my life that I'd rather not remember."

They sat there for a moment in quiet and sipping on their coffee while Jake contemplated how he was going to phrase his next question. He finally decided to go directly at him and not beat around the bush.

"If you don't think it was a suicide, who do you think killed him?"

"I dunno, but if I was to make a guess…I'd say that the captain or one of the lieutenants might be able to help you on that. But I guess now with both Captain Powell and Lieutenant Hatcher gone, it only leaves you with Lieutenant Preacher. And, good luck with that," he finished, snuffing what was left of his cigarette in the ashtray.

They sat in silence for a second before Jackson plopped a couple of dollars on the table and started to rise.

"Before you leave, Mr. Jackson," Jake started to ask, looking up from the legal pad he had been taking notes on, staring directly into Jackson's eyes… "Is there anyone that can corroborate your whereabouts on the days that both Senator Powell and Colonel Hatcher were shot?"

"Nope," he quickly shot back. "But, if I wanted to do either of those two in…I'd a had plenty of opportunity in the desert. With that, he tipped the bill of his hat, and walked past the bar and out the door.

CHAPTER 70

"Sonovabitch," exclaimed Sully, when they were out the door and clear of earshot. "Do you believe that?" he continued.

The parking lot was now full and another three motorcycles had parked in the space alongside Jake's car. The Fairlane was gone, replaced by a Chevy truck.

"Sounds to me like there might have been a cover up." responded Jake, closing the car door before starting the engine.

"I didn't see anything mentioning a suicide in the personal records we brought back from St. Louis," said Sully.

"I don't think the records said that," responded Jake. "My guess is that the records just indicate that Lieutenant Warner died on active duty. We would have assumed that he was killed in action. Would have glossed right over it."

"Yea, you wonder how many other times a serviceman gets done in by one of his own and they call it killed in action."

Ten minutes later as they were headed north on I-95 toward Quantico, Jake called the office.

The call went directly into voicemail but just as Jake started leaving a message, Lynn picked up.

"FBI Office of Special Crime," the voice on the other end of the phone said.

"Lynn...Jake...hey do me a favor. The files we brought back from St. Louis...Pull the record on a Lieutenant Thomas Warner. I want to know how he died, where he's from, any next of kin... Anything you find that looks interesting. Do a full record search. Oh...and pull the record for a Steven Jackson also. He'll be in that same group of files. Call me back. We're heading north out of Richmond but we're going to make a short stop at Quantico."

It was still early when they got on I-95 North and they made it to the Quantico Exit in less than two hours. Jake had called ahead and spoke with Chuck Embers to let him know that they would be stopping by. The FBI laboratory and ballistics testing area was at the far side of the base. Jake stopped at the checkpoint and showed their credentials before being allowed to enter the hallowed grounds of the FBI's training ground for new agents, also the location of the FBI's Behavioral Analysis Unit, otherwise known as the B.A.U., the FBI's criminal profiling experts.

Chuck was waiting for them with a fresh pot of coffee when they walked through the door into his ballistics testing laboratory. With his white lab coat, he could easily have been mistaken for a doctor with the dignified swagger, the short haircut, graying at the temples, the wire rimmed glasses.

"Well if it isn't the bobsy twins," he said, looking over the top of his wire frames. "To what do I owe your visit to my humble abode?"

"Yea, this is humble all right," laughed Sully, looking over at the Electron microscopes and other high tech equipment purchased by the great taxpayers of the United States of America.

"Hell Chuck...You have a new Christmas present in here every time we stop by. What's the latest crime solving toy you got here?"

"I'll never tell," he joked. "No really. What can I do for you boys today?"

"We just came from Richmond," said Jake, sitting down in front of a microscope and peering through the eyepiece, not knowing what he was even looking at. "We met with a man who served time with both Senator Powell and the colonel who were killed in the past eight months."

"Yea..." said Chuck, waiting for Jake to get to the punch line.

"Well, according to our source, he says that he believes these two murders have something to do with another officer who was killed during the first Gulf War."

"How so? What's the connection?"

"According to this Steve Jackson, the Army ruled the death of this other officer as a suicide. Jackson doesn't buy it. He doesn't think there's anyway that this Lieutenant would have killed himself. He thinks he was murdered and there was this cover-up. I'm not sure where this is gonna go but he thinks it's related to the two killings up here."

"And you came to me because..."

"What do you know about the way the Army investigates murders or suicides of their own personnel?"

"I'm not sure. During peacetime, if they death occurred on an army post, they would do their own investigation. Usually one of the doctors on post also serves as the medical examiner. They do their own forensics. If something looks suspicious and they need help, they consult with their civilian counterparts. If it was something that they thought we could help out with, they might call us in. Usually, the military doesn't like to bring us in unless they have to. During war times or in situations like you're talking about...well, I guess...it's a judgment call. Where did this murder or suicide take place?"

"That's where it gets problematic," answered Jake. According to Mr. Jackson, after their quick deployment to the Persian Gulf, the battalion was on a ship headed back to the U.S. and got diverted to the Philippines after Typhoon Thelma battered the island. From my recollection, there were over 5000 deaths attributed to the mudslides and flooding. You can imagine the chaos that was going on. Supplies were limited and the island must have been a mess. Supposedly, the lieutenant was found in a shack at the edge of town with an exit hole in the back of his head. His service pistol was lying next to him. No note, no witnesses. With everything else that was going, on, they declared it a suicide, bagged the body and shipped it back for burial. You can imagine that they didn't preserve the crime scene... Here's where it get interesting. The officer who ruled it a suicide was none other than our Senator Powell, then Captain Powell, the Battalion Commander."

"Hmn," said Chuck, taking a sip from his coffee cup. "Sounds to me it would have created the perfect opportunity. Problem is," he started to say... "How do you prove it? How many years we talking about? Hell that was back in 1991. That's almost eighteen years."

They sat in silence for a few moments before Jake finally asked the question he had been thinking about on the entire trip up from Richmond.

"What do you think about an Exhumation Order?"

"What? Dig the body up after all these years?" exclaimed Sully.

By the time Jake and Sully left Quantico, weekend traffic was already starting to back up on I-95. It was five thirty when they reached the I-395 connector that would take them into D.C. Jake had called ahead to let Lynn know they were stuck in traffic and wouldn't be back before she left the office for the weekend. He asked her to leave the information she had obtained on Lieutenant Warner and Steve Jackson in an envelope on his desk. Jake pulled into the parking garage next to the Hoover Building just after six. After dropping Sully off at his car parked on the third floor, he continued up the ramp to the fourth floor, finding a parking space close to the elevator. The garage was almost empty, everyone leaving early to get a jump on the weekend. He took the elevator to the lower level, walked through the double doors into the Hoover Building and passed through security. Like the parking garage, the building was almost empty. The elevators were open when he entered and punched the button for the top floor. He found the envelope Lynn had left for him on his desk, grabbed it, checked to see that she had locked his desk and left without checking his phone messages. It had been a long week.

CHAPTER 71

Saturday, November 29

Temperatures had risen gradually throughout the week, finally reaching the high fifties by mid afternoon on Friday. The weather forecasters had predicted warm temperatures, clear skies with no chance of rain for the weekend. Jake had the motorcycle itch. Seeing all the bikes parked outside the Bark n' Dog got his adrenaline pumping. He couldn't wait to get the bike on the road again. It had been more than a month since he'd ridden the Low Rider and after hearing the weekend forecast, he had planned on taking the bike for one more road trip before putting it up for the winter. Before going to bed, Jake set the alarm on his cell phone for 5:30 a.m. with full intentions of getting a good night sleep before going for an early morning run. But, the night dragged on and it was after two a.m. when Jake finally drifted off to sleep. Not a restful sleep. He tossed and turned all night long, going in and out of strange dreams. He dreamt that he had been buried alive in a mudslide, probably attributed to the conversation earlier with Steve Jackson. In the dream, he was attempting to scream but nothing came out. Finally, he managed a high pitched squelch and jolted straight up in bed. He had thrown the blankets to the floor and his skin was sweaty and clammy. It was only 5 a.m. when he glanced at the digital clock on the table by the bed. He was exhausted but his mind was racing. He knew that no matter how long he laid there, he wasn't going to be able to go back to sleep. Finally, he turned off the alarm and got out of bed. It was still dark outside. The high thin cloud layer had blocked any light reflected from the moon or stars overhead. Jake grabbed his robe hanging on the back of the bedroom door and headed upstairs. Pete was lying in his dog bed next to the fireplace. Jake tried to be as quiet as possible but the boards beneath the carpet in the stairwell creaked with his full weight of one hundred eighty pounds. Pete heard him on the stairway. He stirred only enough to open his eyes and recognize Jake before closing them again. *Yea, be that way,*

Jake thought. *The life of a dog...eat, shit and be happy.* After starting the coffee, Jake checked the front porch to see if just by the luck, the morning paper had been delivered. *No luck.* Only an idiot would be up this early in the morning. Before going to bed, Jake and Sam had planned on running five miles before Jake jumped on the Harley for the rest of the afternoon. It had been three weeks since the Marine Corp Marathon and he hadn't run more than a couple of times since. The older he got, the longer it took to whip his body back into shape. With over an hour to go before Sam got up, Jake filled a bowl with Cheerios, a sliced banana and skim milk, grabbed a cup of coffee and settled into the Lay Z Boy to read Vince Flynn's latest novel, "Act of Treason".

"Hey old man... Whaddaya reading?" Sam said, bouncing down the stairs with her wet hair rolled up in a towel. She had gotten in the habit of wetting her hair a soon as she got out of bed to get rid of the bed head and wrapping it in a towel until she had the time to blow dry it after her first cup of coffee.

"Just started reading the latest Vince Flynn novel," Jake replied. "And don't steal it before I get done with it."

Sam had the nasty habit of picking up whatever book Jake was reading before he had the chance to finish it. She was a speed reader so normally that didn't cause a problem but there had been times that he waited patiently while she finished the book before handing it back. He was also a nut about not bending the pages back for the bookmark and had reminded her numerous times to use something else for a bookmark.

"Hey, what do you think about some hill work this morning? I need to stretch out my hamstrings."

"Okay with me," he replied, not looking up from the novel that had totally engrossed him for the past hour.

"I was thinking that we'd do about fifteen miles this morning," she said, teasing to see if he was paying any attention to her.

"Yea, fine."

She startled him when she threw a pillow at him that she had picked up from the couch.

"You're not paying a damn bit of attention to what I'm saying."

CHAPTER 72

Sunday, November 30

The five mile run Saturday morning followed by a road trip on his Harley to Annapolis, Maryland later in the afternoon gave Jake plenty of fresh air. He didn't have any trouble falling asleep Saturday night, having slept through the evening news in his Lay Z Boy with Pete sound asleep on his lap. At nine p.m. having floated in and out of sleep for the past three hours, he had turned off the television and headed downstairs to his room. After a good nights sleep, he woke at seven Sunday morning, jumped out of bed, grabbed a robe and headed upstairs. Sam was still asleep. He fed Pete and let him out the backdoor while he started the coffee. Within minutes, Pete had completed his business and was back at the door whining to be let in. Jake poured himself a cup of coffee and let Pete in before going back downstairs to review the files he brought home with him on Friday. He took a sip of his coffee and opened the envelope. Lynn had placed two separate files in the envelope; one was labeled Steven Jackson and the other, Lieutenant Thomas Warner. He picked up the lieutenant's file and opened it to the first page.

The page was a summary of Lieutenant Warner's career in the Army. He was from Coshocton, Ohio, a small town, seventy miles East of Columbus, the Capital of the State. Graduating from high school in 1984, he enlisted directly in the Army. A year later, the Army selected him for officer training, sending him to the University of Akron the following fall where he graduated with a degree in horticulture in June of 1989. While at Akron, he was a four year ROTC cadet, the Commander of the Akron detachment during his senior year and went on active duty on September 23, 1989. After Infantry Training he was assigned to the 24th Mechanized Infantry Division at Fort Stewart, Georgia. His unit was put on readiness and deployed to the Gulf in December of 1990 in anticipation of Iraq's invasion of Kuwait. As part of the U.S. ground forces, he participated in the attack on the Iraqi Forces on February 24, 1991, pushing the Iraqi ground forces out of Kuwait. When the cease-fire was declared at 8:00 a.m. on February 27th, the 24th stayed in Kuwait as part of the peace keeping force until receiving orders on October 30, 1991 to return to the states. Unfortunately, the unit was diverted when Typhoon Thelma made a direct hit on the City of Ormoc on the island of Leyte on November 5. The 24th landed in the Philippines on November 9, 1991. Lieutenant Warner's date of death was listed as November 12, 1991. Just three days after landing in the Philippines. No cause of death was listed. Next of kin was a Katherine Warner, mother. There was a mailing address and a telephone number. Other than a copy of the lieutenant's DD214, there was no other information in the file.

Jake opened his laptop and Googled in the name Katherine Warner and Coshocton, Ohio. He got over two thousand hits. *Well that was useless*, he thought. He decided to call the telephone number that was on the sheet of paper lying next to the laptop.

"Oh Jesus," he said aloud. This was not something he wanted to do. How do you call a mother about the death of her son almost eighteen years after he's been buried? He looked at the time on his cell phone. *Good*, he thought, *I need another cup of coffee and it's only 7:30 a.m. and that's way too early to call anyone on a Sunday morning.*

CHAPTER 73

Early Monday morning, Jake and Sully were sitting outside Director Avery's office waiting patiently for him to get off the phone. Jake wasn't known for his patience and he hated waiting for anyone talking on the phone. He was just about to leave a message and head back downstairs when the director's office door opened and Director Avery ushered them into his office, closing the door behind them.

"Good weekend, gentlemen?" he asked, directing them to the two seats in front of his desk.

"I think Director Preacher has been feeding us a line of shit," exclaimed Jake, not even responding to the director's question. "The sonovabitch is covering his ass."

"That's a pretty big charge Jake," responded Director Avery. He crossed his arms and leaned forward, his elbows resting on the top of his desk. "At this point, what do you have? Just the word of a disgruntled Marine."

"Army," Jake corrected him.

"Army, Marine, whatever. You just can't go barging into the Deputy Director of the Central Intelligence Agency's office and accuse him of a murder that took place eighteen years ago. Dammit Jake. Get me something I can work with. What was the motive? Why'd this guy remain quiet for so long and now...all of a sudden...he decides to come forward with this? What's in it for him? And if any of this is true, how does that fit into the killing of Senator Powell and Colonel Hatcher?"

"Look Mike. I don't disagree with you but I think we need to follow up on what he says. I think it's all connected." Jake didn't want to go into details just yet but he thought that things were starting to make sense.

"Whataya gonna do?" asked the director.

"I'd like to fly to Ohio tomorrow. I placed a call to Lieutenant Warner's home yesterday afternoon. Seems his mother died shortly after the lieutenant but I spoke with his uncle. I didn't go into any detail with him over the phone. Obviously he wanted to know why the FBI would be calling him. I left it that I would get back with him today. I wanted to speak with you first. I've already got Lynn checking on flights. Sully and I can get to Columbus, Ohio tomorrow morning and be back here by tomorrow evening. We can rent a car at the Columbus airport. We'll be driving to Coshocton, Ohio. I did a MapQuest yesterday. It's a pretty direct shot east from the airport. U.S. Air flies in there early in the morning. Coshocton's only about seventy five miles from the airport. We should be able to get there by noon."

"What do you expect to get from talking with this uncle?"

"Not sure but we're missing something and I think it makes sense to meet with him. According to this Steve Jackson, Lieutenant Warner was somewhat of an outsider with the other officers. "Didn't fit in," were his exact words," Jake said, holding his index and middle finger up on both hands indicating quotations. "He said the lieutenant seemed troubled about something a couple of days before they found him dead."

"Didn't say what it was that troubled him?" asked the director.

"No. He said that when he asked Lieutenant Warner what was bothering him, he told him there was something he had to deal with. "And you don't think by that statement that he was contemplating suicide?"

"Not according to Jackson. He said Lieutenant Warner was always talking about his family and writing letters home. He wasn't the kind of guy that would kill himself."

"You feel the same?" asked the director, looking directly at Sully.

"Yes sir. I do. I'm with Jake on this. When I sat there Friday listening to Jackson, I got the distinct impression that Lieutenant Warner knew something, was going to tell someone about it but was killed before he had a chance to talk to anyone."

"Made matters pretty simple when Senator Powell as the ranking officer, called it a suicide," said Jake. "Who was going to argue with him?"

CHAPTER 74

Tuesday, December 2

At six thirty Tuesday morning, Jake was sitting in National Airport restaurant drinking a cup of coffee and reading the New York Times. He had already received his paperwork for carrying his weapon, passed through the security checkpoint and checked in with the gate attendant. Sully had called that he was running late. It was a short flight. Their plane was not scheduled for departure until seven twenty, arriving at Port Columbus and hour and a half later. After their last flying fiasco trying to get back from St. Louis, Jake directed Lynn to book them on a direct flight from Reagan National to Columbus. Lynn booked them on a U.S. Airways flight and reserved a car for them at the National car rental lot. In and out on the same day, directed Jake, when Lynn was making the reservations to Ohio. He hated spending a night out of town after September 11, 2001. The current regulations didn't even allow for carry on baggage to include shaving cream, mouthwash or a myriad of other normal things you take with you on an overnight trip. And, checking baggage was a joke. Last year on a trip to Reno, Nevada, someone mistakenly took his bag from the baggage carousel while he was checking his voicemail and he had to wait until six o'clock the following morning before the airline recovered his bag from a home in Lake Tahoe. Another hour and he would have had to attend a business meeting in sandals wearing a Hawaiian shirt and cargo shorts.

At six forty-five, Jake paid the bill and sauntered over to the gate. Sully hadn't shown up yet but that was par for the course. It didn't look like the plane was going to be full. They were flying on a commuter jet but with the number of people milling in and around the gate area, it looked like the plane was only going to be half full.

Sully finally showed at seven just as the boarding announcement was being made. With the limited number of passengers, the plane was boarded and ready by seven fifteen. After closing the door and quickly checking the passenger manifest to ensure that everyone was on board, the flight attendant announced that they were free to move around the cabin and spread out for comfort. Sully jumped across the aisle to the empty seat by the window, leaving Jake room to sprawl out. Five minutes later, they were wheels up as the plane bounced once before lifting off the runway. Jake glanced out the window at the terminal that quickly passed below and then the Pentagon that sprawled for acres as the plane continued to climb into the blue sky, heading west to Columbus, Ohio.

CHAPTER 75

Within fifteen minutes of landing in Columbus, Jake and Sully were walking through the front doors of the terminal on their way to the Shuttle bus that would take them to the National car rental lot. Like most larger airports, the car rental lots in Columbus are no longer on airport grounds but within a short driving distance of the airport. They found the National Shuttle waiting for them, the driver slouched down in his seat reading a magazine.

"Good morning gentlemen," he said, closing the door when they were seated and shifting the bus in gear. "If you have your reservation number with you," he started, "I can call it in. That way, the car will be waiting for you when we get there."

Jake reached in the inside pocket of his suit, pulled out a copy of the reservation and handed it to the driver, who called the reservation desk, before handing the paperwork back to Jake.

"Where you boys from?" the driver asked politely, trying to make conversation.

"Washington," responded Sully. "D.C," he added quickly.

"You here on business or pleasure?"

"Ah...business," responded Sully.

"Well, welcome to Columbus. I hope you have some time to relax a little while you're here. We're not D.C. but I've been here all my life and it's a pretty nice place to live."

Sully had never been to Columbus but Jake had been there about ten years earlier. His younger sister, Ann, had graduated from Denison University, a small Liberal Arts College in Granville, Ohio, just thirty miles east of Columbus. Jake and Rachael had flown in with Sam to attend Ann's graduation ceremony. That was the last trip the three of them had taken together before Rachael passed away.

After a five minute bus ride passing several areas under construction, they drove into the National Car Rental lot. The rental vehicle was waiting for them when the bus stopped in front of the rental building. It only took them a couple of minutes to sign the paperwork and get the keys. Not knowing what kind of weather they were going to have when they landed, Lynn had requested a four wheel drive SUV. Fortunately, it didn't look like they were going to have any difficulties with the weather. The sun was shining, the skies were clear and the temperature was in the high fifties. Sam had given Jake a copy of the directions to the Sullivan home that she pulled off of MapQuest before he left the office Monday evening. He pulled them out of his briefcase, threw the briefcase on the backseat and glanced at the directions before driving out of the rental lot.

"What we looking for?" asked Sully, putting on a pair of sunglasses and buckling his seatbelt.

"We're on Steltzer now. We need to pick up 670N to I-270 toward Cleveland, take the New Albany Exit for Highway 161 East which turns into State Route 16 about thirty miles east and then stay on that for another thirty miles to Coshocton. Looks like a pretty straight shot from there."

"What time are we supposed to meet with…What's the guy's name?"

"John Sullivan," responded Jake. "About noon. It shouldn't take us more than two hours to get there but I wanted to give us plenty of time for any traffic. Lynn said they're working on the highway and there may be some traffic delays."

Jake followed the construction signs out of the airport finding the 670N exit toward Cleveland.

"Tell me about your conversation with Mr. Sullivan yesterday," asked Sully.

"Didn't say much. Played it pretty close to the chest. I can't say I blame him much. I'm not sure how I would react if someone from the F.B.I called me asking questions about something that happened almost twenty years ago. I think it's natural to be suspicious. He was polite…Answered my questions…but, ah… Didn't volunteer anything. He said he was working today. Some factory in Conesville that we're going to pass along the way. He made a point to mention three tall smokestacks. But, he didn't want to meet us there. Was concerned about people talking. Said the town was pretty small and everyone knows everything about everybody else and didn't want to start any rumors. He only lives a couple miles from the factory. He said he could get out of there for lunch at noon. We're meeting him at the house."

"I just hope this isn't another wasted trip," responded Sully. "We need to hit one out of the park."

Forty-five minutes later and thirty miles into the trip, Jake saw the exit to

Granville, Ohio, causing Jake to think back to the last time he was there. He checked his watch for the time and assured that they were ahead of schedule; he took the exit and entered the village, driving past the Granville Milling Company on Main Street. His mind flooded with memories. His younger sister, Ann graduated from Denison University, a small liberal arts college sitting on a hill overlooking the village. He had flown into Columbus with Rachel and Sam. They had rented a car and met Jake's mom and dad for breakfast at a little restaurant in the village before attending the spring commencement ceremony. So much has happened in the past ten years. Rachael had died. Both Jake's mom and dad perished in a plane crash on their way to Mexico to celebrate their thirty-fifth wedding anniversary. Jake had tried to stay in touch with Ann, his only sibling but Ann was busy and had her own life to live. After graduation, she had gone on to law school before taking a job as an Assistant District Attorney in Pittsburgh, Pennsylvania.

"What are we doing?" asked Sully, realizing that Jake had turned off the highway.

"My sister Ann graduated from the University here ten years ago. I just wanted to see how the town has changed since that time. It's a pretty nice little village. Reminds me of a small town in Massachusetts. If I remember right, I can take a right at the next light and it will eventually take me back to the highway. Won't add more than five minutes to our trip and we've got time to spare."

"Works for me," said Sully. "Maybe we'll even find someplace to grab a bite."

"There's a nice little spot right in the center of town, if it's still there. A real hometown diner." He took a right turn at the light and started looking for a place to park. "There it is," he said nodding to the left side of the road. "Aladdin's. Has real down home cooking," he added. "It's not even eleven so we shouldn't have any problem getting a table." He pulled into an open spot directly in front of the restaurant and shifted the car into park.

"What, no parking meters?" asked Sully.

"Hard to believe it isn't it?" responded Jake.

They stopped in front of the restaurant to look at the specials that were handwritten on a sign sitting in the middle of the sidewalk.

"Spaghetti with meatballs, Italian bread and a drink for five bucks!" exclaimed Sully. "That's got to be a steal. I don't think I'll need a menu," he said.

They entered the restaurant and let the door close behind them. A sign by the cash register indicated that it was seat yourself. It was early so the lunch crowd had not yet arrived. They was a long bar with plenty of empty stools running the entire length of the restaurant but Jake was looking for a little privacy. He selected one of the booths lining the right wall. They no sooner sat down when a young girl in her late teens or early twenties walked from around the counter, took their drink orders and handed them a menu with the lunch specials.

"Probably a Denison student," said Jake, when she had left the table to fill their drink order.

A couple of minutes later she returned with the drinks and took their orders. They both decided on the Spaghetti special and placed their orders. While they were waiting, Jake called the office and checked his voicemails. Only a couple of messages and nothing urgent he had to take care of before they got back to Washington.

The waitress returned shortly with their orders and they ate in silence. By the time they had finished lunch, the restaurant had started to fill up with the locals. The four men sitting in the booth behind Jake were discussing the election results. It was obvious to Jake from their discussion that they were probably Denison professors. It seemed by the tone that all four were happy with the results, Barack Obama, the Democratic candidate and first African American, having been elected by a majority of the electoral vote.

They finished lunch and Jake left a five dollar bill on the table for a tip, taking the check with him to the cash register to pay the bill.

Back in the car, they continued east on Broadway, heading out of town.

"What's up with that pink building on the right?" asked Sully, pointing to an old colonial styled two story building with a walk out covered porch extending the entire width of the building.

"From what I'm told," Jake said to Sully. "The Buxton Inn is supposed to be haunted. Something about an old Civil War colonel and some lady with keys walking during the night. Patrons have seen her and heard the keys rattling while she walked through the halls. We didn't stay there so I don't know if there's any truth to the matter or not."

"That's enough to keep me from sleeping there," responded Sully. "I don't need to see it first hand to believe it."

"I hear it was also part of the Underground Railroad back in the days," continued Jake. "There's a pretty neat bar downstairs with booths cut into the old limestone basement walls."

They continued east on Broadway, passing through a tree lined residential area. A kaleidoscope of colors flashed up ahead with the tree branches extending over the road, their fingertips barely touching. Off to the left, an old mansion sat back off the road. A six foot wrought iron fence surrounded the property, stately maples in various shades of fall colors lining the driveway from the road to front steps. Majestic columns spanned the entire width of the stately mansion. A handwritten sign attached to the front gate indicated that the Columbus Polo team would be having a polo match at two in the afternoon on Sunday in the field directly in front of the mansion.

"That's pretty neat," commented Sully. "I've never been to a polo match. I thought they only did that over in England."

Two miles down the road, they merged back onto State Route 16, heading east toward Newark, Ohio.

"How do you suppose it got a name like that?" asked Sully.

"What are you talking about," responded Jake, checking the passenger side mirror as he merged right into the traffic pattern.

"The county name. Who the hell came up with the name "Licking County? I mean come on... Lick...ing? What the hell was he thinking about with a name like that?"

"You got too much free time on your hands," laughed Jake, shaking his head.

Jake checked his watch for time and kept his speed below the sixty mph highway limit. They drove past, Newark, Ohio, a sign on the road, indicating it was the County Seat. Up ahead, as they were approaching Dayton Road, Jake pointed out an office building on the right side of the road.

"See that building up ahead," he directed Sully's eyes to the right. "That building is the corporate headquarters for the Longaberger Company. The building's been designed to look like a woven basket, handle included. The Longaberger Company makes baskets and kitchenware. They sell their products nationally. The baskets are collector's items. I've seen some of them on eBay go for a couple hundred bucks a basket."

"They'd better be full of food or booze to be worth that much," responded Sully.

Once outside the corporation limits, Jake set the cruise at sixty. Other than a couple of blinking caution lights at road intersections, they didn't have to stop at any traffic lights the entire forty mile stretch from Granville to Coshocton. They drove past rows of standing corn still waiting to be harvested. As they were nearing Coshocton, the road narrowed to two lanes. Just up ahead, a large white cloud hung over the trees, obscuring the bluebird sky on the right side of the road. As they rounded a curve in the highway, Jake could see the three tall smokestacks for the Conesville Power Plant that John Sullivan had talked about on the phone. Thick white smoke billowed from the top of the center stack, filling the sky.

"Wow," he exclaimed. "Look at that. Tree huggers would have a heyday with that. You'd never get away with that in Washington."

Jake checked the directions again, looking for the next turnoff.

"Sullivan said that when we get to the factory, we have about another mile before we turn right. It's a township road. He said it was paved but watch out for the potholes. There it is," he said confirming the road name on the sign before turning right onto Krebs Road.

Another mile playing tic tack toe with the potholes and Jake slowed the SUV before turning left by the mailbox with the name Sullivan painted across it onto a gravel drive. The drive was rutted with the freezing and thawing over the last couple of weeks. He was glad that Lynn had requested a four wheel drive vehicle. To be on the safe side, Jake took his foot off the gas pedal and pushed the button on the dash above the steering wheel from two high to four low. The light on the shift indicator blinked a couple times as the four wheel drive was engaged. Immediately, the SUV shifted down as all four tires churned in the soft pavement, throwing mud behind as the vehicle lurched forward. Another hundred feet and the driveway turned ninety degrees to the right before opening into a clearing. In the middle of the clearing sat a century old clapboard sided farmhouse and a couple of barns in dire need of painting. Jake continued to move the vehicle up into the driveway alongside the house and parked next to an old Chevy pickup that looked like it had recently parked there, steam still coming off the top of the hood from the engine. Jake reached behind him to get his briefcase before opening the door and stepping out. He was careful where he stepped, trying not to sink in the soft mud. The wheels had thrown mud up high enough to coat the side panels and splatter the windows.

Before they could even get to the walkway leading to the front door, a man who appeared to be in his late fifties with a green John Deere cap came out of the house and stood on the porch.

"Sorry about all the mud, fellas" he said, as they walked toward him. "We've had a pretty rough autumn so far. One day it rains, and then it snows. Two days later, it's in the fifties again. I haven't had a chance to grade the driveway. I've ordered a load of gravel but seems like there's bigger orders than mine to fill. Suppose they'll get here sooner or later."

"Mr. Sullivan?" Jake asked, extending his hand.

"Yea…but ah…call me John."

"Jake Hunter," he said, grasping Sullivan's hand. I'm the agent who spoke with you on the phone. This is Agent Gilmore," he said nodding to Sully who had walked up behind him on the porch.

"Come on in," he said. "You said you wanted to talk about Tommy."

Jake and Sully followed him down a short hallway toward the kitchen. The smell of wood burning permeated the air. Before they could even get in the kitchen, a big black Labrador brushed up against Jake, sniffing at his pant leg. *Must've got a whiff of Pete*, he thought.

"Hey, git away. Go lay down." Sullivan ordered the dog, pointing to the dog bed in the corner of the kitchen. "I'm sorry," he said. "I don't know what's got into him. He's almost ten but still full of piss and vinegar. He's friendly though."

"I'm sure he just smells my dog," replied Jake. "My dog does the same thing."

"Have a seat," Sullivan said, indicating a couple of chairs around a wooden table set up against the wall. "What kind of dog you got?" he asked, trying to make conversation.

"Jack Russell Terrier," Jake replied. "It's really my daughter's dog but I live with her."

"Squirrel dog," responded Sullivan.

"Yea, that's what they tell me but he doesn't get much squirrel hunting living in D.C."

"Yea, don't suppose he does," he replied, pulling up another chair. "Can I get you guys a cup of coffee? I just made a fresh pot."

"Sounds good," said Jake, putting his coat on the back of the chair before sitting down next to the table.

"Yea, that'd be great," added Sully, making himself comfortable in a chair next to Jake.

Sullivan grabbed three mugs off the shelf above the stove and filled them with coffee before returning to the table and taking a seat opposite. It was obvious that John Sullivan felt a little awkward and nervous, the tension in the air a little thick. Jake guessed that this was the first time John Sullivan had ever sat across the table from a couple of FBI agents.

"Mr. Sullivan… John," he started, trying to break the awkward silence. "As we spoke on the phone yesterday, we're here to talk about your nephew, Thomas."

"Yea, Tommy," he responded. "He was a good kid. Don't know what got into him. I've been thinking a lot about him since you called. It was a real shock for us when they told us what he'd done. I never figured Tommy would have taken his own life. I've been doing a lot of reading since then and I guess it's pretty bad with the number of young boys who seem to be taking their own life after coming back. You'd think the Army would do something about that. I mean...check them out or something before they put them back on the street. I think we owe them that much. I read something the other day about the soldiers returning from Iraq now. They said they check everyone who had a concussion or head injury. Maybe they finally got it right after twenty years."

"Mr. Sullivan, have you had any contact with the Army or anyone that Tommy served with since Tommy's death?" Jake interjected, stopping Sullivan from pontificating about the Army's treatment of post traumatic stress disorder.

"Well not anyone since them two Army guys came and told us what happened. Or are you talking about since then?"

"In the last fifteen years?" finished Jake.

"Nah, haven't had any contact with anyone since we buried Tommy up in the family plot."

"Tommy's last name was Warner," Jake said. "I understand he was your sister's boy?"

"Yea, Katherine. We called her Katie. She had Tommy when she was seventeen. Katie was still in high school when she got pregnant. She married Tommy's father and they moved in here with mom and dad and me but that didn't last long. Bob, that was his name...He walked out on her after just three years of marriage. Haven't heard or seen him since. She stayed here. I was only fifteen when Tommy was born, so I guess I was kinda like a big brother when he was growing up.

"Mr. Sullivan, let me ask you something," Jake said, stopping momentarily to collect his thoughts. "Was there ever any doubt that Lieutenant Warner...Tommy...took his own life?"

The room became suddenly quiet, only the sound of wood popping in the wood burner could be heard above the stillness. After a brief moment, John Sullivan, realizing the impact of Jake's question, put his coffee cup down before responding.

"You think that maybe that's not the way it happened?" he asked. "You think there was more to it than what we've been told?"

"It's possible," Jake responded. He wasn't sure how much Sullivan knew about the shootings of Senator Powell and Colonel Hatcher and wanted to be cautious before opening up a door he couldn't close. He decided to side step that issue and proceed down another path.

"Mr. Sullivan. Would you by any chance have any of the letters that Tommy sent home while he was in the Army?"

"Well, Katie had a box of old letters, pictures and whatnot. I'm not sure what's still in there. Here, let me go get that. It'll only take me a minute or two. It's just upstairs."

While he was gone, Sully refilled their coffee cups and grabbed a couple of chocolate chip cookies from a cookie jar on the counter.

Jake took the opportunity to pull a file out of his briefcase and set it in the table in front of him. He pulled a small pad out to take notes and scribbled a couple of thoughts down while waiting for Sullivan to return.

Before Sullivan returned, Jack noticed a pack of gum lying next to the mail that was neatly stacked in the corner of the table. "Look here," he said to Sully, picking up the pack of Blackjack gum. "Where have we seen this before?" he finished, dropping the pack of gum in his jacket pocket.

A couple of minutes later, Sullivan returned setting a cardboard box down in the middle of the table.

"Here's what I kept after my sister died. You know it's been almost twenty years. Little by little, I gave some stuff away and threw some in the trash. I got rid of all her clothes down at the Goodwill store but figured I'd keep what's in this box. Mostly pictures, family things. You know the things you seem to pass down and a few letters. It's been a long time since I've even looked in here. I'm not really sure what's left. Here, you're free to look at anything that's in here," he said, pushing the box toward Jake. "I don't know how it's going to change anything but help yourself," he continued, turning away from the table. "If you don't mind… I'm going to run down to the barn to check on the cows before I head back to the factory. I got a couple due to drop a calf any time now and I want to make sure they're all right."

"Take your time," responded Sully.

"Oh, and ah, help yourself to the coffee and them there cookies in the jar," he said smiling at Sully who had cookie crumbs on his chin.

The cardboard box was about two feet wide by two feet long and almost a foot and half high. Jake had to stand to be able to see over the edge. He pulled out an old Bible bound in a worn leather cover, opening the book to read the inscriptions on the inside cover. "Katherine Sullivan," First Holy Communion, Dated May 19, 1953. Love, Mom and Dad. Jake set the Bible aside and pulled out a package of envelopes, yellowed with age. A rubber band wound tightly around them broke when Jake tried to take it off. Jake noticed the letters were marked with an APO. *Letters from Tommy*, he thought, even before taking them out of the envelopes. Something else in the box caught his eye. He set the handful of envelopes down and reached into the box, lifting a wooden framed picture that had obviously been taken some time ago. He blew dust off the glass and looked at the faces of the six happy people smiling out at the camera. He recognized John Sullivan from the prominent nose and eyebrows even though he was much younger in the picture. *The years had been kind to him,* he thought. On the other end was a woman who appeared to be a couple of years older than Sullivan. Jake guessed that that was Katherine. Sitting in the front was an older couple that Jake assumed may be grandparents. Between Sullivan and Katherine was a young man dressed in an Army uniform. The nameplate above his pocket said Warner. *Tommy,* Jake thought. *Good looking kid.* Next to Tommy was a young girl in a red white and blue dress that appeared to be ten or twelve years old. Jake turned the picture over. On the back was a hand scribbled note:

Akron University Graduation/Commissioning ROTC

Grandma, Grandpa, mom, Tommy, Sadie and Uncle John

May 27, 1989

"Hey. What do you make of this?" Jake exclaimed, handing the picture to Sully.

"I wonder who Sadie is," muttered Sully, after looking at the picture and reading the caption on the back. "Nobody ever mentioned there being another kid in the family."

"We didn't ask," replied Jake. "And his records only indicated a next of kin. He had his mom listed there."

He continued to sort through the box, separating out the pictures and letters. Jake was just starting to read one of the letters postmarked in October of 1991 when John Sullivan returned, taking off a pair of knee high rubber boots and leaving them in the entry off the kitchen before entering the room.

"Whatcha got there?" he questioned Sully, reaching for the photo. "Oh, yea.

I remember this like it was yesterday," he said, sitting down at the table opposite Jake and holding the picture with both hands. "Boy that was a day. That's the day Tommy graduated from college and became a Lieutenant. We were so proud of him. That's the last picture we took with all of us together. I almost forgot about that. Boy it was hot that day. We even sat under a tree but there wasn't any breeze that day. I think it almost hit ninety that afternoon. I thought Sadie was going to have a cow. She kept asking how much longer?" he said, shaking his head.

"Who's Sadie?" Jake interrupted.

"Well, Sadie's Tommy's kid sister…half sister. Like I said earlier, Tommy's dad ran off when he was just little tyke. After seven years and no word from Bob…that was Katie's husband's name, mom and dad helped Katie get her marriage annulled. But… Katie didn't date anyone for years. She had a part-time job down at the diner. You might a passed it on your way here. Mom watched Tommy while she worked. After a couple of months, Katie met some guy and wouldn't you know it. Got pregnant. Well in them days and being Catholic, there was no way she wasn't going to have the baby. Mom and dad weren't none too happy. But…just like Tommy's dad…He was gone. That's when Sadie was born. She was just the cutest little thing. She followed Tommy around like a little puppy dog. That boy couldn't do anything without Sadie trying to tag along. She even dressed like him. Used to wear his hunting clothes when they were too small for him. They were still a little big on her but she rolled up the sleeves and put rubber bands around the pant legs."

"Her name is Sadie Warner?" Jake asked, starting to take notes on his pad.

"No. She uses Sadie Sullivan. Same as mine. Katherine went back to using Sullivan after the marriage was dissolved. Tommy's official records were never changed but the kids used Sullivan. That is up until Tommy went in the Army. Then being that all his official records had Warner on them, he went back to Warner for the Army. Kids never had a real dad. I pretty much filled that role."

"Where's Sadie now?" asked Jake.

"Don't really know exactly," he replied. "She stopped in here bout end of October. I tried to get her to stay for awhile. I think she could have got her old job back at the Wal-Mart the other side of town. She stayed about a week and then said she had to get back. Never said where back was. I think she was out east somewhere."

"You have any way of getting a hold of her?" asked Jake.

"No. She calls once in a while but I don't know how to get a hold of her. Leastways, she never gave me any number to call her. She said she lost her cell phone. Tommy's dying was pretty tough on her too. I did my best after Katie died but it was hard enough to keep the bills paid if you know what I mean. I wasn't always there for her when she probably needed it most."

"John," Jake started, waiting for Sullivan to stop talking and look at him. "Would you have a more current picture of Sadie? Something taken in the last couple of years?"

"No, can't say as I do. Pretty sad huh?"

"Don't beat yourself up," said Sully. "I'm sure you did the best you could."

"What's this have to do with Sadie?" he finally asked. Jake was a little surprised it took him this long before he asked the question.

"Sit down John," Jake said. "Let me see if I can make any sense out of this."

For the next twenty minutes, Jake went into detail telling Sullivan about the killings of Senator Powell and Colonel Hatcher. He went so far as to disclose that Tommy was under Senator Powell's command when Tommy died. Without disclosing any names, he repeated what he had been told by Steve Jackson regarding Tommy's untimely death in the Philippines.

When Jake was through, Sullivan sat there for a moment reflecting on what he had just heard before looking up at Jake. "So, that's why you asked me about whether Tommy would have taken his own life?" he asked, the pain of what he was thinking visible in his eyes.

"Yea, that's about right," responded Jake. "Which leads me to the following question?" Jake stopped here to think about how he wanted to phrase his next question before continuing.

"Do you think there's any possibility that Sadie put two and two together?"

"What do you mean? What does Sadie have to do with any of this?"

"Any chance that Tommy said anything to her about what was going on over there in Iraq?"

"Christ, I don't know. I mean they did write back and forth. And Sadie was looking through some of her mother's boxes last Christmas that I had stored up in the attic when she was getting the Christmas ornaments down."

"How old is Sadie now?" asked Sully.

"Well, hell, she was born in ah... 76...1976. That makes her thirty one. Yea, she'll be thirty one on December 18."

"Ah dammit...," he said, getting up from the table, shaking his head in disbelief over what he had been hearing, the full impact of what Jake had been saying, now playing heavy on his mind.

"So what?" he said, turning to face Jake. "You think that Sadie has something to do with the killings of this senator and this other guy? Christ, she was only thirteen years old when Tommy died."

"I don't know." Jake responded. "But I would feel a whole lot better if I could talk to Sadie and assure myself that she was no where near Washington when both men were shot."

"How is Sadie with a rifle?" queried Sully.

"Crack shot," was his immediate response. When she was thirteen, she could shoot the piss out of a bulls eye with a twenty-two at a hundred yards. Tommy taught her how to shoot. Hell, she led her college team to two championships before she quit school. But that don't mean she killed no one."

"What kinda car is Sadie driving?" Jake asked.

"Don't know. She had some little foreign jobby when she was here last. I think it might have been a Toyota, Nissan...something small like that. Kinda blue-gray if I remember right. We never talked about the car. I don't know if it was her car or not."

"You wouldn't recall whether she Ohio plates or some other state?" asked Sully.

"No idea. I remember it had four doors because she got her jacket out of the back seat when we went to dinner."

"Sadie have an Ohio driver's license?" asked Sully.

"Yea, well she did anyway. I remember she had to get it renewed last year."

"Coshocton the County seat?" asked Jake.

"Yea."

"Do you have a phone book I can look at?" asked Jake.

Sullivan left the kitchen and went into the other room returning shortly with a phone book he handed to Jake. After a couple of minutes flipping between the yellow and white pages, Jake found what he was looking for and punched the number into his cell phone. After four rings, someone finally picked up the phone.

"Ohio Bureau of Motor Vehicles," the voice on the other end said.

"Jake Hunter, FBI Agent," he said. "Let me speak with the office manager please."

He waited patiently, listening to country music while he was on hold for another couple of minutes before someone finally picked up on the other end. After several minutes of discussion, trying to get his point across and dealing with the government bureaucracy and all the other red tape relating to the privacy laws, Jake got confirmation that there was a picture of Sadie Sullivan in the Bureau's records. The picture was taken when she renewed her license a year ago. Jake asked the manager to make a copy of the picture for him and he'd be down to pick it up.

After closing the cell phone, Jake asked Sullivan if he would ride with them to show them the way to the Department of Motor Vehicles. On the way, Sullivan was notably silent. Finally, breaking the silence, he asked what they were going to do.

"We're going to get your niece's picture out there and try to locate her. At this point," Jake started, "She's only wanted for questioning. If there's anyway you can think of contacting her without making her suspicious…now's the time to speak up."

"I don't know. Like I said, she never left me a number. When we talk, she's the one to call me."

After a combination of left and right turns, Sullivan directed Jake into a parking lot near a typical government building, brick and glass. The manager was waiting for them when they walked through the door and had already made copies for them. She had enlarged the picture to show a likeness of Sadie Sullivan on a five by seven sheet. Jake showed the picture to Sullivan.

"Is this a pretty good likeness of Sadie when you saw her last month?"

"Yea but her hair was shorter. It was cut down to about here," he said, demonstrating on himself that her hair length was cut just below her ears. "Kind of boy-ish."

Jake asked for a copy of the license as well which included her approximate height, weight and eye color. "Keep this to yourself," he said, extending his hand and thanking the manager for all her help.

The fax machine was broken in the motor vehicle office so they drove to the County Sheriff's office just a short distance away so that Jake could fax a copy of the picture to his office. He decided to call Lynn before faxing the image to let her know what he was doing.

"Hey," he said when she picked up just before the call went into voicemail. "I'm faxing a picture over to you in a couple of minutes. "You might have to lighten it up a little to get a clearer picture. I'll stay on the line to make sure you get the photo. It will probably be a little grainy since I had to enlarge it from a driver's license. Have one of the computer boys clean it up a little. Make a number of copies and circulate it around the office. Let everyone know that we think her hair may be a bit shorter. We need to speak with the girl in the picture. Right now she's only a person of interest wanted for questioning."

Jake paused while he listened to Lynn repeat what he had just told her. "Yea," he said, "She may be our shooter. And Lynn,...after you do that, have the phone company do a trace for the last month on any calls placed to the number I'm going to give you from outside the seven-four-oh area code." Jake then read off the number to John Sullivan's home from his BlackBerry. "I need you to also book another seat for us tonight on our return flight." Jake looked at Sullivan while he was talking and received the nod he was looking for. "Book another ticket for a John Sullivan. He's coming back to Washington with us."

CHAPTER 76

It was raining when the Shuttle driver parked the bus in the off load area in front of the doors leading to the passenger ticketing area at Port Columbus. After talking with Lynn and faxing the picture of Sadie Sullivan, Jake had driven back to the farm so that Sullivan could pack a bag and get his neighbor to feed the dog and cows while he was gone. Jake told Sullivan to tell the neighbors that he was just leaving town for a couple of days. Jake didn't want to put alert the neighbors in case Sadie called any of them looking for her uncle. On the way back to Columbus, Sullivan was quiet for most of the trip, looking out the window at the landscape that passed by the window. Jake imagined what was going through his head. Sully fell asleep in the front seat soon after they left the farm which was fine with Jake. It gave him some time to put his thoughts into perspective.

The airport was busy when they checked in at the U.S. Airways ticket counter. Without any luggage to check, they used the self service kiosks to get their e-tickets before proceeding to the TSA service desk where Jake and Sully received clearance to carry their handguns on board. Jake checked his watch. With over an hour to kill before they were going to begin boarding, he decided that it was probably a good idea to get some dinner before going to their gate. Tired of eating fast food, he passed up the Wendy's burger joint and Quizno's sub shop for a sit down meal at Max and Erma's, a full service restaurant in the main terminal building just before the security checkpoint leading to the departure gates. The sign at the entrance said to seat yourself so Jake selected a table in the roped off area outside the entrance to the restaurant so that he could watch the people walking through the gate area. After placing their drink orders with the waitress, Jake passed menus to Sully and Sullivan.

"Order what you'd like," he said, nodding in the direction of Sullivan. "This ones on the Federal Government."

"Not really hungry," was Sullivan's reply. "Maybe I'll just get something to drink."

"Better eat," said Sully. You won't even get any water on this flight. And you can forget the pretzels. You'd think that the pretzels were responsible for putting the airlines in bankruptcy. Now they even charge for checking a bag. Nothing cheap about flying anymore."

"Gotta eat something," said Jake, scanning the menu.

"Well, maybe just a sandwich then," Sullivan replied. "Suppose I should eat something."

"What's it gonna be like?" he asked, after putting down his menu and looking up at Jake.

"What's what gonna be like?" Jake asked.

"Flying. I've never been on a plane before."

"You're shittin me," responded Sully, looking totally perplexed. You've never flown before?"

"Never had cause to. Why go up in a damn plane when you got a perfectly good set of wheels?"

"You got a point there," said Jake. "But in our line of work...well sometimes...we just don't have the time to be driving where we need to go."

When the waitress returned with their drink orders, Jake opted for a Cobb salad while Sully decided to get his cholesterol fix for the day by ordering a cheeseburger and fries with a side of onion rings. John Sullivan kept to his original thought by ordering the soup and sandwich combo.

"What happens when we find her?" Sullivan finally asked, trying to keep his voice down.

"Right now, we just want to talk with her," Jake replied, in hushed tones.

"I'm just afraid that something's going to go all wrong," he said. "If Sadie's done any of what we talked about at the farm, she's not gonna want to give up easy like. She's pretty strong willed. She's always been pretty independent. Had to be. She lost everything before she even had a chance to be a teenager."

"That's why I want you there John," Jake said, looking directly into Sullivan's eyes so that he could see that Jake was sincere. "I think that if we find her. Well, I think that just hearing your voice and knowing that you're there...Hopefully, she'll come in and talk with us."

"God, I hope so," he muttered under his breath.

They ate in silence when the waitress returned with their food order.

CHAPTER 77

After finishing dinner, Jake paid the bill with his FBI issued Visa credit card, leaving a twenty percent tip. It was going to be a relatively short flight but with the amount of water Jake had drank during dinner, he decided to visit the men's room before heading toward the security checkpoint leading to the B terminal. The TSA officer manning the checkpoint had to tell Sullivan to remove his shoes three times before he finally heard him. Jake had forgotten that Sullivan hadn't flown before and obviously didn't know that he had to remove his jacket, shoes and anything else that would set the metal detector off. It took him two tries and removal of his western belt with the bull rider buckle before he finally was cleared through. After putting their shoes and belts back on and picking up their carryon's, they proceeded down the terminal to gate B-19. They arrived at the gate just as the attendant was announcing that the plane would be boarding in another ten minutes. Sullivan walked over to the window and watched the red and green blinking lights on the planes that were landing and departing. A small plane was parked at the end of the causeway leading from their gate. The light was on in the cockpit. Sullivan could see two people wearing headphones that appeared to be talking and moving switches. Two men jumped out of a gasoline truck parked next to the plane, uncoiled a long hose, sticking the nozzle into the underside of the plane and began refueling the plane. He could see men busily moving baggage from a trailer to the open baggage compartment on the plane. Sullivan was amazed at the amount of coordination that was taking place to get the plane prepared for takeoff. When the gate attendant announced that anyone who needed assistance or anyone with small children could board, the rest of the passengers in the gate area rose and started toward the open door. Sullivan made his way through the crowd to stand with Jake and Sully, waiting for the announcement that would allow them to board. After several women with small children walked down the causeway through the gate toward the plane, the attendant announced that the rest of the passengers could begin boarding.

Sullivan fell in line in front of Jake, handed the gate attendant his boarding pass and looked back toward the terminal one more time before walking into the causeway. The U.S. Airways commuter flight to Washington was a small plane with two seats on one side of the aisle and one on the other. Jake's and Sully's seats were over the wing on the right side of the aisle. Sullivan sat on the other side of the aisle, a row ahead of them.

Within minutes of boarding, with the plane only half full of passengers, the door to the plane was closed and the causeway was pulled back from the plane. The pilot started the engines and the plane was backed away from the gate. Jake noticed Sullivan paying attention to the flight attendant, listening to every word she said as she went over the emergency instructions. He saw Sullivan looking up at the ceiling for his oxygen mask when she got to the part about the mask automatically dropping down. *He really hasn't flown,* he thought. *That's hard to believe in today's world.*

It was only five thirty but looked much later with the dark clouds and low ceiling. Jake watched the rain bounce off of the wings and puddle on the tarmac. He put on the headset that had been provided by the flight attendant and tuned the radio so that he could hear the conversation between the pilot and the air traffic controller. When the pilot responded to the controller, Jake was surprised to hear a female voice. Over the past several years, he had noticed that more and more pilots were female. Their plane was number five in order of takeoff. As they taxied toward the active runway, Jake looked back toward the terminal to count nine more planes in line behind them. Within minutes, they received their orders for wheels up. Without delay, the pilot pushed the throttle forward increasing the rpms, sending the plane rolling down the active runway, the terminal passing quickly by the windows of the commuter jet. Jake looked over at Sullivan who sat erect, his eyes closed, knuckles of both hands white as he gripped the arms on either side of his chair. His lips moving. "Hail Mary…"

CHAPTER 78

An hour after takeoff they were entering Washington airspace. The pilot flashed the buckle seat belt warning indicating that all passengers were to remain seated until the plane came to a complete stop at the gate. Jake slipped his BlackBerry into the pocket inside his jacket. He had been taking notes and drafting emails that he would send upon landing. Sully had been sitting quietly for most of the flight, looking out the window, trying to recognize landmarks as the plane started descending.

Jake looked over at Sullivan who had released his tight grip on the handrails. It appeared that he was starting to relax and enjoy the flight. Fifty miles out, the pilot dimmed the cabin lights and banked the plane setting it on a course for its final approach. The noise of the ailerons rolling out to slow the planes descent and the thud of the wheels being lowered and locked caused Sullivan to increase his grip again. Small beads of sweat broke out on his forehead and he stared straight ahead, praying that he would walk on solid ground again. Jake smiled. *Not bad for his first flight.*

After exiting the plane and walking through the airport, they took the elevator to the short term parking garage. They decided to meet at the office at nine the next morning Sully got off on the third floor. Jake proceeded to the fourth floor where he had parked earlier that morning. Sullivan stayed with Jake, happy to be on solid ground again.

After locating the car, Jake threw their bags in the trunk of the car, paid the parking fare and decided to give Sullivan a quick tour of the Washington nighttime skyline. He took the George Washington Parkway and crossed over the Potomac on the Arland D. Williams Bridge passing by the Thomas Jefferson Memorial. From there he took Independence Avenue toward the U.S. Capitol and turned down Pennsylvania Avenue to the Whitehouse. Sullivan was awestruck, never having had the opportunity to be in the Nations Capital.

"You'll see more of the city in the next couple of days," promised Jake. For now, let's get you to the motel so that you can get a good nights rest. With no argument from Sullivan, Jake left the city, crossing over the Arlington Memorial Bridge where he picked up the George Washington Memorial Parkway again. Traffic was light at this time of the evening and five minutes later, Jake was on I-395 heading in the direction of the motel.

Jake had asked Lynn to reserve a room for Sullivan at the Comfort Inn just down the road from his townhouse, convenient to the Beltway.

"Thanks for the tour," Sullivan said, as they continued in the direction of the motel. "It really is a pretty city. Lots of history. I guess a lot of the decisions we have to live with every day are made right here."

"Yea, I don't know if that's good or bad," responded Jake with a snicker.

It was only a short trip on the expressway before Jake took the King Street Exit onto Van Dorn. Three traffic lights later, he pulled into the entrance to the Motel and stopped the car under the overhang directly in front of the entry. Jake opened the lid of the trunk to retrieve Sullivan's bag and together they approached the front desk. The desk clerk, a pretty blond woman, who appeared to be in her middle thirties looked up as they approached the counter.

"You have a reservation under the name Jake Hunter," Jake said, laying his credit card on the top of the counter.

"Yes, sir. I have a single with a king size bed?" she said as a question, swiping Jake's card through the machine while looking at Jake and Sullivan. "One or two cards?"

"Just one," Jake smiled, handing the card she gave to him to Sullivan.

She gave Jake a copy of the invoice and directed them to the elevators.

"I'll be by to pick you up at eight," Jake said, as they walked toward the elevator. "I've stayed here before. They have a pretty good breakfast. I think it opens at six a.m. Here's my card," he said, pulling a business card from his wallet. "Call me if you need anything. Otherwise, I'll see you in the morning. Get some sleep. Tomorrow is going to be a long day!"

CHAPTER 79

Wednesday, December 3

At five a.m., Jake rolled over and turned his alarm off. It was useless trying to sleep. For the last hour, he had been laying awake rehashing in his mind the events of the previous day. He thought about the look on John Sullivan's face when he realized what Jake was insinuating when he asked about Sadie' shooting ability. Jake hoped he was wrong but the more he thought about it, the clearer it became.

He got out of bed and put a robe on before heading upstairs to make a pot of coffee. Pete was already at the back door, pacing back and forth.

"Hold your pants on," said Jake, flipping on the floodlight to the backyard before turning the deadlock in the door. The door was barely open when Pete shot through the opening and jumped from the deck to the yard, clearing the hedges before hitting the ground and running to the fence. Pete would do his business and be back at the door within a couple of minutes.

"I wish I had your energy," Jake shouted after him, before closing the door. He flipped the switch for the light over the kitchen island and filled the coffee pot at the sink. While Jake waited for the coffee to brew, he went into the den. The phone light was blinking on the desk, indicating that there were three messages. Jake had gone right to bed when he got home the night before without listening to the messages. He clicked on the message board and listened. Two telemarketers and a dating service. "That's all I need," he said aloud, erasing all three messages. The dating service call did get him to think about Jillian. He hadn't spoken to her in over a week. Their relationship was starting to heat up and Jake wasn't quite sure what he thought about that.

Less than a mile away, John Sullivan sat in his room, watching the local news station and flipping through the USA Today that he found outside his door when he opened it earlier. He still had over an hour before Jake was supposed to pick him up. He had gone downstairs to the lobby earlier and had taken advantage of the breakfast that had been provided to the guests staying at the Comfort Inn. He drank a couple of glasses of orange juice and tried a plate of scrambled eggs with sausage. After a couple of mouthfuls of the eggs, he decided that the powdered eggs didn't hold a candle to the fresh eggs he got every day back home on the farm. He pushed the eggs aside and settled on a bowl of oatmeal and a donut before heading back to the room with a banana and a cup of coffee. He didn't get much rest during the night, the thoughts of Sadie out there somewhere, kept running through his mind. He couldn't believe that his niece could do what Jake had alluded to. He sat back on the bed and closed his eyes. A tear ran down his cheek. He had to find her before something drastic happened.

CHAPTER 80

It was eight a.m. when Jake pulled the SUV under the overhang of the Comfort Inn. Sullivan was waiting for him at the front door.

"Morning," greeted Jake when Sullivan closed the door and reached for his seatbelt.

"Good morning," responded Sullivan. "Pretty morning," he reflected. "Not a cloud in sight. Looks like we're in for a nice day," he went on, trying to make small talk.

"How'd you sleep last night?" asked Jake.

"I've had better nights. Took me a while to fall asleep. I'm not used to sleeping in motel rooms. There were some teenagers sitting outside in the hallway last night talking until midnight. The walls are thin enough to hear their entire conversation. I was awake by five. That's the time I usually get up to feed the cows before I head off for work. My schedule is pretty routine. Been doing the same thing for the past thirty years. You kinda get used to it after that amount of time."

"Yea, I know what you mean," responded Jake. "I haven't had to rely on a clock to wake me up for a long time now. I set an alarm just as a back up but usually I'm up before it goes off."

"So what's on the agenda for today?" asked Sullivan, anxious to get down to business.

"We're gonna head down to D.C. FBI headquarters is right downtown in the heart of the city. I've got to meet with the director for a bit and bring him up to speed. After that, we'll set out a plan to try to find your niece."

Traffic was rush hour at that time of day, bumper to bumper as they made their way into the city.

"I couldn't stand to drive in this traffic every day," commented Sullivan as they got stuck behind the same traffic light for three exchanges. A traffic jam at home means you have to stop at a blinking red light."

After almost an hour of horns honking and road rage drivers, Jake pulled into the parking garage finding an open space on the third floor.

"We don't even have a parking garage like this back home," commented Sullivan. "Don't suppose we need one though. Plenty of on street parking."

Jake signed Sullivan in at the Security desk on the first floor getting him a visitor pass to hang around his neck.

"Now I feel official," he joked, following Jake into the elevator. Jake pushed the button in the elevator for the third floor and they rode the rest of the way in silence. When the doors opened, Jake led Sullivan down the hallway and through a set of double doors with the words FBI Special Crimes Unit written across the top. Lynn was sitting at her desk talking on the telephone and motioned for Jake to stop before going back to his desk. They stood there for a couple of seconds while she finished her call. When she hung up the phone, Jake introduced Sullivan to Lynn. She extended her hand which he took and shook it casually.

"Director wants to see you," she said, looking directly at Jake. "His exact words were to…and I quote, "Tell him to get up here as soon as he steps foot into the office."

"There, I told you," she smiled. "My obligation is complete."

"Tell you what," he said to Sullivan. "Lynn here will get you a cup of coffee and put you in a room where you can watch the television or read some magazines. I've got to run upstairs and brief the director. Shouldn't be too long. He's usually running late for another meeting so it's usually in and out in a few minutes."

"Any word from Sully?" he asked Lynn, walking past her to his desk to pick up a couple of files before taking the stairs to the top floor.

"Yea, something about having to stop off at the cleaners on his way in. Said he'd be in before nine. Said he couldn't wear the same suit three days in a row."

Jake left Sullivan in Lynn's hands while he played his voicemail messages before leaving to meet with the director. He skipped through the first two but listened to the third message in full. It was a call from Steve Jackson that came in last night. Jackson said he had forgotten to mention something to him and thought it might come in handy.

Jake bounded up the back stairwell the two flights of stairs to the fifth floor. Fortunately the stairwell was empty and he didn't knock into anyone, taking the stairs two at time. Whenever possible, Jake chose the stairs over the elevator. He actually thought it was quicker and it gave him a chance to work on his cardio system.

He opened the door at the top of the stairwell and entered the hallway, slowing just enough to catch his breath before entering the director's outer office.

"Good morning, little lady," he said to Sandy. He's expecting me. Mind if I go right in?"

"Actually Jake, he's on the phone with the Loren French. Should only be another minute or two. Care for a cup of coffee?"

"That would be great," replied Jake. "I was in such a rush to get up here that I didn't even stop for a cup."

She left the room to walk the short distance to the private lunch area off the outer office while Jake waited on the director to finish his call with the director of Secret Service. Loren French was relatively new as the director of the Secret Service, having moved up through the ranks to lead the Whitehouse President's detail before getting the director's post early last year. Jake had worked with him on a couple of occasions over the last year and found him to be professional and capable.

While he was waiting on his coffee, Jake walked to the window that overlooked the Mall that ran the entire length from the Capitol Building to the Washington Monument. It was still early but the Mall was already full of people walking, flying kites and a couple of kids throwing Frisbees while their dogs tried frantically to grab a Frisbee out of the air. *Only in America*, he thought, smiling to himself.

CHAPTER 81

"Hey Jake. Come on in. I didn't know you were waiting for me. The director shook Jake's hand and motioned for him to have a seat before almost closing the door on Sandy who held two full cups of coffee in front of her.

"Whoa, hold up there," she hollered before he let the door close in her face.

"Thought you might want a fresh one too, Director," she said, handing him the hot mugs.

"Thanks Sandy," he said, taking the steaming cups from her hands. "Please pull the door closed behind you on your way out," he said. "Oh I'm sorry Jake, here throw those files up here on the corner of my desk," he continued, indicating for Jake to clear a chair in front of the director's desk to sit.

"One of these days, I'm actually going to get through some of these files. I was just finishing up a call with Loren French," he said to Jake after taking a sip of his coffee. "You've worked with him before, haven't you?

"Yea, great guy. From what I hear, he's doing a pretty good job in his new role. The guys all seem to think a lot of him."

"He's professional and not an egotistical son of a bitch like the guy he replaced. Oh well, he's gone so... Good trip yesterday?"

"Yea, I'd say so," replied Jake.

"I understand you brought a visitor back with you?" he prodded.

"Yes. I thought it was important. I really think we're on to something now. Let me bring you up to speed."

"Well lay it out for me but you better give me the abridged version for right now. I have an appointment with the Senate Finance Committee in an hour and I've got to review my notes before I show up over there. With gas over four bucks a gallon, I'm asking for more money to buy a couple more of the Tahoe Hybrids and I'm not looking forward to the drilling I'm gonna get from some of those guys. With the amount of discord in the Senate and House after that seven hundred billion dollar bailout program, they're looking at every request with a fine tooth comb.

For the next ten minutes, Jake gave him the short hand version of their trip to Ohio.

"So what are your thoughts?" the director asked when Jake was finished.

"I want to take another run at Director Preacher."

"Well let me caution you Jake. You can't go in there half cocked again. You need to be cautious. You start making accusations and he'll lawyer up on you. Talk with… What's his name…Steve Jackson? Hell, take him with you if you're sure he's not involved in either of these two shooting. But, warn him to keep his mouth shut. Let's see if the director starts to sweat a little when he recognizes Jackson."

"Will do," responded Jake, standing and heading for the door. "Jackson left me a voicemail yesterday. I'll call him back this morning and see what else he's come up with. Sounds like he might have some additional information that may prove useful."

"Good luck," responded the director, pulling his suit jacket from the back of his chair. "Keep me posted. I don't want to be surprised."

With that, Jake left the office, handing his empty cup to Sandy on his way out the door.

"Thanks for the coffee," he winked.

CHAPTER 82

"Hey Sully…New suit?" Jake teased Sully when he returned to the office.

"Don't be a wise ass," replied Sully. "What'd the director have to say?" he asked, sitting on the corner of Jake's desk.

"Just wanted an update on our visit to Ohio. Oh by the way, Jackson left a message on my voicemail yesterday. Says he has some information that we might want to hear. Let's go in the conference and I can put him on speaker. I don't want Sullivan to hear what he has so say. It might prove prejudicial if it ends up that his niece is the shooter. I've got Sullivan in the break room watching the TV. He'll be all right for a little longer."

Jake replayed the message to get Jacksons phone number before the two of them grabbed a cup of coffee and headed for a conference room.

"Let's not let him know we have Lieutenant Warner's uncle in here. I'm not sure Jackson's not involved in this yet and I'd rather keep him in the dark with what we know about Warner's sister. He never mentioned anything about Warner's sister when we met with him last week so I'd guess he either doesn't know Warner had a sister or he doesn't think she has anything to do with killing Powell or Hatcher."

"Good point," said Sully. "Let's just hear him out. See what he has to say."

"Oh, by the way, interjected Jake. "Director thinks it wouldn't be a bad idea if we took Jackson with us to see Director Preacher."

"Kinda like old home week, huh?" joked Sully.

"Yea. Could be interesting but he's got to keep his mouth shut."

"How you gonna play it with him on the phone?" asked Sully.

"First, I'll let him tell me what he called about yesterday. Depending on what he has to say, I'll decide if it's the proper time to suggest that he visit the director with us. He may not be willing to come up for that. I got the impression that Director Preacher isn't one of his favorite people."

"No argument from me on that," responded Sully. "As a matter of fact, without a good alibi, I might even think he'd be our best suspect as the shooter."

"He's not out of the water yet," said Jake. "We really haven't checked him out and he has as much a motive as anyone for wanting those three out of the way."

Jake punched in the number Jackson had left on his voicemail and they waited. After three rings Jackson answered.

"Yea," he answered, with a tone in his voice like the phone call was disturbing something he was doing.

"Mr. Jackson...This is Agent Hunter. I've got you on speaker phone. I'm returning your call of yesterday. Sorry I didn't get back to you earlier. I understand that you have some additional information for us?"

"Is this call being recorded?" asked Jackson.

"No. I'm not recording it. I just have you on the speaker so that Agent Gilmore can hear what you have to say as well. There's only the two of us in the room."

"All right. I understand. Well after I spoke with you last week, I got to thinking a little. I didn't tell you that Lieutenant Warner seemed to be upset about something when we got on the ship that took us to the Philippines. I don't know what it was. He didn't talk about anything, leastways not to me. But, it seemed that he steered clear of the other officers. Actually, kept a lot to himself."

"Was that unusual for him?" asked Jake.

"Well, he didn't hang with the enlisted guys. As an officer, he wasn't supposed to but he was friendly. Once we got on the ship, it was almost like he went out of his way to be alone."

"And you don't have any idea what precipitated that behavior?" asked Jake.

"Pre-cip what? What the hell does that mean?"

"You don't have any idea...why he was acting differently?" rephrased Jake.

"No. I don't have any idea why he acted like that. I just remember it was right after we left Iraq."

"Okay," responded Jake. "Mr. Jackson. Would you be willing to join us this week when we meet with Director Preacher?"

"What? Me meet with that sonovabitch? You got to be kidding! I've got nothing to say to that motherfucker."

"Actually, I don't want you to say a word. I would like you to go with me and Agent Gilmore. I want to see the reaction we get from him when he realizes who you are."

"In that case, count me in. What day we talking about?"

"I'm going to try to set it up for tomorrow morning if we can."

"Okay, tomorrow works for me. Can't go Friday. Friday I got to go to the VA clinic in Richmond."

Jake told Jackson that he would call him back after he spoke with the director's assistant. He'd give him the time and location where they could meet. It would be easier if they all rode together, Jake assured him. Jake knew there was no way that Steve Jackson would ever be allowed to drive into Langley unaccompanied.

CHAPTER 83

After finishing the call with Steve Jackson, Jake and Sully went into the break room where John Sullivan was waiting for them.

"Get you another cup of coffee?" offered Sully.

"No thank you. My eyeballs are floating in coffee now. Anymore and I won't be able to sleep for a week."

Jake pulled a chair up and sat across from Sullivan while Sully leaned against the counter, eating a jelly filled donut and washing it down with a cup of coffee.

"John... Let me tell you where we're at," Jake said. For the next five minutes he told Sullivan that pictures of Sadie had been circulated among the FBI, the DC police and all the local jurisdictions along the I-495 Beltway. The picture of Sadie had been released to all the local news channels and the cable networks. Beginning at noon, the news people were instructed to display the picture of Sadie and report that at this time she was only a person of interest. Anyone who recognized her picture was to call the FBI hotline and talk to the FBI agent manning the phones. There was no mention of her being a suspect in the killings of Senator Powell or Colonel Hatcher. Jake was hopeful that Sadie would see the news channel and come in on her own. Either that or someone would recognize her picture and call the FBI hotline that had been set up to receive the calls. Jake asked John Sullivan to remain there for the duration of the day. He wanted Sullivan to be there if they brought Sadie in for questioning.

"We'll order lunch for you in a bit. Lynn will get you anything you need. Make yourself comfortable. If you need to make any phone calls, Lynn can get you an outside line. It may be a long afternoon," cautioned Jake. Before he left the break room, Jake checked his watch. It was almost noon and he decided to stay in the break room with Sullivan to catch the first part of the noon broadcast. Picking up the remote from the table, he aimed it at the television mounted from the ceiling in the corner of the room and tuned to the local network. He muted the TV until the picture of the afternoon anchor appeared. Turning the sound back on, the newscaster in an elevated voice announced that the Federal Reserve Chairman had just lowered the short term interest rate by a quarter of a point.

"Big deal," joked Sully. The market's gone all to hell, foreclosures are at an all time high and he thinks that dropping the rate a quarter point is gonna turn the country around. Where the hell do they find guys like that?"

"Factories are all closing down," added Sullivan. "Shipping all the work overseas where they can get cheap labor. Nothing's made over here anymore. China…Japan. That's where we get everything now."

They were still discussing the economy when Sadie's picture appeared on the screen.

"Hey, turn it up Jake," demanded Sully, plopping down onto a couch.

Jake increased the volume on the remote until the announcer's voice could be heard clearly over the speakers… "Local authorities are looking for Sadie Warner, a thirty one year old Ohio woman, approximately five and a half feet tall, about one hundred thirty pounds with blue eyes and short brown hair. The woman is only wanted for questioning at this time. Anyone seeing this woman is asked to call the FBI hotline at…" Jake had muted the volume again to listen to Sullivan.

"You think that will work?" he asked, when Sadie's picture disappeared from the screen.

"If she's in the area, someone's bound to recognize her. I just hope they take the time to call the hotline," Jake replied.

"Yea, sometimes people don't want to get involved," added Sully. "They're afraid that they'll be brought in for questioning and have to go to court to testify. People are funny like that. And then, we'll get a bunch of crank calls too. Looney tunes who think it's funny to call here and send us on a wild goose chase."

"I just don't want her to get hurt," said Sullivan.

"Me either," said Jake patting Sullivan on the shoulder as he left the room.

CHAPTER 84

The phone rang three times before it was answered by the Deputy Director's personal assistant.

"Director Preacher's office," the voice came over the headset.

"Good afternoon, this is FBI Agent Jake Hunter. How are you today?"

"Fine sir. How can I help you?"

"I'd like to see the director tomorrow afternoon," Jake responded.

"May I tell him what this is regarding?" she asked.

"He'll know," replied Jake, a smile forming on his face.

"I'm going to put you on hold for a minute, sir. I'll see if he's available."

Jake waited patiently, scribbling notes on a sheet of paper for a couple of minutes before she was back on the phone.

"I'm sorry Agent Hunter. The director is in meetings all afternoon tomorrow."

"In that case...just let the director know that I'll be by tomorrow afternoon and I can wait for a break in his meetings. It's really important that I speak with him tomorrow."

"I'll let him know sir."

Jake hung up the handset and played back the messages in his voicemail from the day before until Steve Jackson's voice came on the line. He jotted down the number left by Jackson and cleared the line, immediately punching in the ten digit number.

On the third ring, Jackson answered.

"Yea, go ahead," said the voice on the other end of the line.

"You always answer the phone that way?" asked Jake.

"My line. What's it matter?" replied Jackson sarcastically.

"This is Agent Hunter."

"Yea, I recognized your voice," he said. "What's going on?"

"We're going to be paying Director Preacher a visit at his office tomorrow afternoon. Wanted to confirm you still want to go along?"

"What? Me at CIA Headquarter? You'd better believe it. I thought you were kidding earlier. I'd love to see the look on that bastard's face when he sees me! He's liable to shit right there in his own office. What time?"

"We don't have an appointment but it's not going to be a surprise visit. I left word that I'd be stopping by in the afternoon. I'd like to be there about one o'clock. You'll be coming up 95. Shouldn't take you more than three hours at that time of day so if you leave Richmond by nine thirty, you should have no problem getting there by twelve thirty. You can leave your car in the Park and Ride Lot ride off the exit and ride in with us."

"I'll even wear a nice jacket and shave in the morning. I'm really looking forward to this," he said, before hanging up the phone.

CHAPTER 85

Thursday, December 4

By the time Jake entered the office Thursday morning at 8:30, there were over fifty calls from people indicating that they had seen someone who resembled Sadie Sullivan in a McDonald's restaurant in McLean, Virginia, a local Wal-Mart in Tyson's Corners, a movie theatre in Rockville, Maryland, the lobby's of several hotels, numerous gas stations and a number of other locations from as far away as Frederick Maryland and all other parts surrounding the I-495 Beltway. Some of these were obviously crank calls but Jake needed to follow up on anything that even remotely lent itself to a hint of legitimacy. Having worked the Freeway shooter several years earlier, he knew that there would be an overwhelming response when Sadie's picture was broadcast on the networks the previous day.

Jake had spoken with Director Avery on Wednesday evening before leaving the office and requested help in following up on these calls. By the time he arrived at the office Thursday morning, the director had assigned five additional agents to help with the calls. Jake had called Lynn on his way to the office and sequestered a conference room at the end of the hall with conference tables and a bank of telephones.

Before meeting with the other agents, Jake poured himself a cup of coffee in the break room. He had left home without having any breakfast and was starting to feel a little low on sugar. Someone left a box of Krispe Kreme donuts in the break room with a sign to help yourself. Jake grabbed a couple of donuts, rationalizing that he'd run another mile on the treadmill that evening. Between bites of donut, he asked Lynn to gather the team for a quick briefing in the conference room. Jake had arranged for a car to pick up John Sullivan at the motel and bring him by the office by nine a.m. He wanted to spend a few minutes with the agents before Sullivan arrived. Sully was just finishing up a call and motioned that he'd be in as soon as he had hung up the phone.

Jake knew all the agents by name. He had worked side by side with a couple of them on the freeway shooter case and felt comfortable with the group. Jake waited a couple of minutes for Sully to join the group before closing the door and turning on the computer, projecting the picture of Sadie Sullivan on the white board at the front of the room.

"Please have a seat so that we can get started," he said, waiting for the various conversations to end and everyone to settle into a seat around one of the conference tables.

"First, I'd like to bring you all up to speed on what we're looking at." For the next fifteen minutes, Jake brought everyone up to date on the shooting of Senator Powell and Colonel Preacher. He discussed the meeting in Richmond with Steve Jackson and his concern for the protection of Director Preacher.

"The woman we're looking for is known as Sadie Warner. As per the description that was disseminated yesterday afternoon…and I have additional copies here for anyone who did not get one…," he continued, handing copies of Sadie's picture and description to the agent sitting in the first row. "She is approximately thirty one years old, about five foot six and one hundred thirty pounds. At this time, we are looking for Sadie Thomas for questioning. Contrary to what has been broadcast across the networks to the public, I have reason to believe that she may be involved in these two shootings. Agent Gilmore and I traveled to Ohio earlier this week and spoke with her uncle. He has returned to Washington with us and will be joining us shortly. I wanted to meet with you before his arrival to answer any questions you may have without his hearing our entire discussion. What we have right now is strictly circumstantial evidence. My concern is that if she is responsible for the killing of Senator Powell and Colonel Hatcher that her next target is the Deputy Director of the CIA, Director Preacher. She is an expert marksman with a rifle, having shot competitive on her college team. To my knowledge and I have no reason to doubt his word, John Sullivan has not spoken to his niece since sometime last month when she visited him briefly in Ohio. Until my phone call to him on Sunday, he had no reason to believe that his niece was involved in any illegal activity. Obviously, he is concerned for her welfare and doesn't want to see any harm to her. Currently, Director Preacher has a team of FBI agents assigned to him for protection but we all know that a determined shooter will find a way to get to his or her target. I want to find her before that happens. If she is not responsible, we're back to square one. But, right now, everything points to her."

"Questions at this point?" he said, opening the floor for questions or comments.

"What's Director Preacher's role in all this?" asked Shane Menser, a young agent, recently assigned to the D.C. office.

"At this point, mere speculation," Jake responded. Preacher, Senator Powell and Colonel Hatcher served together during the First Gulf War. There is some thought that they were involved in the death of a lieutenant at the end of the First Gulf War before they returned stateside. But," he continued... "I want to repeat that it is mere speculation. We have no proof of any of this. This information doesn't leave this room. The woman we're looking for, Sadie Warner, is the surviving younger sister of this lieutenant. She may be in possession of information that we do not currently have."

Jake looked around for more questions. Hearing none, he continued; "I've got about fifty leads so far from phone calls received since we first started showing her picture. Some of these are obviously bogus but you know the drill. Everything has to be followed up as if it was accurate. I don't know how much time we have but if she's here in D.C., I would guess that she's seen her picture on the television and she's probably laying low. Also, if she's the shooter, this moves up her time table. The clocks ticking on her ability to finish the task before we find her. I'm going to be meeting with Director Preacher later this afternoon but so far he hasn't proved to cooperative. If there are no questions, I'm going to split up the information on the calls we've received so far. Please follow up on these and call me if any of these look promising. Lynn will be handing out additional calls as they are received. Jake and Sully left the room, closing the door behind them.

"What are you going to tell Preacher this afternoon when we meet with him?" asked Sully.

"Well, it ought to be interesting to see the expression on his face when he recognizes Steve Jackson. That in itself may tell us something. If he's implicated in the killing of Lieutenant Warner, seeing Jackson might cause him to come clean. I don't know though. He's been in the business of keeping secrets and covering up actions since he joined the CIA. Might just be another day at the office as far as he's concerned. On the other hand, seeing Jackson might just rattle him enough."

John Sullivan was waiting for them in the visitor area outside Jake's office when they got back to the squad room. Lynn had already given him a cup of coffee and he was leafing through a magazine, his mind on something else.

Discarding the magazine when he saw them approaching, he asked, "Any luck on anybody seeing her?"

"Actually, we have had quite a few calls," responded Jake, a note of encouragement in his voice. "I've got a team of agents following up every call we've received. Most of them will not pan out but you never know what's valid unless you check them all."

"What can I do to help?" he asked. "I feel sorta helpless. There must be something I can do besides just sit around here and wait."

"Well, actually there is," Jake responded. "I was thinking last night about having you interviewed on the news. You've seen those newscasts where a family member is asking for help in finding a lost child or pleading for someone to please return a kidnapped kid?"

"Yea, he responded, a glimmer of hope visible in his eyes.

"I can do that."

"If she's here in the D.C. area, unless she's holed up somewhere without access to a television, she's bound to have seen her picture," Jake said. "It's been shown almost every hour or two since we first turned it over to the networks yesterday afternoon."

"What are you thinking?" asked Sully.

"Fox News," responded Jake. "I think if we get Fox Breaking News Desk to do an interview with John here and he asks Sadie to turn herself in to us, maybe…just maybe, she'll call or turn herself in. Maybe just seeing her uncle will be enough to come in."

"I suppose it's worth a try," commented Sully. "You want me to give them a call and see if they'll meet us here say in an hour or so?" he said, checking his watch for the time.

"Yea, maybe they'll tape it for the noon news," replied Jake. "That way the other networks may pick up on it and carry it on the six o'clock news tonight."

"I'm on it," Sully said, leaving the room to place the call.

"Don't forget we have to be out of here by noon for our meeting at one," Jake hollered after him.

"What else? Anything else you can think of?" asked Sullivan. "I feel like there must be something else I can do."

"I know it's tough, but hang in there," said Jake. "At this point, a lot of it's up to Sadie. If she's in the D.C. area, it's pretty much up to her," he continued, not wanting to think about the alternative.

CHAPTER 86

Fox News was delighted to get the call. Within minutes, they sent a reporter and camera crew over to the Hoover Building. They set up in an empty conference room, moving the conference table and chairs to the far wall to give the reporter space to conduct the interview. Sullivan appeared nervous, crossing and uncrossing his arms in front of his chest, waiting for the reporter to begin the interview. After checking the sound recording and adjusting the lighting to minimize the shadow effect, the reporter was ready. When the cameras came on the reporter started immediately with a recap showing the picture of Sadie that had been broadcast earlier before turning the camera to John Sullivan and introducing him as Sadie's uncle. Acknowledging Sullivan's nervousness, she carefully asked him leading questions, ending with Sullivan asking Sadie to call the FBI.

"Good job," the reported said when the cameras were turned off.

"You did good," said Jake, patting Sullivan on the shoulder, and walking him to the door.

"Agent Gilmore and I are going to be out of the office for the next couple of hours. If you want, I can have somebody drop you back at the motel or you're welcome to stay here until we return. I can get Lynn to order lunch for you if you decide to stay here."

"I think I'd rather stay here in case she calls or comes in. I want to be here when she does."

"Understand," responded Jake. "In that case, make yourself comfortable. It may be a long afternoon."

CHAPTER 87

Sully ran into the corner deli to get drinks and a couple of sandwiches for their lunch while Jake waited for him in the car. They weren't expected to meet with Steve Jackson for another hour and it was less than a half hour drive to where they had agreed to meet him in the Park and Ride lot. Jake wasn't sure how long they would have to wait in Director Preacher's outer office until he had a break in his afternoon schedule. He knew Sully couldn't go more than a couple of hours between eating and he had only eaten the one chocolate frosted donut since getting up at six that morning.

"Pastrami on Rye with a slice of Swiss," announced Sully when he returned to the car. Got a couple bags of chips too. Plain or barbecue?" he asked Jake.

"Doesn't matter to me," said Jake, checking his side mirror before pulling into the line of traffic and heading toward the 395 Interstate in the direction of McLean. "My greatest asset is my flexibility," he added.

"Yea," quipped Sully. "You're about as flexible as my ex-wives."

Jake smirked but didn't want to touch that one.

That ate their sandwiches, mostly in silence, listening to the news on the radio until Jake pulled into the Park and Ride lot and found an empty space near the front. He backed into the space, a habit he had picked up while attending the FBI academy.

"You know, I'd sure like to get this case closed, but I hope we're wrong on this one," said Jake, shutting off the engine while they waited for Jackson to show up. "That John Sullivan seems like a pretty nice guy. I really hope his niece isn't tied up in this thing."

"Somehow I got the sick feeling that she is," said Sully, a rueful look on his face.

"Hey, isn't that Jackson's Fairlane coming down this way?" Sully asked, looking toward the car turning into the parking lot and heading in their direction.

"Yea, that's him," said Jake, getting out of the car to motion to Jackson, who continued in their direction, pulling into the empty space next to Jake.

The Steve Jackson that emerged from the Fairlane was a steep contrast from the disheveled man they met in Richmond earlier in the week. Jake and Sully walked around the front of the car, greeting Jackson when he stepped away from the car.

"You clean up nicely, don't ya," snickered Sully with a hint of sarcasm in his voice.

"Yea, well I thought it might make more of an impact. I've been looking forward to this since we spoke."

Jackson had taken a razor to his face and his hair was cut, neatly combed. He was wearing an open collar shirt with a blue blazer and charcoal gray slacks, cordovan loafers. Jake could sense the military bearing in the man that stood in front of him.

"Thanks for coming," he said extending his hand.

"No…Thank you," he replied, shaking Jakes hand before climbing in the back seat.

From there, it was only a fifteen minute drive to Langley and just before one in the afternoon when Jake stopped at the security checkpoint.

The guard stopped them at the gate and Jake rolled down his window as the guard approached his door.

"Good morning sir," he addressed Jake. "Do you have an appointment?"

"Director Preacher is expecting us," said Jake.

Sully handed his ID and Badge to Jake to give to the guard while Jake asked Jackson for his driver's license.

"If you wait here a minute I'll get you cleared and get your visitor badges," he said, returning to the guard shack and picking up the phone to make a call to the director's office. He returned shortly thereafter, passing their identification back to them and handing Jake three visitor passes on lanyards to hang around their necks.

"Do you know the way to the director's office?" he asked.

"We've been there before," responded Jake.

"Have a great day sir," he said, returning to the guard shack. He pushed the button, raising the gate, letting Jake pull through.

Jake drove to the parking lot, pulling into a visitor space in front of the building where the Deputy Director's office was located. They locked the car and mounted the steps leading into the Administration building and stopped again at the receptionist desk. The receptionist took their names and called upstairs, offering them a seat while they waited.

Within a few minutes, the elevator bell rang, the door opened and the same tall blond that had met them before stepped out of the elevator and approached them.

"Lisa, right?" Jake said, extending his hand.

"Yes," she smiled. "Nice to see you again Agent Hunter."

Jake reintroduced Sully and introduced Steve Jackson.

"As I said to you on the phone," she said, walking toward the elevator. "The director has a busy schedule this afternoon. I don't know when he'll be able to meet with you but he knows you're coming. I'll let him know you're here."

"We understand," replied Jake. "We can wait on him. I'm sure he'll take some time to meet with us," he said, following her into the elevator.

When the elevator door closed, she pushed the button for the third floor and the elevator rose, the bell ringing as it passed the second floor before stopping on the third. When it opened, they followed her out of the elevator, taking a right down the corridor to the end of the hall through the double doors into the same waiting area that they had been in a month earlier.

"I'll get you gentlemen some coffee," she said, leaving them to find a seat in the waiting area outside the director's inner office. She returned shortly with a tray holding three coffee cups, steam rising from the hot coffee, sugar packets and a bowl of miniature creamers.

"Oh, this is great," commented Jake. "Thank you Lisa, that's very nice of you."

"I'll let the director know you here," she said, smiling and returning to her desk behind the counter. Jake watched her make a call and speak into the phone. He wasn't good at reading lips but from the length of the call, he was sure she had spoken with the director. Jake checked the clock on the wall above her desk. *One o'clock*, he thought.

Two o'clock came and went and there was no sign of the director. It was obvious to Jake that Lisa was uncomfortable with the amount of time the director was making them wait. She asked if they would like refills on their coffee but other than Jackson, Jake and Sully declined. Jake took advantage of the time by writing notes in the pocket notebook he always carried with him. Sully and Jackson busied themselves by talking and reading magazines from the racks alongside the coffee table. They found a common interest in fishing and before long were exchanging fishing stories and laughing.

At three thirty, Jake watched Lisa take a call, speaking quietly into the receiver.

Hanging up the phone, she came from behind the counter and approached the three men sitting around the table.

"I just spoke with the director. He said to tell you that he had one more call to make and he would be with you shortly."

"Thank you, Lisa," Jake said, smiling outside but ready to ring the director's neck.

At three forty-five, Lisa took another call from the director and announced, "The director can see you now."

She led them toward the director's office, opening and holding the door for them as the three of them passed in front of her and entered the director's private office. When all three were in, she closed the door behind them. The director looked up from his desk and invited them to take a seat. If he recognized Jackson, he was good to cover because he acted as if he had now idea who he was.

"So, gentlemen… What brings you here today? I'm sorry you had to wait so long but ah…I have a pretty busy schedule today as you can imagine. As a matter of fact, I only have a couple of minutes to give you today. I have another conference call that I can't be late for in less than a half hour."

"A half hour should be more than enough," smiled Jake, pulling his notebook out of his jacket pocket. Fortunately, the long delay had given him plenty of time to think about what he was going to say and what he wanted to accomplish with this meeting.

"Director, talk to me about a Lieutenant Warner," he said, stopping and letting the silence sink in before continuing. "I understand that you served together under Senator Powell's command during Desert Storm," he concluded.

"Lieutenant Warner…Yea, Yea…Boy, that was a long time ago. "I'm not sure what you're getting at," his lack of patience erupting. "What the hell does that have to do with the murders of Senator Powell and Colonel Hatcher?"

"Let's just say I'm playing a hunch." Jake answered.

"Look," he demanded, staring at Jake. I don't have the time to waste while you play your hunches," he shouted, his face reddening with anger. "I suggest you spend your time tracking down the idiot that took the lives of two good men."

Taking advantage of the discomfort displayed by Director Preacher, Jake interjected: "I'm sorry. I don't remember if I introduced you to Mr. Jackson, here. I believe you know each other already."

"Jackson," repeated the director, looking over at Jackson, who was thoroughly enjoying this encounter. "Yea, I remember you, now. You were in Warner's unit."

"Yea," was all that Jackson said.

"Warner was a quiet guy," the director said, regaining his composure. "Kept to himself. Who knows what demons were flying around in his head before he decided to end it."

"I just thought you might want to know that we're having the lieutenant's body exhumed," Jake said, looking directly into the director's eyes.

"What the hell for? Christ, it's been almost twenty years. The guy was a loose canon. What do you expect to find? A suicide note? He didn't leave one. He disappeared one night and they found him dead the next day."

"You didn't find that odd?" asked Jake, looking up from his notes.

"What's odd about that? The guy was a loner. Kept to himself most of the time. He was always more comfortable around the enlisted guys. I think the fact that Senator Powell, Colonel Hatcher and I went through the academy intimidated him a little."

"There's a possibility that the lieutenant's death wasn't suicide," Jake said, starting to really enjoy the discomfort he was witnessing on the director's face.

"What's that supposed to mean?"

"You're a smart man, Director. Think about it," Jake said.

"I don't like what you're insinuating," said the director, rising from his chair and walking toward his door.

"I'm not insinuating anything Director," responded Jake, following him to the door, now opened, the director standing red-faced ready to explode.

"Enjoy the rest of your day," Jake said, winking at him as he passed in front of him and headed for the elevator.

"Thanks for the coffee, miss" said Jackson to Lisa, who was busy typing on the keyboard in front of her computer.

"You struck a chord there," said Sully, when they were in the elevator descending to the first floor.

"Fuckin prick" was all that Jackson added.

CHAPTER 88

Friday December 5

John Sullivan had spent two days at FBI headquarters waiting for Sadie to call or show up. His pleas on the television for her to come in for questioning went unanswered. The FBI agents assigned to the hotline had spent the last two days following up every lead, returning phone calls and meeting with everyone who had claimed to have seen Sadie. Calls to the hotline had stopped coming in. The television stations were no longer displaying her picture. Sullivan had asked Lynn to make him a reservation to return to Ohio on Saturday morning. He had been away from the farm for three days now, he told Jake. He couldn't afford to take any more time off and he had asked enough of his neighbors to feed the cattle and take care of the dog. He was disappointed that they had not been able to locate Sadie but had high hopes that something would turn up. "But for now," he told Jake, "It was time to go home." Jake understood. He felt bad that things had not turned out the way he had hoped.

Jake left the office early Friday afternoon, dropping Sullivan off at the Comfort Inn on is way home. They shook hands and Jake promised to keep him informed of any future developments.

Several weeks earlier, Jake had gone online and ordered a couple of theatre tickets to the opening show that evening of "A Christmas Carol" at the Lansburgh Theatre. The Ford Theatre, the historical theatre where President Lincoln was killed by John Wilkes Booth was closed for renovations. Until its rescheduled opening sometime during 2009, all theatre productions were being held at the Lansburgh.

Knowing that the afternoon traffic would be busy with everyone trying to get a jump on their weekend, Jake had arranged to be at Jillian's house at five o'clock to get to the Theatre for the 7:30 opening.

After quickly looking at the mail, he took a shower, glancing into the fog free shaving mirror hanging on the shower wall. Jake had shaved that morning but by early afternoon, he was already developing a five o'clock shadow. He quickly ran the razor over his face before toweling down and splashing a little after shave on his face. Picking a dark gray suit, white shirt and burgundy print tie, he dressed quickly, matching his cordovan wingtips to his tie.

He had let Pete out the back door to get a little exercise before jumping in the shower. Pete was now standing at the door, whining, expecting to be fed.

"Too early, buddy," Jake said letting him in and bolting the door.

Before leaving, he phoned Sam, leaving a voicemail that he was taking Jillian to the theatre and would be home late. He reminded her to make sure to feed Pete when she got home. Jake was almost out the door when he remembered his handgun, still holstered in his shoulder holster on his bed. He thought about leaving it home but then his better judgment took over and he ran upstairs to grab his gun. Slipping on the shoulder holster holding the Sig Sauer .40 SW gave him a sense of security.

Jake hung his suit jacket in the back seat and backed out of the driveway. Turning left off of Van Dorn towards the Beltway, he decided to take the freeway to Jillian's, thinking that it would be quicker than trying to fight the traffic on Van Dorn. Fortunately, he made the right choice and was parking in her driveway by four forty-five. Jillian had a last minute emergency at the office and was running a little late. She let him in the side door and invited him to make himself a drink while she finished getting ready.

Jake poured himself a glass of red wine and relaxed in front of the television, watching the Fox News Network. Before he knew it, Jillian was standing in front of him in a beautiful black silk dress, matching pumps, diamond earrings and necklace

"Well, what do you think?" she asked Jake, twirling in front of him.

"I think you look beautiful," he said, grasping her hands and pulling toward him, giving her the slightest peck on her check so as not to disturb her lipstick.

Noticing the weapon hanging on Jake's side, she remarked, "Do you have to carry that thing everywhere you go?"

"Don't have to but the day I don't is going to be the day I wish I had," he replied.

"Traffic is going to be slow, so we better hit the road," he said, draping her coat over her shoulders.

Traffic wasn't as bad as Jake had expected. They took the I-495 Beltway toward Washington, crossing over to I-395 just before Alexandria. Following I-395, they crossed into the city over the Fourteenth Street Bridge. Turning right onto Pennsylvania Avenue, Jake continued east toward the U.S. Capitol. He turned left onto 7th Street heading north to D. Street. After waiting several minutes for the light to change, he turned left onto D Street, taking an immediate right turn onto 8th Street and turned midway up the block into the Colonial Parking Garage, finding an empty space on the fourth floor.

After locking the car, they took the elevator to the ground floor and left the parking garage turning right, her arm draped lightly through Jakes. Walking slow so that she would not trip in her three inch heels, they looked like two young lovers out on the town. Seeing the long line in front of the ticket window, Jake was thankful that he had purchased their tickets online.

Jill left Jake standing in the lobby while she used the ladies room before going to their seats. While Jake was waiting for her, he noticed Director Preacher coming through the front door, a woman, who Jake assumed was his wife, walking alongside him.

The director noticed Jake, and approached him on his way toward the seating area.

"You're not stalking me are you Agent Hunter?" he asked, a hint of sarcasm in his voice.

"No sir," replied Jake. "Just here to enjoy the show."

"Very well, then," he said. "Enjoy the show." Without introducing his wife, the director walked past Jake in the direction of the seating area.

"Who was that?" Jillian asked Jake, returning from the ladies room and noticing that Jake had been speaking with the man.

"Just one of the three stooges," he replied, smiling at her

"Ready?" he said, offering her his arm. "Ready," she replied, reaching for his arm and walking with him toward the usher. Jake handed the usher their tickets and they followed him to the upper deck, directly in front of the stage.

Glancing at his watch as they took their seats, Jake noticed that it was almost seven. His thoughts went to John Sullivan and he thought about him for a minute before Jillian, noticing the blank look on his face said, "What are you thinking about?"

"Oh just thinking about a man who is probably sitting in his motel room right now worried to death about his niece." Jake took a couple of minutes to tell Jillian about his trip to Ohio and John Sullivan and his niece Sadie.

"You really think she's involved in this?" asked Jillian.

"Don't know but until we have a chance to talk with her, she's the only suspect we have."

Waiting for the show to start, Jake glanced around the theatre looking for Director Preacher. He finally found him, sitting in one of the private box seats on the side walls, his security detail standing behind him, separating the director and his wife from anyone who approached them from behind.

At seven twenty, the theatre lights were dimmed and the spot lights were directed to the center of the stage where a tall distinguished looking man in full tuxedo came from behind the curtain. He welcomed the audience to the Lansburgh, announced that there were three acts in the play and that there would be a fifteen minute intermission between the second and third acts finally pointing out the emergency exits. With the announcements completed, he walked to the side of the stage, the curtain opened and the show began.

Jake wasn't much of a culture buff, enjoying outdoor and physical activities to plays and musicals but he found himself laughing and having a good time. Maybe it was the company he was keeping, he thought.

At the end of the second act, the curtains closed and the overhead theatre lights came on. Jake and Jillian went downstairs to stretch their legs and get a cup of coffee. The lobby was crowded, everyone else having the same idea. When the five minute warning light came on, they returned to their seats. Before the lights were turned down, Jake glanced over to where the director had been sitting. The director's wife remained seated but he was standing, talking with a couple of the agents that were assigned to his protection. Just as the lights were dimmed for the beginning of the final act, Jake noticed a lot of commotion in the box that he had just been looking at. Letting his eyes adjust to the darkness, he saw the director slumped in his seat, the FBI Agents scurrying around, their MP-5's and tactical lights visible in the feint light.

Jake jumped out of his seat, directing Jillian to stay put. He pulled out his .40 Caliber and ran up the aisle, rushing through the door at the top. Flashing his badge to an usher standing outside the door, he ordered him to get the theatre lights on.

Jake took the stairwell, two steps at a time to the lower level to make sure that no one escaped from the front doors. Pulling out his cell phone, he punched in the speed dial for the 911 emergency number, identifying himself as an FBI Agent.

"Get a squad over here now!" he ordered. There's been a shooting at the Lansburgh Theatre and I need back up. Send the SWAT

He was still on the phone when two of the agents on the director's detail came bursting through the main doors. They had jumped ten feet from the box to the floor below in pursuit of the shooter.

Recognizing Jake as they came through the double doors with their MP-5's raised, one of the agents asked: "Did you see anyone Jake?"

"No, I got down here as fast as I could to block the front door. I called it in. They're sending a medical squad and SWAT team."

"Squad's not necessary," the one agent replied. "Director's dead. One shot between the eyes. The shooter's good."

"I saw a flash," the other agent said. "Just before the director was hit."

"Shot came from the box directly across from where we were sitting. I'm sure it was a muzzle flash. Didn't hear anything so he's gotta have a silencer."

"There are too many people in here," Jake said. "I don't want this to turn into a shooting match. Innocent people are going to get killed."

"We've got agents on all the exits," replied the other agent. "What do you suggest we do?" he asked.

"Wait here for the SWAT team, instructed Jake. "I'm gonna approach the box from the stairwell and see if I can talk the shooter into giving up." Jake immediately thought of Sadie. If it was her in the theatre box, he didn't want to have to kill her. He thought about getting John Sullivan over to the theatre but there wasn't time. He approached the door to the Box and wrapped his hand around the door handle. He attempted to turn the handle but the door was locked from the inside. *Shooters still in there*, he thought.

"Sadie. Sadie Sullivan. If you're in there…My name is Agent Hunter. I've been working with your uncle John to try to find you. I don't want anyone else to get hurt. It's over. The director is dead. I want you to put your weapon down and come out. Can you hear me?"

Jake listened and waited but didn't hear any response.

Then, he heard shots. Many of them…coming from inside the theatre.

"Dammit," he shouted, running down the mezzanine stairs to the lobby.

Opening the doors, he almost ran into two FBI agents who were coming back into the lobby.

"We got him," said the one Agent who earlier had said he saw the muzzle flash. "He was in the private box, just like I said."

By that time the SWAT team had arrived, covering all the exits.

"Get the manager," hollered the one agent. "Door's locked. We need the key."

"No time for that!" screamed Jake. "Follow me," he said to the SWAT team standing next to him holding a ram bar.

Jake took the steps two at a time followed by the SWAT team. At the top of the stairs, Jake stood aside while the SWAT team slammed the ram bar into the locked door. On the second thrust of the bar, the door burst open. Following protocol, Jake entered the room behind the two SWAT officers. The shooter was laying facedown on the floor in a pool of blood, a scoped rifle by his side. Jake's immediate thoughts went to John Sullivan.

At least three exit wounds were visible on the back of the shooters coat.

Jake knelt down beside the shooter and turned the body over.

CHAPTER 89

Jake left the Theatre after telling Jillian she'd have to catch a cab. The Comfort Inn was on the way and he had called ahead to speak with John Sullivan. Sullivan would be waiting for him when he pulled up to the front doors. With siren blaring and lights flashing, Jake made it to the motel in less than fifteen minutes. He pulled into the driveway of the parking lot where he saw Sullivan standing under the portico. Sullivan saw him coming and waved his arms to get his attention.

"Hop in!" Jake hollered through the open window.

"Where's Sadie?" Sullivan asked. "Is she all right? What's happening?"

Jake hadn't taken the time to explain what had happened at the Theatre when he called Sullivan at the motel to tell him about the shooting.

He pulled out of the parking lot and immediately took a right turn onto the down ramp to I-395 in the direction of Falls Church, Virginia.

Jake didn't know how to answer Sullivan's questions because he wasn't sure what to expect.

"Shooter wasn't Sadie," he said. "From what I know at this point," Jake hesitated. "I have reason to believe your niece is at a motel in Manassas. That's where we're headed. When we get there, I want you to stay in the car until I tell you its okay to get out. Do you understand what I'm saying?" Jake demanded. Sullivan just shook his head, not knowing what else to do.

Twenty minutes later, having traveled the twenty seven mile distance at speeds in excess of ninety miles an hour, Jake pulled into the Red Roof Inn parking lot off Interstate 66. He had called ahead to the Virginia State Police who were waiting for him when he stopped the car in front of the motel entrance.

Two Virginia State Police Troopers followed him into the motel where he identified himself as an FBI Agent to the desk clerk and got directions for the location of the room. Bypassing the elevator, he found the stairwell and bounded the stairs to the third level, troopers following. Jake knocked on the door to room 340 and hearing no answer, slid the key pass into the door slot. Getting the green light, he pulled the door handle down and pushed the door open. The television was blaring, the newscaster reporting on the shooting earlier that evening at the Lansburgh Theatre. Sadie Sullivan, lay on the bed, her mouth duct tapped and her hands and feet tied. She had been struggling for sometime to get released but otherwise was unharmed.

EPILOGUE

Monday, December 5, 2008
FBI Headquarters
Washington D.C.

"So…What do you think?" asked Sully, standing at the edge of Jake's desk early Monday morning. "Do you think he really killed all three of them?"

"Appears that way," said Jake, not looking up from the report he was finishing. "That's how I'm writing it up. The way I see it, the father came back to make it right after deserting them for all these years. The letter we found in his pocket from Lieutenant Warner to his mother laid it out pretty good. The senator, Colonel Hatcher and Director Preacher executed nine prisoners that they were told to release. Lieutenant Warner even though he didn't take part in the killing, by his own admission stated that he did nothing to stop it. He was going to go to the authorities. They must have found out about it and killed him, making it look like a suicide. The lieutenant's father got a hold of the letter, stalked the three of them, taking them out one at a time. Must have been his way of making it right after walking out on him when he was three years old. According to Sullivan, Bob Warner was one of the best marine snipers in Viet Nam. He had the motive and the ability. Chuck Embers said the same rifle was used in all three killings. The only prints on the weapon are from Bob Warner. Warner was shot by the FBI immediately after killing the Deputy Director. There wasn't anyone else in the box with him. We have his written confession for all three murders."

Signing his name to the bottom of the report and looking up at Sully, Jake finished, "I don't see any reason not to call this case closed, do you?"

"Nope, I'm good with it."

Happy the man whose offense is forgiven,
whose sin is remitted.
O happy the man to whom the Lord
imputes no guilt,
in whose spirit is no guile…
Psalm 32

LaVergne, TN USA
27 December 2009
168124LV00007B/50/P